Sun Damage

Also by Sabine Durrant

Having It and Eating It
The Great Indoors
Under Your Skin
Remember Me This Way
Lie with Me
Take Me In
Finders, Keepers

CHILDREN'S FICTION

Cross Your Heart, Connie Pickles
Ooh La La! Connie Pickles

Sun Damage

A Novel

SABINE DURRANT

HARPER

NEW YORK • LONDON • TORONTO • SYDNEY

HARPER

Excerpt from MARNIE by Winston Graham.
Copyright © 1961 by Winston Graham.
Reproduced with permission of the Licensor through PLSclear.

Excerpt from THE GRIFTERS by Jim Thompson.
Copyright © 1963 by Jim Thompson.
Reproduced with permission of the Licensor through PLSclear.

Originally published in Great Britain in 2022 by Hodder & Stoughton.

HarperCollins books may be purchased for educational, business,
or sales promotional use. For information, please email the Special
Markets Department at SPsales@harpercollins.com.

FIRST U.S. EDITION

Library of Congress Cataloging-in-Publication Data has been applied for.

ISBN 978-0-06-327768-7 (pbk.)

23 24 25 26 27 LBC 6 5 4 3 2

For Mabel

There was little glory in whipping a fool—hell, fools were made to be whipped. But to take a professional, even if it cost you in the long run, ah, that was something to polish your pride.

Jim Thompson, *The Grifters*

I suppose you'd have seen her as a quiet girl.

Winston Graham, *Marnie*

Chapter One

It was the English voice that caught our attention—the sub schoolgirl French, grappling with an order for a demi-carafe. We were close to the bar as usual: you tend to pick up most there. She was at a table in full sun—rookie mistake, one of her shoulders already going red. Fresh off the plane, always a bonus. A British Airways tag hung from the leather straps of her powder blue Longchamp bag (genuine logo, I'd checked), and the paperback in front of her, spine unbroken, was part of a three-for-two airport deal.

What other tells? New mani-pedi—the neon pink all the posh Brits were wearing that year—and on the sand next to her, a brand-new sarong, still furled in its store-packaged ribbon. Also present: signs of the mild agitation people display on the first day of a holiday, an eagerness coupled with a daunting sense of vacancy, of a big hole waiting to be filled. When Sean went to the bathroom, I kept her in my line of vision as she scrolled through her phone, then held it up, small lips pursed, for a selfie.

"Debit card: L Fletcher Davies," Sean murmured, his chair sinking a little into the sand as he slipped back into his seat. "Address on luggage: 11a Stanley Terrace, W11."

"Lulu," I countered. I couldn't help myself. The four letters were strung in gold on a chain around her neck.

He smiled, pleased with me, then jerked his chin at my phone, saying time to get trawling.

I looked at him: *Really?*

I wish I could say it was conscience that initially held me back, or at the very least foreboding. But I'd be lying. We shouldn't even have been there. The "Picasso" napkin ploy had gone to plan, and Sainte-Cécile-sur-Mer would have been two days behind us. Except I'd gotten ill—some kind of virus that left me wasted and bedridden in the hotel. It was searingly hot. Music, a soft jazz, swam against the murmur and shuffle of waves. Sand slid silkily between my bare toes. I wrinkled my nose, one shoulder raised in a reluctant shrug. But I'd gotten the mood wrong. His smile had gone. "Ali," he said, and I could feel the cold of him like steel across my cheek.

It wasn't the money. There was enough in the hotel safe to get us where we wanted, even—a new, dangerous thought—*go our separate ways*. No, my hesitation was the problem; he'd taken it personally. He liked us to be in sync. Two parts of the same smoothly functioning machine.

And, maybe, he was right. She was the perfect mark. Tourists usually are. The south of France may not be India, where eighty rupees pass through a person's fingers as easily as eight, and where you could say I'd become who I was. But a fish out of water is a fish out of water whatever water it's out of. Isolation makes mugs of us all. We all make our worst decisions when we have a lot on our mind.

I adjusted the strings on my bikini top, pulling the knot so tight it bit at my neck. I'd been for a swim, and the towel between me and the wooden seat was damp. I tasted salt on my lips, felt the loss of the heat-heavy afternoon. It was me who'd begged for one last day on the beach. I'd been holed up in the hotel room. I wanted to be out in the sun. Maybe I'd snag a Jet Ski. Maybe even get to read the book I'd found on a train: the Trojan siege told from the perspective of the women. I forced myself to smile, hold his gaze. It was one of his tests. After a few long seconds, his jaw relaxed and he gave a small nod. Was that even a wink? I felt a flood of relief. My hands, I realized, were shaking.

I picked up my phone and got to work. Facebook, Insta. Didn't take long to find what we needed. A double-barreled surname is a gift.

Sean flapped open his newspaper—a four-day-old *Sunday Times*. I could feel his eyes on me above the pages as I got to my feet.

Raoul's was one of several casual bars that fringed this small crescent bay—sand under foot, director's chairs, umbrellas, a bustling trade of goat cheese salad and *steak haché* carried aloft on oval trays. It was drawing close to lunchtime and the tables were filling up, sun-dazed adults wandering up from the beach, trailing towels and small kids. Boats were moored out on the buoys now, their occupants swimming or bobbing ashore, pushing their dry clothes ahead of them in inflatable tenders. All these shiny happy people, all these creatures from another planet. This was the rush, the razzle-dazzle hour. It'd be quiet again by four.

I screwed up my eyes as I walked from shade into brightness, worked my way through the tables toward her. When I reached the back of her chair, I crouched down. The sole of one of her striped espadrilles still bore the price tag. Heat rose up from the sand. I could smell the coconut of her suncream.

"*Mademoiselle?*" I straightened up. "*Je viens de trouver . . .*" I dangled a sliver of cotton decorated with glass beads and metal charms. "*Mademoiselle, est-ce que c'est à vous?*"

She turned to face me then and, seeing her close up, I felt the stirrings of recognition.

"Oh God." She blushed. "I don't understand."

Her voice was unknown to me. But the shape and position of her features, the *essence* of her face, were familiar. We looked alike, that was it: the same nebulous

4

green/gray/blue eyes, the same pale skin, the same fine, straight hair.

"I don't speak French," she said.

She hadn't noticed anything. But then I'm never really noticed. It's why Sean chose me: the way I edge through the world unremarked, unwanted.

"Oh, you're English!" I let out a small, exhausted exhalation of relief. "Me too. I just found this—did you drop it?"

She looked at the bracelet and at her wrist.

"Er, I don't . . ."

She looked again, more thoughtfully, at the bracelet.

"Oh . . . yes!"

She extended her hand.

"Thank you!"

I hardened toward her then. It's not true you can't con an honest person, but it's easier emotionally when they're not. Hell, Sean was right. It would have been a mistake to pass her up. She was just like the rest of them: out for themselves.

"Let me," I said, pulling back the tiny clasp with my fingers and holding it so as to attach it to her wrist.

"Thanks," she said, and I bent over her, feeling her eyes skate over my head as I secured it. I studied her hands. Mine were steady again now that I was working. A pebble-shaped burn on the pulse point, quite recent, still red. Calluses on the back of the knuckles, a tiny ladder of white scars on her left index.

Don't look; *observe*. Sean taught me that.

"There," I said when I was done. "Don't lose it again."

She swung her wrist to admire the flash of junk. "I won't."

I straightened, tensing as his footsteps drew closer, small shivers of movement in the sand.

"Lulu?" His tone was both surprised and cautious, as one might gently admonish a small child. "It is Lulu, isn't it?"

I turned then in time to see him loom into view, the full force of him. His dark hair was still damp, tousled, and his tan brought out the sharp blue of his eyes. He was sporting just the right amount of stubble (too much, and he can look a bit shady), and the careless lope of his walk gave you the impression he was both taller and broader than he really was. He was secretive about his age. I guessed him to be about forty, but he could pass for ten years younger. Ray-Ban Aviators attached to the top of his white T-shirt, revealing a triangle of muscular, smooth skin.

"Or—" He took a step back now. "Am I wrong? Sorry. I thought I recognized you."

He looked at me, and then back to her. His smile was lopsided, boyish, diffident.

She had twisted around completely in her seat to fix him, her fingers toying with the letters on her necklace. The strap of her meshy pink bra slipped out from under her tank top.

"No. No. Yes. I am Lulu . . . Who are you? Do we . . . ?"

I wondered if he'd noticed our resemblance. Probably. The more similar someone is to you, the less objectively you weigh them up. Perhaps he knew we'd have a head start.

His teeth dug into his lower lip.

"Val d'Isère?" he said, tentatively. "I'm John Downe."

"Val d'Isère?" Her eyes were searching his face. "Were you a guest at the chalet? No. I'd remember. The Bar d'Alpine? Um. Oh God. Le Petit Danois! Carrie Bowman's last-night party?"

He tapped his forehead, a small dramatic movement, a magician producing a bunch of flowers from his sleeve. "Carrie Bowman's last-night party!"

"Oh my God. That's so weird. *Yes*. How do you know Carrie? Were you part of the Marlborough crowd?"

"Yeah. I *adore* Carrie."

He had moved around so she no longer had to strain to see him. His smile was full now, interested, engaged. He still had those manners he was brought up with. But it was more than that. In the full beam of his attention, you felt warm, like you were loved.

"John Downe." She was gazing at his face as if restoring it to memory. "Of course. God. Sorry, it was the end of a long season. I was wrecked that night."

"Weren't we all!" he said.

I rolled my eyes. "John. Honestly!"

She looked from him to me, and back again. A pause and she said, "So, you two here on holiday?"

"Yes, I suppose you could call it a holiday." He hooked his arm around my neck, squeezed it. "Ellie's on her way home from a course in Florence, and I've come out to join her for some R & R." He poked me in the ribs. "She's totally gassed to have the chance to spend time with her big embarrassing brother."

I watched the twitch in her zygomaticus major, the muscle on the side of the mouth that's impossible to control. The involuntary movement caused a tiny quiver in her lower lip. She was pleased, but also satisfied at being proved right. He was older than me, yes, but in her judgment, way out of my league. I leaned into him sideways, feeling the support of his chest. He reached his arm across my shoulders. My big brother. I felt suspended for a moment, safe.

"So, what kind of course?" she asked.

I felt Sean tense. I knew, fresh from the Picasso sting, he was thinking history of art. But I'd seen her Instagram feed—the bread stretching from bowls of fondue, the ceremonial racks of sacrificial lamb, the totteringly flamboyant meringues. And I'd run my thumb over the scars.

"Cookery," I said. "Italian pasta."

"Not Mansaro's?" she asked.

Sean's breath brushed across my neck.

I shook my head. "I *wish*. Nothing so grand. Nonna's Kitchen?" I'd plucked the name from the ether. "Basically, homemade pasta."

"How wonderful." She looked amused. "It makes me hungry just thinking of it. Wouldn't one just love to tuck into a bowl of Nonna's homemade pasta?"

"Come on then, we should probably . . ." Sean hooked one thumb back at our table. "Order food before the rush." He reached his hand out to shake hers. "Lovely to see you again, Lulu." The way he said her name; it lingered in his mouth.

We began to move away. Our bare feet sank into the sand. The waiter with the lazy eye, the one who had snuck me a free croissant with my morning coffee, was standing aside to let us pass. A small boy had run up, his splayed feet sending little cascades. Disembodied sounds reached us from the beach like the chatter of birds. A woman somewhere screamed.

"Unless . . ." I wish I hadn't turned so quickly because I caught the eagerness in her eyes, the vulnerability. My jaw slackened—in appeal or warning. But it was too late. Sean's hand was pressing into my back, his thumbnail sharp against my skin. He released me, and she gestured, fingers fluttering, at the empty seats to either side of her.

". . . you'd like to join me?"

Sean always said the secret of a good con is working out what someone wants and delivering on that desire, but it's not as easy as it looks. I mean, for starters, it's not like people always know what they want. And sometimes they don't want what they think they want,

9

or don't think they want what they do. You often have to wade through wishes and hopes, regrets and self-delusions, even to get near.

Take Lulu Fletcher Davies. At this stage in the game it wasn't what she could give us but what *we* could give *her*. She was on her own, bored, hoping for an experience Sainte-Cécile-sur-Mer had so far failed to deliver. Handsome, friendly John Downe was here to provide it. The artistry was in the details. Human beings are hard-wired for self-protection. If he'd simply approached, claiming to know her, he'd have activated her defenses. Which is why a little sister was vital to the act. The business with the bracelet wasn't just an excuse for an "in." It proved our honesty. I was trustworthy, so was he. We'd leapfrogged her guard. When he moved toward her, she was already willing him to be part of her social circle; she was meeting him halfway.

The best grifters always work in pairs.

As soon as we sat down, she started blathering away—keen, now *she'd* caught *us*, to entertain. I memorized the details. She was an actor really—she'd had a small part in *Downton Abbey*, and had we seen that ad for Argos?—but it was so hard to get auditions, and cooking paid the bills. She was addicted to Instagram; she was trying to cut down, feel more centered, you know, in herself. In two days' time, she was starting a job as a private chef in Provence. She'd worked in the same house the year before, only for different people—

a really cool young couple, Olly Wilson, the guy who started the food delivery service, and his wife, Katya, the fashion designer? Did we know them? Heard of them? No? Maybe?

"Anyway, so Katya told the owner about me, and somehow I've got roped into doing it for the people who are renting the Domaine this year. I said yes because I wanted to get away—life can be so samey; I needed a change. They're in publishing, and I've always quite wanted to write a novel, so . . . and I've scored a couple of nights with the house to myself at the end. But, I mean, the money's *nothing*. It's loose change. And I'm missing a party I really want to be at—Boo Watson's? Do you know her? She was at St. Mary's with me, but her brother Will was at Marlborough . . ."

Sean wasn't sure, but the name was familiar.

I'd been smiling to show I was engaged. Now I picked up her book, a bestseller about two sisters growing up in war-torn Sudan, and asked her how she was finding it. I'd cried when I'd read it, but I'd seen the unbent spine and caught the fleeting upturned quiver of her nose so, before she could answer, I said, "I gave up, too hard to get into."

"I *know*, right?" She slipped off her espadrilles, getting comfortable.

"I mean give me a good magazine any day."

She pulled out the copy of *Vogue* I'd already spotted in her bag. *Tra-la.*

11

"Ooh," I said, as if it was an enormous bar of chocolate she'd produced, or a small puppy.

I could feel Sean's eyes on me, approving. He'd taught me how to do it, reflect a person back at them. People like others to be the same, for their lives to mirror theirs, and I was good at that. The more closely you align your interests or opinions, the more likely they are to trust you. The Chameleon Effect, he told me it was called, or Egocentric Anchoring. Human nature would be another term for it.

When our order came, she ate like a woman who loved her food, cracking open claws, pulling at the flesh, sucking greedily at shells. She said no to the bread—some sort of intolerance—but she scarfed down the chips, chomped at the char-grilled chicken. "These prawns," she said, bringing a quiver of pale pink to her mouth, "are as good as the ones in Ibiza last summer." Her lips glistened. "Have you been?"

"No, but I really want to," I said.

"Oh my God, you *must*. Todd, my ex, and I had a ball. You'd *love* it. It's just one long party."

The breeze dropped; the heat sank and turned to something solid like jelly. She changed into her bikini, using the cubicle out back, and we took our coffees down to the beach. Sean persuaded her to take his sunbed and he sat between us, facing the sea, cross-legged under the umbrella. She lay down before undoing her sarong, unfolding both sides like a fancy menu. Closing her eyes, she let out a small sigh. Her eyelashes were blue-black against her freckled skin. Her stomach was pale and curved. Sean leaned back and caught my eye. He was enjoying himself. It had begun to bug me how much he liked to get one over on a certain kind of woman. Revenge on the society mother who'd ignored him? Or on the fiancée who'd ditched him? Either way, he didn't like women to be *better* than him. It was important, around Sean, to lay low.

On Lulu, I was looping back and forth. I'd felt bad because she was a failed actor, and then OK again because it seemed like a hobby. She was loaded, that was obvious: even without parents who lived in Dubai "for tax," I'd seen the price tag on the espadrille. I liked her appetite, the way she ate, her zest, but then she'd say something snooty about Essex girls or "the French," and I'd think, you deserve what you get. I thumbed through her magazine: expensive clothes and ridiculously strapped sandals—another world. It contained a free sample of face cream. I peeled it out of its metal foil. It smelled of hot plastic.

As her energy dropped, she started moaning—about her mother, who was interfering, and her friend Boo, who was irritating; even her ex-boyfriend, Todd, who, to be honest, did sound quite the creep: "He was waiting outside the bar when I came out, to see if I needed a lift home, and I'm like 'are you fucking kidding me?'" But none of it seemed to trouble her. As she droned on, with her eyes closed, I studied her uncreased face, just

13

flickering, and found myself wondering what it must be like to be her, to live inside her skin. She had grown up loved, cosseted. And for some reason, in that moment, I felt a skewer of such intense curiosity, such a painful kind of longing to feel that for myself, I had to look away.

The sun had lowered into a pinky haze on the horizon, the water melted to liquid silver, when the waiter came down with our bill. Brown seagulls were teasing the waves. Up at the bar, they were raking under the tables now, clearing and clattering, getting ready for the evening shift. Sean had started preparing our escape, and Lulu was leaning on her side, her elbow doing the heavy lifting, her eyes watching his mouth as he seeded thoughts of the following day: a plan to take a boat out to the islands, where we could find a quiet bay, swim, get away from the crowds. There was a lovely hotel with a restaurant, though stick-in-the-mud little sis Ellie here wasn't keen. His arms rose lazily to encompass the emptying beach, the pockmarked sand, and then paused in midair, as if welcoming the waiter into our midst.

"My treat," he said, scrambling to his feet. "Definitely on me."

Lulu tried half-heartedly to protest. "No, no, I ate so much. I drank all that wine."

But Sean had ducked out from under the umbrella and, reaching into the back pocket of his navy shorts, produced the CDG black leather holder he'd filched from the American student in Madrid. He handed his credit card to the waiter, then keyed in the number and stood back, entirely nonchalant.

I watched him. He'd timed the mention of the boat trip just right; not actually inviting her, but leaving the possibility hanging that we'd meet again, that the relationship had a future. The bill he'd treated casually—hadn't even checked the amount—and how deft his fingerwork with the wallet: the way he flipped it open with the thumb of one hand, cursory, practiced, as blasé with the contents as any arrogant hedge fund manager or whatever he'd told her he was.

The waiter—the older one with a crucifix nestling in his salt-and-pepper chest hair—was having trouble. He apologized in French; Sean, unconcerned, told him it didn't matter. The waiter tried a second time, and a third, and then, shaking his head, handed the card back.

Sean tutted in frustration. "Damn. It's got damp, I think." He rubbed it on the side of his shorts and then looked at it closely. "I dunno." Flicking open the wallet. "The other's Amex and I'm not sure that you . . . ?"

I took up a handful of sand and let it run out through my fingers.

The waiter shook his head.

I breathed in slowly and pushed myself up. "I'll go back to the room," I said. "Get my wallet."

Lulu stirred into life then. "No," she said. "Stay there," she said. "It's fine. Let me." Finding her card in a dinky burlap purse ("LOVE" spelled out in silver beads), she slotted it into the machine. She didn't even glance at the bill, still scrunched in Sean's hand, with its itemized list of our day's expenditure: the early morning *grands crèmes* and sunbeds, and the ice creams, the aperitifs, the cocktails, the rosé, the food, *les petits cafés*.

"Pay me back another time. Tomorrow."

"You're a doll."

"Or," she began, "I don't know if you're doing anything later. I mean we could go back and shower and then . . ."

"Sorry to be a wet blanket," I said. "John—you know we've promised?"

He nodded slowly. "Damn."

I explained, underlining the weight of this *previous commitment*, about the aunt who lived up in the hills with whom we'd promised to have dinner. I was sorting my stuff while I talked, handing back the magazine, and her fancy lotion, not looking at her, not quite ready to see her disappointment. Sean was dusting the sand off his legs and shaking his hands through his hair. Lulu flapped her sarong out, rolled it and rewrapped it, and then the three of us walked back up the beach, around the side of the bar, and to the road.

Sainte-Cécile is on the far left of the French Riviera as you look at the map, a fair hike from St. Tropez, not far from the fleshpots of Marseille. Which is not to say it doesn't have its own grandeur. Monopoly villas scatter the dark green hillside above and rows of white yachts line the harbor, the occasional Russian oligarch holed up on the horizon in a vast gleaming canister. We were around the headland from the main port, in the blue-collar, low-rent end of town. The hotels that lined the main drag, a dusty, utilitarian stretch, were mainly modern boxes with ragged outbuildings, though a few had palm trees and patches of grass, maybe even a fenced-off pool. I thought Lulu would head for one of those, but she stayed with us—moaning again about that impending job of hers—until we reached the flat, unprepossessing entrance of La Belle Vue.

"Oh, you're here too?" she said as we went through the sliding doors. The small reception area was sometimes unattended, but that evening a neat blond young woman was sitting behind the desk. It was hot in the room and she was fanning herself with a Hertz rental car leaflet. "Were you also late to book?" Lulu said. "I don't know whether there is a convention in town, or whether it's just the French's absurd obsession with August, but when I tried there was just *nothing*."

It wasn't good, her staying here. Too close for comfort. "Beggars can't be choosers." I tried to speak softly. The receptionist, pausing her fanning, looked up.

"I'm this way," Lulu said, pointing to a fire door on the right leading to a staircase.

I gave her a careful, damp hug and turned to the back door. My skin felt sweaty and tight; in my head I was already crossing the courtyard toward the annex

17

and our quarters overlooking the car park. I would run a shower. It was all right. It was over. Our day on the beach was gratis. All expenses paid. The best kind of scam when the victim doesn't even realize they've been scammed. Tomorrow, Lulu would find a note; a family crisis that meant we'd suddenly had to leave. By the time she read it, we'd be gone. On to the next place. We'd talked about Monte Carlo.

But Sean hadn't moved. One hand was propped against the wall, the other roaming beneath his T-shirt, massaging his chest, the pressure of his palms both efficient and sensual.

"I mean, I don't know what time we'll be back tonight," he said. "But maybe if it's not too late and you're still up for it, we could have a nightcap?"

"Oh. Well." She brought her hand to the back of her hair and twisted the clip, turning her hair into a fresh knot. "I'll probably have supper at Raoul's, so . . ."

A couple of mosquitoes were floating up and down against the glass of the back door.

"We'll be lucky to escape from Aunt Marie," I said. "You know how she talks."

Sean still hadn't looked at me. "I don't suppose at her age she'll be looking to pull an all-nighter."

I knew he had sexual encounters. Usually, he kept them discreet.

"She doesn't live that close," I said. "A longer drive up into the hills than we always remember."

I was expecting him to step toward me then. He didn't, and I felt fresh alarm. Was this a new form of punishment?

I put my hand against the glass and pushed. The door swung open more easily than I expected, and I knocked over a pot of geraniums. The earth as it spilled looked like ants.

I could hear them laughing as I bent to scoop it up.

Chapter Two

It's possible you've heard of Sean. Full name: Sean Wheeler. He's gained some notoriety, what with being in the papers. But, equally, maybe you haven't. When someone has power over you, it's easy to lose perspective, to think of them as a bigger deal than they are.

We'd been together at that point for three years. The day we met, in Anjuna, a hippie hangout in Goa, I'd been at a low ebb. If it hadn't been for him . . . I don't know. That day was the beginning of something, or maybe the end. Whatever you want to say about him, I owed him a lot.

Not to be self-pitying about it, but my childhood was a shit show. Fourteen addresses. Eleven schools. Not that I'm blaming the system; all those demons, they come from inside. You only have to look at my sister, Molly, and how differently her life has worked out, to see that.

Joy was in her early teens when she had us, and it was fine when her own mother was around to help. There's a picture of the two of us in matching dresses and matching socks, matching bows in our hair. But our nan got cancer and after that Joy did her best, but it went wrong by degrees. There was weed and booze and different boyfriends, and one, Pete, liked her to stay over at his place. In the end it was a neighbor who ratted her out. Police broke down the door and we were taken away and bought toothbrushes at Superdrug—that's what I remember anyway. I got to see my file once and it described mouse droppings and dog excrement in the bedroom, and how the neighbor pushed packets of biscuits through the letter box. Yet that's not what sticks in my memory. I remember being in the park, pushing Molly on the swings and still being there as it got dark, keeping her busy scrubbing the little rocking pony things with a packet of wipes; a cardigan hanging on the jungle gym that smelled of someone else's washing powder. And the sound of the planes at the emergency placement that first night; counting them in every three minutes, and worrying about Pete's dog, and if he'd been taken away too.

It was push-me pull-you after that. We'd have a few months "with Mum," and urgent referrals and spates of temporary care. Foster families. Some with their own kids, some not. Different smells. Different food. Fish sticks. Dumplings. Rice 'n' peas. You'd go to school thinking everything was normal and then be picked up at the end of the day by a woman you'd never seen and taken somewhere else. There were review meetings and contact meetings and toasted sandwiches at Costa for dinner. I'm not sure we were always that clean—I remember trying to wash my shirt in the bathroom after a girl told me I stank. I used to get into fights, defending Molly from kids in her class, and I got a note in my file that said I didn't know how to deal with emotions, though I think maybe I was never given the chance to try. One thing you learn when you're in the system—your version of events is only your opinion.

Eventually, we were taken in by a couple in Hastings, who were open to the long term. It was a chance for a new start, our care worker said. We were lucky, she said, to be placed together. I wanted it to work, so I don't know why I fought so hard to make it fail. The settee had a weird texture, like bristly velvet, and the seats were molded so it only fit three people. Usually none of them was me. It was a bungalow and it had windows you could only open at the top, like a freezer compartment in a fridge. Food was hard; I got it into my head I was being poisoned. And there were so many rules—at home, at the new school. I got in with a bad crowd, like the boys down at the arcades—though it was the good crowd that did me in: the girls with their lacy bras and their holidays in Tenerife who'd taunt you for wearing the wrong Nike trainers. It was one of them who persuaded me to break into a teacher's house. Of course, they took off, leaving me to take the rap. The betrayal made you feel crackly inside, like you could start a fire, which was something I later did.

Permanent breakdown, they call it. It all happens so quickly, when they want you gone. Molly stayed. She was calling Mrs. Ormorod "Mum" by then. Better off without me, that was their conclusion. I think it's what hurt most of all, the feeling that, all the time when I thought I'd been protecting her, I'd been making her life worse. I still see her. We're still in touch. But I think—well, I kind of know—that she'd rather we weren't.

Fairlight House, where I was sent next, had a padded "quiet" room and locks on the fridge, and all the house parents had training in how to restrain a child without being accused of sexual assault. I gave up on school and spent most of my time in town with the older kids, begging for cigarettes, getting into trouble with shop-keepers and security guards. I began to drink too much—it helped with the panic attacks and the loneli-ness, the last of which, frankly, was a bit unfair. I mean, I was never on my own. I was surrounded by people *all the time*. But then that's psychology again. It's a joke. I'd think, I want to go home. And then I'd think, where the fuck is home?

At eighteen, I got a new social worker, Karen, who found me supported lodging for transitional care-leavers, basically a studio apartment, and started trying to talk to me about vocational training. One day, she mentioned this charity in Nepal, and said I could get funding. She said it would be character-building, and I had this idea then that maybe I could really build a new character—you know, properly start again. But when I did get out there, I felt even more myself, more of an outsider. The other volunteers, "off to uni" in September, wanted to know where I'd gone to school, where I lived, to place me. For them, it was less about character-building—or even well-building—and more about full moon party nights and white-water rafting, and I'd soon had enough. I hitched a ride to Kathmandu and cut loose.

For a couple of years, I scratched together a legitimate living. I'd get a bed in exchange for odd jobs—an ecolodge in Siem Reap, a houseboat in Srinagar. But it was a tough, lonely existence. I began to develop a hatred for those backpackers, and one night, after I'd seen a noisy group leave a restaurant without paying, I followed them, and later, nicked a wallet from one of their bags. I told myself it was only tit for tat. Even the richest of them, I'd noticed, weren't averse to hiding market jewelry up their sleeve or swiping a bottle behind a barman's back. I got more ingenious after that—as the months and then years passed. I pretended to be their friend, went from "borrowing money" for a phone call to incorporating misdirection into an engineered situation where they'd "break" or "lose" something precious ("look after this gold necklace while I have a quick swim"). They'd literally throw cash at me to ease their guilt. When I started dealing dodgy weed, I'd tell myself it was practically a public service—a load of travelers getting their kicks from nothing more damaging to their health than oregano. It made me feel I was getting my own back at the Nike-taunters at school. Anyway, what did it matter? I was only proving them right, being the lowlife they'd thought I was all along.

That day in Anjuna three years ago, I was running out of steam, down to my last rupees. A trick, one I now know as "The Flop," when you engineer an accident involving a small vehicle—in this case a moped—had gone wrong. There's a knack to it, like a footballer's dive; the aim is to maneuver your body out of the way, but to use a prop, a bag or stick, to create impact, and your best acting skills to ape moderate injury. Cry or hold a limb at the right angle, and people nearly always pay you off—they're in a hurry, or their insurance is dodgy—but in this case, I'd misjudged it. The guy was an arsehole, and I was sitting on the side of the road in the straggled outskirts of town, nursing not a generous payoff but a bleeding leg and a bruised ego, when I saw a man in a polo shirt leaning against a tree. He crossed over and produced a tube of antiseptic cream from his cross-body canvas duffel. We got to talking, and he ended up buying me a vegetable roti in one of the shacks that lined the main drag. He was older, but handsome—the sort of looks that made you think you were the only one who'd noticed—but when he brought out his wallet to pay, I saw the photograph of a blond. I'd had a few bad experiences with married men and, as soon as I'd eaten, I cut and run, taking the exit that led under a tarpaulin straight from the restroom to the street.

Anjuna was above my pay grade and I was crashing upcountry forty minutes away, in a cheap room at Mapasa. Limping down the side of the road to the bus stop, I saw a figure standing in the corrugated shadow between Prakesh Tea Stall and Lakshmi Sweets, a foot gently resting on a heap of rotting marigold garlands. He waited until I reached him and used his hands to push himself forward. He was grinning. "You might need this," he said, holding out my brown leather purse. I felt for the strap around my neck, pulled it out from under my T-shirt. The strap dangled, empty.

He'd been watching me, he said. I had talent, soft skills, a capacity to build trust, an instinct to blend in. I was just the right sort of mousy, the right sort of invisible. I was raw, but I had potential. I shouldn't have let that couple get away with giving me so little to replace my dead mother's wedding ring. "Why these losers and vagrants?" he said. "Why fake weed and not fake cocaine? Why waste your talents and your time?" He'd had a partner who'd gone south (metaphorically speaking) and he needed a new one. In his line of work, women had an advantage. No man, he told me with a sideways glance, thinks a woman could be smarter than him. He looked at me hard as if holding me up to the light; nodded as if he liked what he saw.

"We're the same, you and me. We could make it work."

We're the same. It wasn't true. He came from money— country estate, boarding school, "family connections" (severed). But it worked. The next day, I met him back at his hotel—a large bland resort with a spa and three pools. He fed me breakfast and asked me questions about myself, nodding at the answers as if, yes, he knew exactly what I meant. He hinted at a similar back story. He himself had always been unwanted. He took my anger and twisted it, made it sound useful, an advantage. "Outsiders like us," he said, "what a perspective we have on the rest of them, what an *edge*." For the first time, I felt strong, as if I'd found some place I belonged, that this profession he said I was already part of was my own secret family. We went to his room and had sex, quick and clinical, like the signing of a contract. First and last time. I didn't mind. That's foster care for you; you get used to thinking of love as a transaction. Afterward, he laid out his proposal. He was down in Goa for some R & R, but he was heading back up north to the Golden Triangle, Taj Mahal, Jaipur, Jodhpur: what he called the retiree circuit. Rich pickings were to be found in Rajasthan: tour groups and wealthy Americans. He told me to imagine how much money I could be making, to picture a hotel suite with a queen bed, 500-thread sheets, and a fully stocked minibar. Then he explained what he had just done. Picture this; imagine that—they're persuasive techniques. Visualization, he said, releases oxytocin; bends the listener to the speaker's will.

"Stick with me," he said, opening up his arms to encompass a whole new world. "I'll teach you everything I know."

Chapter Three

He wandered in ten minutes after I'd left him in the foyer and perched on the end of my bed, legs apart, palms tapping a rhythm on his outer thighs. His eyes were sharp; his mouth loose. He didn't speak, didn't even look at me for a full minute. At last he said, "Maybe we shouldn't scoot off so quick." He raised his chin and breathed in sharply, still not catching my eye. "Maybe we should play this one out."

My chest was tight and I cleared my throat. I'd kept the curtains drawn and it was hot and airless; above my head dozens of flies spiraled silently. I'd spent too long in that bed. The maid had changed my sheets, but it still had that sickroom feel. I felt the walls press in.

When I didn't answer, he started talking about "the angle," as if it was something we'd already discussed. Once we were out on the RIB, he said, we'd mention how we'd hoped to charter a yacht and sail to Corsica.

We'd find a beauty to show her in the port. Get her juices flowing before we tell her we're a few grand short—what do you think, five, ten? She wants an excuse to give up on that cooking job; she only needs a small nudge.

One thing he'd drilled into me was the importance of planning. Every project—the "antique" furniture in Jaipur, the "genuine" diamonds in Delhi, the weight-loss program in Barcelona—was mapped out in detail. The "Picasso" napkin had been plotted frame by frame. We'd heard about the mark, Jamie Nicholls, from a connection in Madrid, had followed him first to Nice and then Sainte-Cécile, where we'd spent several days buttering him up. When we *mentioned* the artwork on the walls of the auberge—the missing goat woman, worth four times the price being asked—we already knew about his private income. When, ultimately, Nicholls absconded with the piece itself (after ponying up the purchase price in exchange for a percentage of the profit), it was as predicted. We knew about the scandal at Eton, when he'd passed off a friend's essay as his own; we knew about his failed art history degree, and that he'd do anything to prove himself to his bullying bastard of a father. Nicholls wasn't any old victim. He was profiled, chosen, fit for purpose.

Occasionally, yes, you'd be caught on the hop. In Marrakech, the owner of the empty building we'd decked out as a shop had arrived on the scene days before we were due to sell the business on. On that occasion, Sean had kept his cool, put on a crisp white shirt, met with the real owner in secret, negotiated a deal. More recently we'd had a bit of a disagreement around Nicholls. Sean wanted me to sleep with him and had gotten a bit nasty when I refused. There'd also been a complication with Cyril Dutroix, the guy who owned the bar with the "Picasso" in it. He'd gotten greedy at the end, demanding more than his fifty percent cut. This blew up during those two days when I was ill. But Sean, always rising to a crisis, managed Dutroix. He talked about a future partnership, sweet-talked him into accepting the original deal. It was about staying calm, adjusting, not acting on impulse.

"It needs more groundwork," I said now. "We don't know anything about her. I don't like it that she's staying in our hotel."

He shrugged. "Sometimes you have to take your chances."

"It's too risky. What if she checks her card and sees how much yesterday cost? Or she's gone over her limit and the bank gets in touch?"

"Coutts," he said, like the luxury of it was delicious in his mouth.

I was leaning into the headboard; it scraped against the wall when I shifted forward. "Her friends—she might ask them about you. She might already have."

"She won't. She's on a social media detox. And even if she does, it doesn't matter. She's in the palm of my hand." He held it out, cupped, to demonstrate. "She'll believe anything I say."

His voice lacked conviction. Perspiration pearled above his upper lip. In the gloom, he looked older; eyes bloodshot, jowls heavy. I thought: middle-aged man falls for younger woman. This lame old story? Please, no. Not *Sean*.

I said: "We've already been here too long."

"What's too long?"

"What if Nicholls comes after us?"

"He won't." The beige bedcover was made of a thick satiny material; he ran his hand along a decorative swirl.

He was right—Nicholls's sense of inferiority, the problems with his father: he'd do anything to bury the humiliation of spending 60,000 euros on a worthless paper scrap. If the best con is one where the victim doesn't realize it's taken place, the second-best con is where they're too embarrassed or humiliated at the re-alization to do anything about it.

But what else did I have to pull Sean away? "He *might*."

Sean made a sudden movement, levering himself up from the bed. I recoiled—I'd pushed him too far—but he just said: "It's a mistake to think you're cleverer than me. You're not."

He walked through the interconnecting door into his own room, and after a few moments I followed like a dog and stood against the wall. He bent down on his haunches in front of the wardrobe and spun the dial on the safe. Too quick. He always was. He brought out the shoebox, opened the mouth of the blue plastic bag inside it, and added the stash of banknotes he'd taken out for the day. "Have you got the rest?" he said.

I nodded and fetched the backpack. He stood over me as, crouching, I pulled out the paraphernalia, including the fake IDs and the plastic packets containing cheap Indian bracelets. The box was full, and a couple of the packets slipped out onto the carpet as I fumbled to close it. I knew he was still annoyed with me, because he let out a tut and turned his head, as if my clumsiness was too irritating, too *predictable*, to watch.

"I might still meet her for a drink," he said, moving to the window. He pushed the white plastic curtain liner out of the way. A vehicle was revving, and he peered down, narrow-eyed. "Just to see."

"Oh. OK," I said. I tried to sound casual, to keep the unease from my voice. I felt a spasm low in the pit of my stomach. He did things sometimes to confuse me. I didn't understand what was happening.

My hand was feeling around in the bottom of the backpack. Sean was looking out of the window. I was taking my time, and still he didn't turn. I paused; the room suddenly felt very still. One of his feet moved, but he was just shifting his weight, pressing his forehead at a different angle against the glass for a better view.

"Get under their skin," Sean had taught me. "Get so close they drop their guard."

Sometimes he told me he'd created me in his "own image."

It took five seconds to transfer the bag of euros from the shoebox to the backpack. Just a short-term measure, I told myself. Just a little piece of temporary insurance while we saw off this girl.

Chapter Four

That day we first met he took me to the hotel boutique and bought me new clothes—narrow black trousers, tight dresses, silk tops—peeling crisp counterfeit dollar bills from his wallet. We ate lunch at the all-you-can-eat buffet, and in reception he showed me how to use food poisoning to leave a hotel without paying. When I asked if our bill would come out of the manager's own pocket, Sean told me I'd never get anywhere in this business if I cared about everyone I met.

"We'll get you there," he said. "You'll be OK. You're with me now."

Goa has an international airport, catering to the package holiday trade, but we flew from the domestic terminal, a dusty, cracked-tile kind of place. Sean told the flight attendant I was pregnant and, when we weren't allotted seats with extra legroom, charmed her so we were moved to first class. Free champagne. Sean didn't touch it. So much of what he does is for show, though I didn't realize it then. He took no pleasure in the comfort or the free trappings, spent the short flight standing by the toilets. It's a principle with him, getting one over.

In Delhi we stayed in a hotel so smart it had a circular driveway and its own airport-style security: an X-ray machine for luggage, and a man with a metal detector on a stick. On the second evening, over predinner drinks, Sean struck up conversation with Mrs. Williams, a Texan widow. She was "India mad," on her eighth trip in as many years. I watched as he flirted, coaxed, drew her out. He kept his cards close, but he dropped enough clues that intrigued her: references to "high-net-worth individuals." She had joined us at our table, when he finally told her we were interior decorators, on a buying trip for some important clients.

Mrs. Williams clasped her hands together. "What kind of important?"

He cast his eyes down at the bar, freeing her imagination. Film stars? Royalty? The exquisite agony of not knowing. What a coincidence, she said. She herself was here for the same reason, having decided, after all these years, to do the ranch up *her* way. Sean's jaw dropped in surprise—as if he hadn't overheard her talking about it in the foyer the day before. The Texan widow was oblivious. Now her husband was dead, she was going to redecorate the whole place. Did we have any tips?

"I'm sorry. It's all promised elsewhere." He gave Mrs. Williams a conspiratorial roll of the eyes.

When we met at breakfast, he had softened: we might be able to spare the odd piece. Two days later, he was showing her photos of colonial daybeds and dressing tables. He had papier-mâché dance masks and giant ebony-carved elephants. Paintings: Balakrishna with a pat of butter; Damayanti in the forest; Krishna with consorts. Wall hangings and carved panels. The cost ran to thousands of dollars. One Indo-Persian hammered brass tray alone worth over £2,000. *None* of it was available to Mrs. Williams. Unless . . . well, oh, maybe . . . oh, she was dreadful: yes, OK.

We stayed in Jaipur for several months, repeating that con six or seven times. It became more sophisticated, progressing from photographs to a warehouse of props and an "authenticator" called Advik, a bespectacled railway worker as interested in history as he was in making a quick buck. The "shipping costs" alone soon covered our accommodation in the Emperor Suite.

If Sean understood rich people's greed, it was because he had inside knowledge. It was personal. He'd had a job in the family import-export business after leaving school, but had been caught embezzling. His girlfriend had left him, his mother had disowned him. You could still feel his humiliation. After that he'd never gone home. Hatred had sharpened his instincts. He taught me how to sniff out gullibility (boredom, loneliness, *need*); how to profile, how to *listen*. On quiet evenings, we played dice and cards, and he demonstrated speed and misdirection. He described classic tricks: the Dry Cleaning scam, and the Drop Swindle, Change Raising. But most of all he talked about people—their weaknesses and veniality.

"The true con doesn't force anyone to do anything," he would say. "We don't steal. They *give*."

No one had ever paid me that much attention. I lived on Planet Sean, hungry for his approval. He was protective. If a mark got too attentive, he'd manhandle him into the street, and that one time I got picked up by the police for shoplifting he was at the station and talking me out of it within the hour. He could be strict. Once I called him by his real name in front of a coachload of tourists and he shaved my head as punishment. Later he brought me a headscarf; pretty, block-printed, and he was tender when he showed me how to tie it. "It'll be useful," he said. "You're recovering from chemotherapy. Tomorrow we'll try a version of the Spanish Prisoner—fundraise for further treatment. It'll be good for your education."

And he did educate me. I got better, sharper. In Barcelona, I found the clients. In Marrakech, I did up our little fake shop. Our relationship became more equal. By the time we had arrived in France, I had persuaded him to give me a cut—twenty percent of earnings, which for the moment he was keeping in a separate bank account. It should have become easier, but it hadn't. We'd started playing tricks on each other. Small but nasty. He'd begun to resent me.

He hated other people. That, ultimately, was the truth of it. I was finding that harder to ignore.

I slept badly. In the hours when I lay there awake, I strained my ears for movement in the next room, alert for each creak of Sean's springs. Maybe he listened out for me. I was coughing a bit, still getting over the chest infection. When I did sleep, I sank into dreams I would rather have avoided. Disjointed images. Sean shredding a passport into the toilet, blood on the cuffs of his white shirt. A tour guide who'd crossed us crying in reception. Her room had been broken into; everything taken. The intruder had left a "present" in her bed.

"Who would do that?" she was sobbing. "What monster?"

I was drenched with sweat when I came to. The curtains were still pulled, but the room was bright. The door between our rooms was wide open—a rectangle of sunlight spread across the carpet. His bed was empty.

He would have gone for breakfast. Raoul's. He was a creature of habit.

I dressed carefully—black bikini under denim shorts and a tank top—and I did my hair like Lulu's, piling it up into a loose chignon, securing it with the tortoiseshell clip I'd taken from her sunbed. The safe was locked so I couldn't pick up the fake IDs or jewelry; not that I needed any of it today. But I went through the room, ticking off my checklist. First rule: carry everything with you except your clothes, leave nothing (possessions, love) you wouldn't walk away from in a second. Bathroom, wardrobe, under the bed, chest of drawers. Your eyes get used to something as part of the background and before you know it you've left it behind. It had happened to me in Jodhpur. I'd left that pale blue T-shirt that had belonged to my sister hanging on the back of the bathroom door. And, of course, once we'd gone, I couldn't contact them to send it on. Mistakes like that stay with you.

At reception was a dark-haired man I hadn't seen before. I slapped on a mild smile, keeping my face slightly averted, and crossed quickly to the entrance. My hand was against the metal bar when he called out.

"*Mademoiselle. Excusez-moi . . .*"

I slowly turned. He was rubbing his hands together, like he was massaging in cream. A badge on his lapel told me his name was Clément.

"The tap of your basin?" he said, getting to his feet. "Many apologies for the inconvenience of the dripping. My colleague has passed the matter to myself. Somebody will look at it as soon as possible this morning."

He pointed at the staircase, with a jerk of his head, and I realized it wasn't just the hair. I'd done my eyes like hers, too, the same cat-like black flick. I can speak quite good French now: all that hanging out with Parisians in Kerala, not to mention those six months in

Morocco. But it didn't seem worth bothering to explain. "Oh, OK," I said. "Thank you."

It didn't surprise me that she'd found something to complain about.

It was hot on the strip. The soles of my sneakers slapped against my feet as I walked away from the hotel. A French family came toward me, the youngest child dwarfed by a pink inflatable in the shape of a flamingo. The air was rich: coffee and salt and diesel, and something faintly savory. In a glass cage outside the brasserie, pallid chickens were turning in horizontal rows on metal spits.

I crossed over when I got to Raoul's. Only a few people were sitting at tables—a pair of young lovers and a man on his own, sitting at a laptop. No sign of Sean, which was odd. I didn't go in, instead I took the passage between Raoul's and the next bar along, walking in the cool shadow of their wooden panels, toward the light.

The beach was already half full; older couples on the orange and white sunbeds, young families on patchworks of colored towels, naked babies in hats crawling. A woman was wobbling clumsily on a paddleboard; farther out the heads of swimmers dipped and fell like seals. Seagulls floated low. The water was very blue today; you could see the line past the yellow buoys where turquoise turned to navy, where the shelf of sand gave way to rock. I'd swum out the day before and had looked down into the blurry depths where the seabed

41

was dark and jagged, quick with fish and leathery weeds.

The sand where it was dry had a satisfying crust, the sun hot on the side of my head, but a fresh breeze came off the water. That mixture of warmth and cool released a memory of the first month with the Ormorods in Hastings; their bungalow near that wide bay, the path down whiskery with long grass. I closed my eyes, listening to the soft collapse of sea on sand, the shove-penny rattle of its backward drag.

I was hardly ever alone, and I felt the acute and sudden thrill of it, a bliss of freedom so penetrating it felt like a thud in the chest. I think it was thinking about Molly; her settled and respectable life in Morden, her husband, her dog-grooming business, her patio garden. I could see if she'd let me visit. It wasn't too late. But even in that moment, even as I was feeling it most strongly, I was aware of the euphoria beginning to slip; overtaken, even as I tried to hold onto it, by anxiety, a sense of my own uselessness.

The canvas of my sneakers was dark where the water had lapped against them. I had the feeling then that I was being watched and I spun my head. Raoul's was almost empty. The man on his laptop was staring not at me but out at the water. Farther down the beach, a group of teenagers was playing racket ball; *tat, tat, tat,* shouting to one another in what I think was Italian. No one on any of the sunbeds paid me any attention. Out in the bay, one of the yachts was making ready to leave;

a figure leaning out of the back, pulling at the anchor; sails were flapping unfurled. A girl in a navy swimsuit jackknifed, with a shriek, off an inflatable float. And then a speedboat hove into view from out of the headland, cutting through the water, churning white, parallel at first, and then growling toward the shore. The engine cut and it bobbed out there, a figure proud in the center, another, a woman, high in the front, waving her arms. She shouted, though I couldn't make out the words. It didn't matter. I was already taking off my sneakers and shorts and tank top and stuffing them into my backpack, zipping it up tight, and paddling out toward them, wading until I was out of my depth and then swimming with one hand, holding my bag aloft with the other, until I was close enough to hurl it over the side.

When I reached the back, Lulu had let down the metal ladder, and I hauled myself up toward her. She was laughing down, her face shadowed by a jaunty red cap. The logo across the brim read St. Tropez. "You found us," she said, though I think it was more that they had found me.

"Hop in," Sean said, standing proud at the controls.

He threw me a towel—a plump navy affair with "FYC" embroidered at one corner—and I rubbed my arms and legs and then wrapped it around my waist and perched on the side. The rubber beneath my bum was so firm it felt solid rather than inflated. I felt suddenly exhausted, and for some reason, tearful.

"Hasn't he done well?" Lulu had sat in the center of the padded seats at the back, her arms stretched out on either side of her, legs out in front—inhabiting the luxury, showing off the glamour. "It's a Tempest 800. The man at the rental gave him an upgrade."

"He's done brilliantly," I said.

I guessed he'd searched the marina until he found a vessel with the key still in it; sometimes the owners just left them like that. Or he'll have waited at the end of a pontoon for someone in a hurry; look official and they'll throw you the key, expecting you to valet-park it. He might even have been tipped.

On his head sat a pair of unfamiliar sunglasses—black, wraparound; expensive. He'd probably found them by the ignition. They weren't as nice as the Ray-Bans he'd filched in Barcelona. But he would be enjoying the feel of them, the chance they gave him to pretend to be someone else. He never passed up an opportunity to do that.

"Right," he called. "Let's go."

He looked magnificent, a winner. Perhaps I'd been wrong to doubt him.

He gave a salute and, shoulders back, revved the engine, curled the boat around, and, nosing between the buoys, headed out of the natural harbor in a diagonal line toward the open sea. Land began slowly to diminish behind us, Sainte-Cécile an even line of low structures dwarfed by the hulk of the hillside—higher than you could tell from down there, stretching up, in a rash of trees and villas, up and beyond to a high expanse of velvety dark green.

He accelerated.

I grabbed a handhold, and I might also have let out a yelp, or maybe it was Lulu who screamed—her hair was streaming loose now, and the red cap was somersaulting in the churn of our wake—because it was to her Sean hurled his next words.

"Don't worry. I know what I'm doing," he yelled. "I won't kill you."

She laughed then and he pushed the speed up another notch, the bow reared, the stern bore down, and the boat bumped and skimmed across the waves. Ears full of the engine, face blasted by salt, hair tangled, I clung with both hands onto the closest handle. The sea raced toward us, surged and parted; white horses streamed on either side. The mainland was thin and distant behind us, the island ahead—a dark shape like a sleeping dinosaur. I closed my eyes, held my face into the wind, and gave myself up to the exhilaration of it. I forgot Lulu. I forgot the fear. I thought, This day is a gift, an apology. *He's done this for me.*

It was twenty minutes before the swell dropped and the water calmed. A lighthouse came into view on the farthest promontory and before it, a series of inlets and small beaches, a few yachts at anchor, sails curled. Sean dropped gears, and we puttered parallel to the shore for a few minutes, until he nodded to himself and steered toward a crease between low cliffs.

The water under the boat lost its color, the light radiating in shafts down to the depths. We were out of the wind now, the air still. I leaned over, trailing my fingers and watching ripples of sand, far beneath, flashes of weed-covered rocky outcrops, darting fish. The boat slowed, started to bob. The engine cut. Sudden silence. The creak and crank of the anchor; the rattle of a canopy. Sean was moving around the deck, giving Lulu instructions. I stayed bent over the side of the boat, watching the shadow of the vessel swell and shrink on the sand below. Let her do it, I told myself. Put her to work.

"There," Lulu said, when the anchor was down, a sunshade on metal struts above us. She was looking bedraggled now, her eyes creased, her cheeks red. Under her arms, her T-shirt was damp with sweat, strands of hair stuck to her forehead. I wondered if she regretted coming.

Sean gestured at the small arc of beach, the debris-fringed sand, the few storm-swept trees, the cluster of rocks, the privacy. "Will it do?"

He kept his eyes on me until I nodded; then I unraveled the towel, spun my legs over the side, and dropped vertically into the water. The cold was enveloping, like a sheath. I paddled for a bit, until I was used to it, then turned onto my back and floated.

I waited for them to join me, and when they didn't, I began to swim toward the shore. Sand gave way to small, jagged rocks; the cracks filled with sinister clusters of black spikes. I'd stepped on a sea urchin before—in Spain during the period when we were selling bogus time-shares—and I didn't fancy doing it again. I changed direction, swam a little way back toward the boat, trod water for a bit, watching them. They were sitting next to each other on the back seat. Her arm lay across the top of the cushion and he was turned toward her. His eyes were behind the wraparound sunglasses now, and he had taken off his top, his chest broad and tanned. Lulu was slight and pale next to him, her shoulders bony. She turned to stare at me, and there was a second or two of nothing before she raised her spare arm in a wave. Sean looked at me, too, but made no sign of acknowledgment.

After a minute, he got to his feet. Lulu leaned over the back, and he stepped toward the helm.

I felt the vibrations of the engine before I heard it, spreading not from the surface of the water but, it seemed, up from the seabed, a low growl. Arms flexed, Sean looked at me over his shoulder. I felt the slap of water against my neck, a choke, the sting of salt at the back of my nose. I shouted and began to swim, head too high, vision blurred, the sun flashing, water in my eyes, my mind full of the rocks and the sea urchins. Then I let my legs sink, watching the boat get smaller, panic changing to anger—an upsurge of fury. "FUCK YOU!" I shouted, moving my arms sideways, spinning in circles, feeling the resistance of the water against my muscles, aware of the ripples wrinkling outward away from me, a dot in an endless expanse of blue.

In Marrakech, he stood over my bed one night and told me my sister was outside, that she needed money for the taxi. I thrust cash at him, everything I had, and threw on some clothes, but when I got downstairs the street was empty—no taxi, no Molly, no Sean. "It was a joke," he said in the morning. "Just a bit of fun." It was punishment—a flexing of muscle. I'd mentioned going off on my own; he was telling me he knew my vulnerabilities.

The engine became a buzz, a hum, and then deepened, became more guttural. On the other side of the bay, another boat was mooring up—a fancy yacht with people sunbathing on the roof, music blaring. A series of sudden waves hit my face. I turned sharply. Sean was swooping down, almost on top of me.

He shouted: "We were dragging the anchor. Thought we'd try to secure it again."

I'd got my own back in Barcelona a few weeks later. I opened my heart over dinner, told him I was in love with him. I watched his face as vanity tussled with reason and won. When he sidled into my room later, with a bottle of champagne and a pack of condoms, I laughed my face off.

Now I glared up at him. "You wanted to scare me," I said.

"Believe me, if I wanted to scare you," he said, "I'd do a better job than that."

He leaned over to pull me up, those wide creases on the side of his face prominent, his eyeteeth visible.

Lulu was unpacking a picnic—a bottle of rosé resting between her knees. I flicked my hands, scattering drops; then pulled a towel from under a bowl, and sent a nectarine rolling.

We ate the picnic—slices of expensive meats and tubs of olives. I thought about the ketchup sandwiches Molly and I used to take up to the rec. No sandwiches here. Something to do with Lulu's allergy. Not an intolerance but more serious: "I'm a celiac. Not being funny, but wheat could actually kill me." Afterward I read my book. I didn't care if it was out of character. I wanted Sean to know he'd pushed me; that it was a consequence of his stunt with the boat.

He didn't like it. "Book club," I heard him say, rolling his eyes. "She's always in trouble for not reading the book."

"Oh Lord, poor Ellie," she said. "Book clubs, they're the worst. Not only having to read the book, but then having to have an opinion on it. Oh my God, what's it even about?" She bent forward to read the back cover. "The Trojans? What the actual fuck?"

I tried to concentrate, but it was hard above her chatter. She talked a lot, but her words seemed preprepared, disengaged from thought, bolstered with ready phrases. "Notting Hill," she said. "Nothing like as cool as it used to be; the movie put an end to that." And, "Rural France: of course, most of it is dead." She segued from fringe theaters—"The Gate's where it's at"—to the possessive tendencies of her ex-boyfriend—"If he can't track me down, Todd rings up my friends to ask where I am."

I looked up from my book. "This Todd sounds a bit controlling," I said.

She laughed, rotating a bare shoulder. "To be fair, we were very close. It all got a bit too much. I needed my space. I mean I'm not saying it's over forever; I just want to try something different. Have a bit of an adventure. You know?"

I returned to my book, as the conversation drifted in and out; hotels she'd like to stay in, houses she dreamed about buying. I wondered if Sean was finding it hard to get a grip—the endless pointless opinions: the best shows on Netflix; her favorite ski runs; where she'd live if she could live anywhere.

"Ellie's natural home is the outskirts of some Indian slum," Sean said. "A fleabag hotel with no Wi-Fi."

I glanced up from the page. "I like a simple life," I said.

"That's because you don't have a choice. Unlike Lulu, who has a proper job—not something you could ever manage."

"I could manage a proper job."

He laughed loudly, looking at Lulu to include her. "As if," he said.

I felt a flash of anger. "I could stick at a job. If I wanted to, I mean."

He stopped laughing. "You can't even cook."

"I can," I said. "Don't forget Nonna's pasta."

"You don't have the resilience," he said. "You wouldn't last a week."

I wanted to punch him. "I would."

Lulu was smiling, looking from him to me and back. "Children, children," she said.

Sean moved on then, to the holiday requirements at his firm, how everyone has to take a hefty chunk, so if they've been up to anything dodgy it'll come to light. "So, with two weeks at my disposal, I fancy sailing over to Corsica, chartering a yacht." His eyes met mine. "Picture this: the blue sea lapping against the boat, the sail flapping in the breeze, dolphins playing in our wake. Imagine how quiet it would be at night, what amazing places you could discover."

Picture this. Imagine that. He was drawing me back to him, reminding me we were a team.

He dipped his finger in his wine and flicked it at me. "But little sis here is refusing to play ball."

"Yeah, like that would really work," I said, closing my book. "Me on my own with you for a fortnight on some tiny two-berth junket. We'd come to blows after the first day."

Lulu leaned back on her elbows and lifted her face to the sun. "Oh my God, Corsica. I can't think of anything nicer. Not gonna lie, I'm gonna kill myself stuck in some house in the hills cooking all day."

Neither of us said anything, let her words rest. I found myself again wishing I could feel what it was like to be her, to have people depend on you, for your transactions to be so normal. Sean was wrong. I *could* manage a proper job. I'd never had the chance, that's all.

Lulu finished the wine and Sean produced a large spliff that I suspected he'd found ready-rolled on the boat. She held it close to the end between her thumb and forefinger, and sucked in with a tight slit of her lips. When she passed it to me, I pretended to inhale.

After a while, she said, "I mean, God, would it kill the stupid bitch to do her own food?"

Later we piloted slowly out of the bay, a breeze ruffling the sunshade, into choppier water, around another dip in the headland, and into the island's sun-baked port— an arc of pretty pink buildings with blue shutters, a few palm trees, a couple of cafés. Sun sparkled. Light glinted. Sean steered for a prominent position at the end of the first pontoon. When Lulu leaped out to deal with the ropes, he shouted instructions, and she shouted back—as testy with each other as any boating couple. I packed our things away in the hold under the back cushions. It was brimming with the real owner's possessions: more fluffy towels, plastic bottles of water, sun lotion, and several pairs of flip-flops, including small ones for children. The sight of them made me feel tight across the chest, like when you've swallowed something too cold. I felt another sort of yearning then, the kind I never know what to do with.

We sat outside a café. You could see the white ramparts of the posh hotel on the headland from there, and the two of them wondered how much it would cost to spend the night. Lulu circled back to the yacht a little while later. "How many does it sleep, the boat you want to charter?" Casual, just making conversation.

"Just two." Sean wrinkled his nose.

"Too small," I said, addressing him. "As I keep telling you."

She was rubbing the calluses on the inside of her palm. "So, you couldn't squeeze in one more?"

Sean was clicking his fingers to get the waiter's attention. "Not unless we paid for a larger boat."

"And how much more would that be?"

"Too much." I rested my foot on the bar of her chair.

"I'll google it." She picked up her phone, then put it back down as the waiter arrived. "No signal."

Sean looked at me—a slight lift of his eyebrows to say that was lucky.

After the waiter had taken our order—three *grands crèmes*—he asked us flirtatiously if we were sisters. Lulu said: "No!" and made a face to suggest she was offended.

Sean had taken a plastic lighter out of the pocket of his shorts and was flicking the tiny metal wheel, shaking it and trying again, failing to get it to work. Nothing to burn, just keeping his fingers busy. It was a tell with him; suggestive of tension.

In front of us, two small boys were leaning down from the harbor wall, poking at the water with sticks.

Lulu kept her eyes on them for a bit and then clasped her hands together, taking a deep breath in.

And then, looking at Sean from under her eyelashes, in a rush: "What if I ditched this job. Frankly, I could make the same money with a single corporate city dinner. I've had such a busy year, one thing after another. My friend Pippa said to me the other day, she said, 'Lulu, you're a workaholic. You never take a break.' Well, how about for once, I put myself first? I know a bigger boat would be more expensive, but I mean, I don't know, what if I, like, contributed? I've never been to Corsica and it would be a laugh, wouldn't it? I mean, Ellie, you'd come, wouldn't you, if there was a third person to break up the fights? Promise I'd take your side. Come on, let's go. Let's do it."

I said, "I'm not sure . . ."

Sean said, "You're a sweetheart, but it'd be pricey. There are hidden expenses—insurance, diesel, berthing fees . . . I haven't really costed it, but—it'll be into the thousands. Maybe five? Ten? God, you're lovely." He gazed at her, as if struck by her beauty, inner and outer. "Would you really come?"

"Yes. And I can afford it." She looked from Sean to me and back again, face alight. "So, shall we?"

I shrugged, raised my arms in surrender. "It looks like I'm outnumbered."

"Right. That's sorted. I'm telling her now." She pulled her phone from her bag and mumbled to herself as she typed. "So sorry to let you down at such short notice, something's come up . . . unavoidable . . . personal reasons . . . best wishes, no, kind regards, Lulu. There. Sent."

She threw her hands in the air, vertical above her head, as if she were at the top of a roller coaster, preparing for the drop. "Fuck," she cried, so loudly the woman at the next table turned to look. "I can't believe I actually just did that." She lowered her voice. "Feels so good."

Sean was laughing. "You're insane."

Chapter Five

Lulu stood next to Sean at the controls as we bounced back across the sound. He put his arm out to save her when we cut sharply into a wave, and after that she leaned into him, her arm across his back, hand tucked into the waistband of his shorts.

Clouds had gathered from nowhere and, when the sun went behind them, the sea was iron gray, flecked with white horses. Sean seemed to be steering more erratically than before. I felt nauseous with each sudden heave. He was pleased, but to me the play felt curdled, overworked. I began to imagine the voyage to Corsica and felt Lulu's disappointment at the loss of it, her sense of our betrayal, as sharply as if it were my own.

Close to shore, a large dark vessel with a tall boxy cabin came up from behind and whooshed alongside us, keeping just outside our wake. Men in uniform. Coast guards.

I straightened, feeling the color rush into my face. I expected Sean to slow, to rear away, but he tipped the prow toward them and raised one hand in a grand, confident salute.

And after a minute, they slalomed ahead of us and away.

I looked at him, shoulders back, the wind whipping under his T-shirt. This was what he wanted. The danger, the glamour. Lulu in her bikini wrapped all over him. I felt a blast of admiration, followed by a trickle of sickening self-hatred. *This.* Other people's lives. Never my own. I thought about the way Lulu worked at the calluses on her hand, her self-conscious fingering of the joint. I wondered whether her references to wild parties and her sweeping assertions about the world came not from arrogance but a desire to seem interesting, to hold our attention. She was just an out-of-work actor, a cook, making her way, trying to make the most of life. Maybe, when she realized we had gone off with her money, her parents would reimburse her. But still, she didn't deserve it.

I thought again about Jamie Nicholls and his wandering hands, the way this time Sean had encouraged his attentions, and I thought with a sudden urgency that maybe it was time to turn my back on this. On him.

Sean slowed when we came close to port, pushed the throttle up and purred in, hugging the channel. The marina was divided into areas, demarcated by size, and Lulu offered suggestions, pointing at spaces next to speedboats the size of ours, but he ignored her advice. Jaw rigid, he turned sharply to the left, motoring slowly down to the farthest point before finding a gap tucked between two large yachts. He nosed the boat in and cut the engine. It was immediately quiet, just the clatter of wires from the sleeping yachts, the gentle creak of a resting boom. He'd chosen well. Tucked in here, between the high fiberglass walls of its neighbors, it would be a while before the boat was found.

It was late afternoon now, but still hot and airless out of the wind. Sean secured ropes and tidied, using a towel to clean the deck, and the controls and the surfaces—wiping away water, salt, fingerprints.

I piled up most of our stuff on the dock—the used towels and the bagged-up remains of the picnic—and got dressed, hitching on my backpack, ready to leave. I looked at Lulu. She was still sprawled on the cushions at the back of the boat. The open harbor was behind her and she was holding her phone up, pouting. The light was translucent. The water clunked against the hull.

"Come on," Sean said. "Stir your stumps."

"Yeah, just a minute," she said.

"It's getting late. I'll go to the charter office before it closes and see if I can get a quote on a 45-footer."

"Lulu and I'll go back to the hotel while you're doing that," I said. "Coming?"

"Yeah, coming," she said, still not moving.

Sean was standing with one foot on the side, poised to leap off. "I might need to leave a deposit."

Her head was bent over her phone. She didn't look up. "I'll give you my card."

"If they've got the right size of yacht available, that is. We might not be in luck."

She didn't answer, still looking down at her phone, frowning now, puzzled.

"That's odd." She looked up. "Carrie just texted, says she doesn't know who you are."

Heat collected in my chest, a tight pressure. Sean was gripping on to the frame that held the sun canopy. His hand slid down the metal pole.

"Hah! There you go, Johnny." I managed a laugh. "You're not as memorable as you like to think."

"It's Will, her brother, you knew from school, wasn't it?" She shook her head. "She must have gotten it wrong." She started typing. "I mean, you were at her party."

Sean stepped down toward her just as I stepped forward. We collided, and he swore. I put my hand on his shoulder and turned him to face me. I could feel his biceps flex as he balled and unballed his hands. What I'd said in the hotel room was right. You can't segue a short into a long like that. Using a convincer from Facebook: it was too flimsy, it had no depth. More important, it could only ever be temporary. Thirty-six hours and counting. This impasse had been inevitable from the beginning. And he knew it.

"Out of the way, Ali," he said.

Ali. He was losing it.

"Let me take a picture of you together," I said. "Go on, John. Go and sit next to Lulu."

I pushed him down onto the back seat. "Come on," I said. "Put your arms around each other. Smile."

I held out my hand for her phone and, distracted, she handed it to me. She was scratching the palm of one hand. "I don't understand—she didn't recognize you in the picture I sent."

I held up the phone, but it was locked. "Lulu. What's your passcode?"

"Um. 170289," she said vaguely. "My birthday."

I thumbed the numbers in. "Smile," I said again. "Johnny?"

This was the moment for his charm. Change the angle. The story. Dance. Sean. *Dance.*

"Hurry up, Ali," he said.

Lulu's eyes were drilling into him. "Were you at Marlborough with Carrie's brother or not?"

"I'm amazed at your memory," I said. "My school days seem *so* long ago. Come on. Lie back. Look like you've just had the best day ever, which, let's face it, we have."

She slid her elbows back into a stiff semi-recline. Her face began to organize itself into a smile, but her eyes remained detached from the process. "You said you were part of the reunion gang—you ski together every year, you said. Why did you just call her Ali?"

What was wrong with him? His forehead was furrowed, his mouth a tiny bit open, saliva stretching at one corner. He was staring past her, eyes focused on the hull of the boat alongside. All he needed to do was delay. Throw his arms around her, make a joke. Kiss her for fuck's sake. Ten minutes, that's all it would take to get us out of here.

The lines running down from his mouth were pronounced; his stubble and his eyebrows tinged with gray. His features were usually alive, active, moving. Motionless, he looked stupid. *Old.*

I thought in the moment he was feeling humiliated. Now, when I think back, I realize I was wrong. He was planning his next move.

Lulu pushed to stand up, but his feet had tangled with hers and she toppled back immediately. "Were you actually at Marlborough?" she said, holding her arms protectively across her chest. "Were you even in Val d'Isère?"

"Does it matter?" I extended my hand to pull her up. "Come on. Let's go and shower and then get a drink."

And then finally his lips broke open. "Lulu," he said, with full contrition. "I'm sorry. I feel dreadful."

"What?" She let out a noise, a bit like a laugh, but more baffled than that; vocal cords that didn't know what to do with themselves.

He looked up at her from under his lashes, pushed his hands together in prayer, a sheepish schoolboy.

"You're right. I didn't. I wasn't. I saw you yesterday at the beach. I liked the look of you. I found an excuse to start talking, that's all it was."

She pulled her chin back, looking down at him. "But . . ." Her mouth was curved like she was smiling, only she wasn't. "But you knew my name."

"It was on your luggage label."

"You knew all that stuff about me."

Her hand lifted to her hair, but then froze there, and dropped. She looked over at me. I tried to smile. A sour taste rose in my throat.

"What about you? Ali or Ellie, or whatever you're called? Are you even his sister?"

A long silence. "This is too creepy." She slanted her eyes sideways and raised her palms, as if stopping traffic—signaling to an invisible witness a disdainful repugnance: *Who are these people?* "I mean, are you two, like, together?" She stood up, mouth tight, and took a step toward the edge of the boat, one foot raised to climb up onto the pontoon.

Sean reached out his hand to grab her elbow. She turned, tried to yank it away. He held tight, and her face clenched as she summoned all her strength to pull again, but as she did so, he must have let go because something went wrong and she lost her balance. Her right foot was already raised, and with the force of that she seemed to topple, quite slowly at first and then more quickly. I didn't hear a crack, but with a hiss of breath, she tumbled and then at the last minute sort of sank to the floor. One minute she was standing, the next she was lying there crumpled, twisted, one arm back, the other under her body, her legs skewed out at an angle.

It hadn't been a loud bang. The boat didn't vibrate; the water didn't slap against the side. I waited for her to get up, to swear at us, but she just lay there on her side, motionless. Her eyes were half shut, glazed: her neck lolled.

I let out a cry and leaped forward. Sean pushed me back.

"Did she hit her head? Is she hurt?" I said. "Oh my God. Is it bad? What shall we do? Is she unconscious? Don't move her. Keep her still. I'll ring for help." I was still holding her phone. "What the fuck—999. What is it in France? Is she all right? Lulu. Are you OK? We need an ambulance. What's her passcode again?" I was shouting at the top of my voice now. "HELP!"

"Shut the fuck up," he said. He put his hand out either to grab me or to reach for the phone, but I pulled away. "It's too late," he said.

I'd seen death up close before, and in that case one minute a body was working and then the next it wasn't, all those complicated processes that sustain life, the pumping and the diffusion, the firing of neurons, just stopped. People talk about the split second between life and death. But it didn't make sense here.

"What do you mean it's too late?"

"She's not breathing, Ali."

"She is. I saw her. Her chest moved. She just needs an ambulance."

"It's too late, Ali."

"It's not." I was trying to get past him, but he was crouched over her, holding me away with his spare hand. I managed to kick him, hard into the flesh just below his waist, and he twisted to grab my foot. I lost my balance and fell into the side of the boat. I lay there, winded. "I saw her breathe," I said. "I saw her chest move."

He bent forward, put his ear down to her mouth, and stayed there for a long minute.

"Yes. OK. Maybe," he said.

I sat up. "Maybe?" My heart was hammering. "What do you mean, maybe? Is she breathing or isn't she?"

"You're right. I can hear something." He sounded drained.

"You can? She is breathing. She's alive." I could hardly get the words out. "Put the towel under her head. Keep her still." I fumbled again for the phone, my hands shaking so much I could hardly hold it. "I'll ring for an ambulance. Or I'll run for help."

"You can't get help." He sounded calm now. "How will we explain this?" He waved his arm to encompass the boat. "And anyway, it's over. She's on to us. It's very simple what we have to do." His voice was low and steady. "Go back to the hotel, wait for me there, order room service as we'd planned. I'll sort Lulu." He stopped talking for a moment while he slotted his arms underneath her body, cradling her like a child.

"Don't touch her," I said. "You mustn't move her."

But it was too late. He'd lifted her up and was gently laying her across the back cushions. It was the gentleness that lulled me.

"I'll do everything," he said. "You don't have to worry. Go on." He flapped his hand, telling me to go. The towel was scrunched on the floor and he smoothed it and then folded it neatly into quarters, making a thick wedge of it. "I'll sort it."

He had his back to me, and my view was obscured. For a second, I thought he was still going to use the towel to cushion her head, and I wished I had suggested not this wet salty one but a clean one from the locker. I had time to remember that the locker was under where she was lying so it would be hard to get to, and to think it didn't matter, that this one was damp but still soft, before I realized what he was really doing: that he had laid it over her face and had put his forearm across it and was bearing down his weight. And it was only then that I realized what he had meant by the words he had just said.

What happened next is a blur. I remember the impact, and the slipping and pulling and choking and biting, my fingernails gouging his chest; his hands reaching for my neck, the scuffle of elbows and knees, hips, nose. I kicked and bit, scratched. But he was bigger than me and stronger. He pinned me on the floor of the boat, one hand around my neck, while with the other he pushed down on the towel. I couldn't have saved her, but I fought as if I could. I kicked out, trying to reach him. Even now, with everything that has happened since, it's important to me to remember that. He let out a guttural groan and turned, his eyes glittering. I thought it was my turn next, but he grabbed me by both arms and threw me roughly onto the jetty. "Go back to the hotel room," he said, chucking out my backpack. "Wait there."

He turned the ignition. At the back of the boat her body was motionless, her head under the towel. I struggled to my feet and tried to get back in. But the gap between the jetty and the boat widened. I toppled forward, and back, and screamed: "I'm going to the police."

And he laughed. "But, Ali," he said over his shoulder. "You were here. You're involved. You did it too."

I shouted his name, screamed at him to come back until the boat was out of sight, until my throat was sore. It was over; did he hear me? He was a monster. I was *gone*. I collapsed then. I was sick—violently, into the oily space the boat had vacated. I raked my fingers along the pontoon until splinters were buried under my nails. Blood in my mouth, I lay there with my face pressed into the wood, willing myself to push myself headfirst into the water, for oblivion.

Time passed. I don't know how much. Nothing happened, no one came. Eventually, I pulled myself up and, after a few more minutes, dragged myself along the jetty. A garbage can stood at the end, and I threw in the towels and the bag of leftover picnic, pressing them down deep. And, somehow, I kept going, like an injured dog limping home, up some steps and across a patch of grass, to the main promenade. I carried on between the cafés and the children's carousel and the stalls selling candied pecans and waffles, my ears buzzing with white noise, to the outer edge of the town, and past the shops and bars and the sailing club around the headland to Sainte-Cécile. I was aware of Sean behind me in the boat, and ahead of me in the hotel, and being incapable of thinking beyond those two images. I remember trying to work out what time it was; morning, evening, night? The light was pastel, either way, the umbrellas on the graying beach scrolled. The brasserie on the corner was playing its suppertime jazz playlist. Two bare-chested men carrying paddleboards came toward me, feet encrusted with sand, and behind them strolled a middle-aged couple dressed for dinner. And I was aware that when the woman looked at me, even though the air was warm, she pulled her pashmina more tightly around herself.

At the entrance to La Belle Vue, another wave of nausea bent me double, and I retched violently in the gap between a pot of red geraniums and the wall, though all that was left was bile. I wiped my mouth and my face with my sleeve and pushed open the door of the hotel.

I was halfway across the foyer, my hand out for the back door, when a voice said: "*Mademoiselle?*"

I stopped and turned slowly around.

The dark-haired man at the desk got partly to his feet, legs still bent, his body craning forward. "Mademoiselle Fletcher Davies, many apologies, but the plumber has not been free today, and *le robinet*, the tap, in your room he was unable to be fixed."

I put my hand out to touch the wall and pressed against it with my palm. I looked down at the floor and noticed my feet were bare, that I had smeared dirt and what looked like blood on the tiled floor.

"But a deluxe room has become available and we will happily move your luggage if you would like to upgrade—with no extra cost, of course." He was holding out a key card and, after a moment, not knowing what else to do, I took two steps toward him and took it.

"Would you like us to move your luggage?"

"No. It's OK." I swallowed to clear the obstruction in my throat.

"The deluxe room is on the same floor as your room, the first floor, with a sea view. Number 47."

"Thank you."

Why wasn't I wearing shoes?

He was watching me, and when I didn't move, he said, "It's a lovely room."

I walked in the direction of the stairs. There was a fire door blocking me, and I stood in front of it for a moment, bewildered, and then forced myself to turn. "Could you let me into my old room?" I said to him. "I left the card inside."

He gave a small bow. "Yes, of course."

He fiddled at the desk for a bit, collecting what he needed, and then he lifted a section of the counter, and came out. He was slight and very slim, with darts on the side of his pressed shirt. He waited for me to pass through the fire door to the stairs and then climbed behind me up the first flight. At the top, the corridor ran in both directions. Panicked again, I bent to rub my bare foot. "Sorry," I said. "I appear to have made a bit of a mess. I'll get some paper and clear it up."

He was ahead of me now, showing the way, and had turned right along the corridor. He stopped three doors in, pushed the card into the slot, turned the handle, and then stepped back. With a small bow, he said, "You are sure you do not need any help with your luggage?"

"No. I'm fine. Thank you."

I got past him and closed the door.

Chapter Six

The bed was made—the sheet pulled tight; on the floor was an open suitcase, spilling clothes. On top of the chest of drawers lay the plastic protective strip from the crotch of new swimwear.

My legs gave out and I was down on the floor, my backpack squeezed against the wall. I could hear a noise, a sort of whimpering, and I realized it was coming from me. I put my hand over my mouth to stifle it.

I couldn't breathe. Someone had tied bands around my solar plexus. I could take tiny breaths only. I wanted to sob, hard, but there wasn't the space. I needed the toilet, and I untangled the backpack and made it to the bathroom. Nothing came out, though I felt a sharpness, a pressure in my bladder. I sat with my head between my legs, my eyes closed.

What had happened? For a moment, my mind was blank, numb, a nothingness, and then images: the white bulge of Sean's knuckles as he gripped the towel; Lulu's limp body. I began to retch again then, but there was nothing left to bring up. Dry heaves.

I got to the basin and drank from the tap, the water slopping across my neck. In the mirror, my face was gray; the pupils dilated. I looked half dead. Except I wasn't dead. Lulu was dead. But that didn't make sense. She couldn't be. It was a mistake. A joke. Roughly, I rubbed off the eyeliner with my fingers and then washed my hands, squeezing the soap over and over again until it slipped from my grasp. I reeled back into the bedroom. Here were all her things. Her clothes. The charger dangling empty from the socket. The mascara wand on the bedside table, loose from its tube. All this stuff couldn't still be here, and her *not*.

My back pocket vibrated. I put my hand in and her phone rested like something alien in my palm. Messages on the screen as if nothing had happened. "Todd," asking for the name of her hotel, and a Send Failure. Her message canceling the catering job hadn't gone through. At the island where she'd written it, she hadn't had a signal. But she did now. She'd have to send it again. The screen flashed—Low Battery—and I picked up the charger hanging from the socket and plugged it in. She was always on her phone; she'd need a full charge, I thought, when she got back.

I'd turned off the tap in the bathroom, but it was drip, drip, dripping.

I began packing then, putting everything into her

suitcase—dresses and shorts, bikinis, sarongs, under-wear, cashmere shawls, the tank top and the white trousers she'd worn the day before, still inside out, knickers attached. Shoes—heels, flip-flops, a single pair of trainers. From the sink, I grabbed her tooth-brush, the tube of toothpaste, a bottle of self-tanning lotion. In the bedside table I found earplugs, an iPad, a silk mask, her passport.

I was working fast, keeping my hands busy. It was a compulsion to clear the space, to get everything she owned in one place, neat, ready. I didn't stop to think. I just kept going. When everything was packed, I sat on the edge of the bed and looked around. Apart from the suitcase sitting in the middle of the floor, the room was empty. It was as if she'd never been there. For a micro-second, my breathing eased. I felt calm, as if I'd done it for her, and then it rose up in me, like a silent howl, the horror of it.

I was fucking mad.

Lulu didn't need her stuff. She didn't need her phone. She wasn't moving rooms.

She was dead. I'd seen it happen. He'd said I was involved. But I *wasn't*. There was blood on my feet, but it was mine. It wasn't hers.

He'd killed her.

I slunk sideways onto the bed, hit my head against the wall. I wanted oblivion. But I couldn't escape my own mind. I wanted to scream—I opened my mouth, but nothing came out.

More images: metal hitting wood, the pull of the anchor, the tug of the rope, the blurred whiteness of her body as she disappeared beneath. The images were inside me. I *was* them.

He'd killed her. I said it over and over to myself.

He'd killed her. And he'd enjoyed it. The hatred that coiled inside him; I'd known it was there. The excitement in his eyes whenever there was a confrontation—in Morocco, and then the other day, here in France, when he left to discuss the "Picasso" payment with the bar owner, Dutroix. His anger with any man who came on to me when it wasn't in his plan; the whiteness of his knuckles as he got them by the neck. Being told what to wear, being locked in my room, his hand on my wrist when I'd told him I wanted to go out on my own. The constant fear. The violence had just been waiting to be unleashed.

He'd killed her, and in a minute he'd be back.

I stood, hooked my backpack over one shoulder, grabbed Lulu's phone from the wall, and picked up the suitcase. I pushed the door with my elbow and got into the corridor. A sound ahead. Footsteps on the stairs. A voice saying, "*Attends.*" I froze. Was I already too late? I turned to duck back into the room, but the door had closed behind me. I didn't have the key. I panicked, sank for a second against the wall, and then remembered the room opposite, the upgrade. I felt in my pocket and there it was, miraculously—the key card. I pushed it into the slot in the door of room 47, and turned the handle. The lock released and, pushing the suitcase ahead of me, I fell in. The door snapped shut behind me. The room was the same size as the one I'd just left, but the window took up one wall, a great expanse of space and light that did something to your nerve endings.

I crossed to look out. The sun was hovering above the headland. On the horizon, low thin clouds were streaked with pink and violet, but the sea still flickered with light. I could see the tables and chairs outside the brasserie on the corner; the concrete blocks that narrowed the road just ahead. People drinking, talking. A woman's voice shrieking: "*Mais non!*" Music spiraled, a motorbike backfired; on the beach a tractor was raking the sand into serried lines. Outside the horror of my own head. Normal life.

It was like a jolt, a physical shock.

It sprung not from low down in my stomach, though my muscles there clenched, but from higher up, from a point behind my rib cage, and spread along my arms and up into my throat.

I could escape not just Sean, but this *life*. I could tell the police everything, and then I could go home. Lulu's death would have some meaning. I could begin again, visit Molly, get a job, find a place. I could be something, *someone* different. I could *change*.

I rummaged in the backpack for my phone. My head had cleared. The police. I had to turn him in. Why couldn't I find my phone? Where was it? What number would I even ring? I threw the backpack aside. I'd go downstairs and find a *gendarmerie*, or ask at the desk. I'd tell them everything: that we'd gone out on the boat and we'd pretended to be people we weren't and she'd found out. And then I'd tell them what had happened next. And they would believe me. He was wrong. I *hadn't* done it. It was *him*.

But then that burst of clarity and elation dispersed, replaced by doubts and questions. Why hadn't I already raised the alarm? Would they think it suspicious that I hadn't? I'd made my way back here, spoken to the receptionist, packed up her stuff. When I'd been in trouble in India, Sean had slipped the cops a bribe, he'd spun them a story. And he'd do the same here. He was more confident than me when it came to authority. He'd throw me in it. And I *was* guilty. I'd been there all day. I'd been part of it. I hadn't killed her, and yet I had approached her at Raoul's. I'd made up the cookery school. I'd stolen her hair clip. And I had a history, a record—those anger issues in my file— and Sean could manipulate people we'd conned to use as evidence against me.

I began to pace the room, trying to think straight. If I could just wait until I was back in the UK, see Molly, get her to help me, and Karen, the social worker who'd always been on my side. And Steven, Molly's husband, he worked for the police—in IT, but he had connections. We'd had our problems, but he *knew* me. He would tell them I wasn't capable of murder.

But how to get there, how to get home, without Sean finding me first?

My passport was in the safe, and I couldn't get to it, but I had Lulu's passport and . . . of course, I had the *money*.

I looked at the backpack, in the middle of the carpet where I'd thrown it.

The money.

Another complication.

How gleeful I'd been the previous evening at my own sleight of hand, slipping the money from the box to the bag, right under Sean's nose. A caper. Cat and mouse. Cops and robbers. Child's play.

I thought again about the look on his face when he'd killed Lulu.

Thirty thousand euros. Would he let me get away with that?

I crossed back to the window, peered down. He could be here any minute. I could feel my heart begin to race. He didn't know I was up here in room 47, but I couldn't stay here forever.

He would take his time. He would ask for me at every hotel—charm the waiters, the concierges. He would take my picture to the railway station, the bus station, the airport. He would get in touch with contacts he knew in other towns, people who hung around transport hubs, widen the net. He might report me missing, have the police search too. There was no escape. He was too connected. He had tentacles everywhere.

I needed to lie low for a bit, throw him off the scent. Where could I go? Where could I hide that he wouldn't find me? Where could I disappear right now and be safe while I made future plans? There had to be *somewhere*. Where was the last place on earth he would think to look?

Lulu's suitcase sat on the floor at my feet. I'd zipped it up in a hurry and a piece of white silk was poking out at the top—a dress, it looked like, or maybe a slip. How delicate her clothes were, how soft they must feel against the skin.

An idea began to form.

I took her phone out of my back pocket, keyed in her code, and looked again at her messages, and then at her unread emails.

It didn't take long to find what I needed.

Rebecca at becksotty2@hotmail.com was looking forward to seeing Lulu at the Domaine du Colombier on Saturday. She and the girls were getting a taxi from the airport and would be arriving at 4-ish so there was no need to worry about lunch. "Or only something light to keep us going till supper. Can't wait. *Gros bisous*, as they say in France. Rebecca x."

I picked the backpack up off the floor and laid it on the bed. l looked more calmly for my phone and this time I found it. It had been in the outside pocket. I had three missed calls from Sean. My finger hovered for a moment, and then I pressed the off button. I removed the SIM card and went into the bathroom to flush it down the toilet. The phone itself I put in the wastebasket.

I splashed my face with water and took a long drink from the tap. Rising, I wiped my mouth with the palm of my hand. Then I stared at myself in the mirror, long and hard.

I looked so like her.

Chapter Seven

I was busy on the internet until the early hours, scouring websites, maps, social media. People walked up and down the corridor, and once I thought I heard the rattling of a handle as if someone was trying to get in. I crouched behind my door, just in case. But after a bit I heard the steps move away.

I lay down for a while, but when I closed my eyes, I remembered the way Lulu had laughed when I'd said "Nonna's Kitchen" and how her top slipped off her shoulder when she flirted with Sean, and how I thought she'd noticed me take her hair clip and yet hadn't said anything. I felt a pressure on my chest, an unendurably heavy weight.

At 6 a.m., I showered. I washed my hair and dried it with the towel. I brushed my teeth with toothpaste on a finger. My shorts and T-shirt were filthy and I had to open her suitcase to find something to wear. I didn't want to. Putting on something of hers felt unbearably intimate, but I didn't have another option. I found a dress still with its price tag, which meant at least she had never worn it. Though she'd chosen it, bought it: that was bad enough. It had tiny mirrors across the front, the sort of thing you'd find in a market in Jaipur, but the label read "EGGNOG, Shoreditch." Her trainers were a size too big, so I stuffed the toes with toilet paper. I found a hat, too, a floppy one that would cover my face.

After that I took the SIM card out of her phone, tucked it inside the book about the Sudanese sisters, and went around the room, checking that I'd left nothing behind, wiping down everything I had touched, including the strings that operate the curtains.

At 7:05 a.m., I pulled the chair to the window and kept watch.

It was 9:37 a.m. when he emerged—an hour earlier than I'd guessed. No lie-in today, then. He was angrier, or more determined, than I'd hoped. I watched him through the gauze, my heart thumping. He was wearing dark gray chinos and a white polo; trustworthy, semiofficial clothes. He rubbed his chin a couple of times—he'd just shaved—tipped his sunglasses from his head to his nose, and turned left, away from the port, in the direction of Raoul's. He was as predictable as any of his marks: croissant and a coffee before he began his inquiries.

I was quickly out then and along the corridor, bumping the suitcase to the bend in the stairs, lowering it the last bit gingerly, step by step. No sound, or movement below, so I continued, slowly, as quietly as I could, to the bottom and hauled it the short distance—five steps at most—until I was this side of the fire door. Through the crisscross of wires in the reinforced glass, I had a view of the entrance and the street. It would take less than a minute to go through one door and out the next. I was hoping reception would be empty. But the neat blond receptionist was sitting behind the desk.

I pulled back, thinking fast. My instinct had been to do a runner, but maybe, actually, it was better this way: no risk of the hotel getting in touch with the police. The fewer alarms at this point, the better.

The receptionist eyed my suitcase as I approached, and with a polite smile asked in perfect English if everything had been all right. I wondered if she looked guarded. Or maybe my own expression had unnerved her. I tried to smile.

I told her everything couldn't have been better. I gave my name and she referred to the computer. "No extras?" she said, eyes on the screen. I shook my head, waiting. I tried to breathe. When you pay in cash, it sometimes alerts suspicion. I didn't want to have to hang around while a manager was called.

She typed for a moment, and then looked up at me. I tried to swallow, but my mouth was too dry.

"Well, you're already all paid up."

"Oh, really?" I laughed lightly.

"Yes, all paid in advance, through booking.com."

"Of course." I nodded. "I'm an idiot. Sorry."

"Do you need a taxi?"

"No." I gripped the suitcase handle. "I'm fine. The walk will do me good."

"You moving on somewhere nice?"

"The Eurostar," I said. "London."

I bent forward and drummed my fingers on the desk. The more you engage a person's senses, the more likely they are to remember you. A message for Sean, for when he asked.

"I'm going home."

Sainte-Cécile was busy; people heading away from the center with heavy bags. Market day. I walked as fast as I could, but I adjusted my gait, pushing my shoulders forward and forcing my legs to take more of a sway. It's important, that. A person's walk is the most immediately distinguishable thing about them. The face you might not recognize until you're up close; the gait you can identify from two hundred yards.

I'd pinpointed a phone shop in advance and I stopped in to buy a pay-as-you-go. I put Lulu's iPad in the trash can outside. The bus station was a few minutes away, on a main road at the back of town—less of a station, more of a stand. A couple of women were hunched on the bench under the Plexiglas shelter, heavy bags of shopping slumped between their legs.

I bought my ticket from the kiosk and stood behind

a pillar at the far end. It was airless, the sun beating on the plastic. I felt hot, my face and armpits damp. My hairline was sweaty under the band of the hat. I should have stopped for a bottle of water, but it was too late now. I couldn't risk breaking cover.

I'd left it as tight as I could, but the coach was five minutes late—five agonizing minutes out in the open—before finally it rolled into the bus stop, heaving to a halt with a noisy sigh. The driver opened the hold for my suitcase, and I climbed the steps.

The bus smelled musty, of old sweat and clothes with cigarette smoke on them. I kept my eyes low and headed past several empty seats, to a row in the middle. It was a trade-off—I could disembark more quickly from the front, but I was less visible here. I told myself to calm down. He couldn't be on the bus. He was still having his precious coffee. And yet I sensed a prickling across my back, was aware of the shortness of my breath, that my hands were trembling.

The engine restarted with a loud diesel clatter, the air filled with vibration, and we rocked into motion. Sainte-Cécile unscrolled past the window—a couple of roundabouts, a supermarket, a parking lot, a long avenue disappearing to the right, dotted with palm trees; glimpses, at the end, of the sea. The bus picked up pace, settling to a noisy cruise, as we drove west for several miles along a divided highway, between industrial parks and open scrubby countryside. We stopped at a mainline station and a few people got off and on. I sunk deeper into the seat, but the only newcomers were two middle-aged Brits, the man in a linen suit, clutching a copy of the *Fodor Guide to Southwest France*. After that, we headed north for forty minutes or so, eventually crossing a river that had carved a deep passage through a ravine—wide and dark and surprisingly full, considering the season. I had a feeling the town we stopped in was famous, that maybe it gave its name to the region, like the Dordogne or the Loire. Maybe not. Geography had never been my strong point. It was Mol who'd loved all that. Capital cities and mountain ranges. The Ormorods had a puzzle of world flags, and she spent hours doing it. I wish now I'd sat down and done it with her. Maybe they'd have kept us together if I had.

It was another half hour to Pugot, where I knew to get off. The bus negotiated a long square, a strip of stubby plane trees and wrought-iron benches, before rattling to a halt at the far end. Most of the shops were closed. One corner of the quadrangle was taken up by a garish Mickey Mouse–themed children's merry-go-round, but it was closed up and had the tragic abandoned air of all abandoned fairground rides.

According to Rome2rio, I had a fifteen-minute wait until my connection, which gave me time to buy something from the bakery-café opposite. I wheeled the bag, bumping it over the high curb and under the trees and across the dry red earth and down again to the road. Two mop-haired men in cap-sleeved T-shirts and baggy jeans were drinking coffee outside the café. Inside, I asked for a large bottle of water—choosing the brand with the widest mouth, which would save me time later—and a ham and cheese baguette.

The total came to four euros something and I held out a fifty-euro note I'd taken from the packet.

The boy with spiky hair and eyeliner behind the counter looked at me, rolling his eyes: *Really?*

"OK, sorry," I said. "How about I also have some of those little sugared choux buns? Five. No, ten." As he counted them out, I asked him a series of questions: Is it always this hot? Is it a family business? How long have you worked here? Didn't really matter what.

As I've said, my French isn't bad. It's quick-fire distraction that matters when you're "Change Raising." Conversational French is all you need to bewilder the victim's synapses, to deflect attention from the fact I'd replaced the fifty-euro note in my hand with a ten.

He took the ten-euro note without looking and handed me the change for fifty.

"*Bon appétit,*" he said, as I left.

I was starving and I'd gnawed the baguette to pieces

before I was even back at the stop. I drank deeply and then tipped some water over the back of my neck. I opened the paper bag and stared at the choux buns, and then I closed it again and stuffed them in the trash can next to me.

Very little traffic. No one else waiting. Even here in the shade, the afternoon had a liquid, dreamy feel. Small beige pigeons pecked in the gutter. I looked at the time on my new phone and then up and down the square, and then back to the phone. The fifteen minutes had passed. It was almost 4 p.m. In the email Rebecca Otty had sent the night before, she'd mentioned a light snack. I should get some food in. And then there would be supper. Lulu might have planned to have gotten there earlier. There had been a bus at 7 a.m., so maybe she had intended to get that one. Or had she been going to rent a car?

And still: no bus. It was quarter past now, half an hour later than the app had promised. I couldn't wait here indefinitely. I'd seen a sign for a station, but I wasn't sure a train went anywhere near Saint-Étienne, and even walking to the station seemed a task. Lulu's suitcase was restrictively huge. I eyed it, wondering whether to set off without it, leave it behind. No, that would be mad. It had clothes and toiletries, and even if I didn't want them, they were the sorts of things I'd be expected to arrive with.

I was standing by a row of redbrick houses, windows shuttered. The pavement was narrow and in shade at least. No one else was waiting. No one else in sight in this corner of the square, though opposite, the two men were still sitting outside the bakery. I left the case where it was, and crossed back.

Yes, they did know the bus I needed and it did run on a Friday—only it left from the street one down toward the river. No, there wasn't another bus that day and they didn't think Patrice, the local taxi guy, was working. He had gone to visit his sister in Toulouse who was pregnant. The older guy, called Antoine, shook his head. Carole's bloke, he was bad news. He'd had several run-ins with him himself. The more Patrice supported her, the better. He shook his finger. "You be careful. There are a lot of bastards out there."

That conjecture led on to more general observations about the state of the world, but eventually Antoine, tucking his hair behind his ears, asked where in particular I was headed and when I said Saint-Étienne, he stuck out his lower lip and gestured to his companion: Pascal, there you go. He's heading there soon.

Pascal was fondling a hefty vape and he brought it to his mouth and inhaled deeply. The puff of white vapor curling from his mouth smelled of caramel.

He shrugged, got to his feet, and the two men embraced fondly. Then the two of us crossed the square again to collect the suitcase, and I followed him along the narrow pavement that left the square at that end.

We reached a patch of wasteland where a few cars were parked and he headed for a scratched white hatchback with a large dent on one side. He threw the case in the boot, and then, clearing the passenger seat of rope and wrappers and an old towel, opened the door for me to get in.

We didn't speak at first. I think I was too busy adjusting to the smell. The caramel from his vape overlaid more savory odors—dog and cheese, and something vegetal like a rotting onion. I know *not* getting into cars with strangers is basic common sense, but I'd picked up enough clues. He had tried to wheel the suitcase for me, and in the exchange about Carole, Patrice's sister, he and Antoine had both seemed concerned about her safety. So basically: decent.

He reversed out of the space and then drove with one hand while, with the other, reached across to rummage in the glove compartment. First cassette: discarded. Second: thrown with contempt to the floor. Third, found satisfactory, he slotted it in. Elton John.

Very "retro," I told him, hoping retro in French had the same positive meaning as in English. I meant the cassette, but it applied equally to the music. He was nodding along to the track—"I'm Still Standing"—and he nodded more vigorously in reply.

We turned left and right and went straight on, mainly downhill, and then he pulled into a small parking lot outside a supermarket, a Casino. He had a message to give someone, he said, but he'd be back in an instant. He set off for the entrance and I waited for a few minutes before, and realizing it was an opportunity I shouldn't pass up, I followed.

I went around quickly, collecting what I needed: bread, salad greens, a package of frozen croissants, a tube of mayonnaise, a jar of mustard, two ready-cooked chickens. I saw Pascal at the back of the shop talking to a man in white overalls. He didn't notice me.

At the checkout, I loaded my provisions in a shallow box that still bore the indentations of the cans it had held. I used the money I'd conned out of the café owner to pay; at least I was keeping it in local circulation.

Pascal had left the car unlocked, but it was too hot to get in so I waited outside. Through the window I could see his phone attached to the portable charger. I stared at it for a while, tempted, and then averted my eyes, training them on the entrance to the supermarket. I'd tell him when he came out to be more careful.

Saint-Étienne was small and compact. It had a center with a church, a Casino, and a *boulangerie*, and a concrete square given over to parking. I had given Pascal the name of the house, Domaine du Colombier, and he seemed to know it, because he drove through the village, out the other end along an avenue lined

89

with trees, turned left into a single-land road, crossed a small humpbacked bridge, and climbed up a hill. Sunflowers in long lines bowed their heads in fields on either side. It reminded me of another puzzle Mol had found—of a painting, though the field in that was filled with poppies. I asked Pascal if the sunflowers were looking down because it was late in the afternoon, whether they raised their faces to the sun at midday, and he gave me a curious look. "No, they are over. Dead," he said. We lapsed into silence after that.

He turned off onto a dirt road, bumped along it for a little while, and then uphill, the road narrowing to a small ribbon between a field on one side and trees on the other. He stopped the car just before some ornate gates, edged by a pair of tall pointed green-black evergreens. We were on a slight incline, the ground on the other side dropping down to a stagnant pond and what looked like a cowshed. I got out. Cicadas hissed.

Pascal had taken out the suitcase and the box of shopping and my backpack and stacked it all at the side of the road. "So, I will be seeing you," he said, giving me a vigorous thumbs-up. He got back into the car.

Through the bars, I could see strips of house—pieces of cream, mauve, dark red. The deep blue of the sky reared above me. I felt suddenly hot, the stitching on the dress scratchy at the bodice, as if the heat had been collecting all day and was at its most intense at this particular moment. I had the old familiar feeling of arriving at a new place, a rising of hope with an urge to destroy it before everything went wrong.

As the little white car puttered away from me up the road, I had to stop myself from running after it.

Chapter Eight

The house beyond the iron gates was long and low, with small windows, the upper ones jostling against an ancient tiled roof. It was both bigger and more cottagey than it had looked on the rental company's webpage, grander but more dilapidated. It appeared to be deserted. The pale blue shutters on the house were closed, and fig leaves as crumpled as old men's hands covered the drive. I thought it was silent, though of course it wasn't. Pretty soon, I'd learn to distinguish between background sounds—the staccato spitting of a distant sprinkler merging with the ticking of the cicadas, the low hum of the pool motor separate from the humming of bees. Within twenty-four hours I'd trained my ears to other noises, too—the crunch of footsteps on gravel, the slap of a sandal on stone—and to discover the spots in the house and grounds where voices carried, even whispers.

For now, though, thinking myself alone, I crossed the driveway in search of the key, which the email had "reminded" me was inside the terra-cotta pot to the right of the front door. I was scrabbling, face in a plant that was blue and long and fluttery, when a voice came out of nowhere.

"LULU!"

I took a sudden, sharp breath. Felt the earth tilt as I stood up. *What was I doing?*

"I thought I heard a car. *There* you are. Thank God. I was about to send out the dogs."

A short blond woman had emerged, scowling, from the left-hand side of the house, wearing an elaborately upholstered swimsuit. As she got closer, I realized she wasn't scowling but wincing; the tiny agony of sharp stones on bare feet. "I've been *beside* myself," she said when she reached me. "I thought you were getting here *hours* ago. Where have you been? I've rung you a million times." She was speaking very fast and gave the impression of barely contained energy and emotion.

"I'm so sorry," I said.

"I thought you'd disappeared off the face of the earth." She made a rictus with her mouth. "And then where would I have been? A houseful of guests and you dead in a ditch."

Her face was still contorted, half smile, half grimace.

"I mean, First World problems I realize, but you know . . . it is . . ."

She dropped her arms and caved her body inward, humble and simperingly grateful.

"... it is my *holiday*."

Her toenails were the same neon pink as Lulu's. Her swimsuit was stiff and unfaded—brand-new. It was covered in hundreds of tiny white anchors. I pulled myself together. "Of course it is." I smiled understandingly.

She straightened. "Is everything all right? I mean, did you break down? Where've you parked?"

"I'm sorry. I've just had a ridiculous journey. No car. I . . . took a taxi."

"Oh." She sighed, making another collapsing shape, and then pulled herself back up. "Oh well. We can add you to our insurance." She frowned again, baffled. "But where's your luggage?"

"It's just out there." I pointed beyond the gate.

"OK. Well, you've been to the house before, of course, so you know where to dump yourself. You're in the *pigeonnier*. We're down at the pool. You can meet my girls on your way past."

She flashed her teeth then, her lips pulling back in a smile. Her eyes were a lovely denim blue and she was wearing matching blue eyeliner and mascara. She'd been pretty when she was young; a slip of a thing in that wedding photo she had posted on Facebook in honor of their recent anniversary. The way she had done her hair—scooping up the front bits and securing them at the top with a barrette—some of the women on the retiree circuit had done that, too; pushing their hair into a bouffant above the forehead as an attempt to harness their lost youth.

"House is open by the way, if there is any kitchen stuff you want to dump. Oh." She clasped her hands to her heart, raised her eyes to the heavens, and, in relief, but also continued reprimand, said: "Thank God you're *finally* here."

She wobbled back around the side of the building, this time with audible *ow*s. I watched her go. I knew she had a cat—a photogenic black Bengal called Arthur—and that she had worked in publishing until she had her first child. I knew she was in a book group, and a walking group; that she worried about her weight, and Southwark Council's arbitrary planning laws, and maybe also—she'd run a 5k to raise money— the plight of Syrian refugees. I had seen inside her house. I knew what her kitchen cupboards looked like, the paint color in the living room, her outside furniture. What did she know about me? In some situations, a mark's vulnerability comes from their insecurity; in others it's their confidence—their certainty in their own immunity. It hadn't occurred to Rebecca Otty that I was anything other than the chef she was expecting.

I crunched back across the gravel and through the iron gate to the road to get my backpack and the suitcase and the box of food. It took two trips, and then finally I was standing outside the front door. I'd faltered, while I'd been in front of her, thought I might run. Staying, it turned out, was only a few movements, a matter of putting one foot in front of the other.

I took a deep breath, filling my nostrils with the warm scent of sage and fig and rosemary, and pushed the door open.

I'd loved the little "shop" in Marrakech; it came into my head the moment I walked into the Domaine du Colombier. The hallway had the same sudden cool, the same smell of ancient wood, the same darkness, as if it were protected by a shroud from the light, like sinking under water. First thing I saw: a large deep-carved oak chest, displaying a round glass lamp and a rough pottery bowl containing lemons. I knew that trick: someone had been "curating" here too.

I stood for a minute, getting used to the sensation of my body inhabiting the space. Houses tell you how to behave. I don't remember much about the flat where we lived with Joy, but the Ormorods' bungalow in Hastings had a thick cream rug that made you feel you had to be careful where you trod, like you were the dirtiest thing the house had ever seen. Fairlight House, where all the surfaces were wiped down, and half the chairs already broken, you stopped even thinking of as "home." It was just floors and walls; somewhere to kick stuff around, to try and find space to be alone.

I wasn't sure what to feel here. The house seemed suspended, like it was holding its breath. There were stairs ahead of me, and an open door to the living room, and to the left a narrow corridor, which I took, pushing open a door at the far end into a large, light kitchen. Terra-cotta tiled floor, blue and white tiles on the walls, copper pans hanging from hooks over the stove, an industrially deep white sink. Coffee machine, kettle, toaster. A vast silver mixer. One shelf displayed a ridiculous quantity of baskets. The room was clean and bare—except someone had left a used tea bag on the side and there was a red-brown stain leaking from it across the counter to the floor. Beyond the island stood a large table and chairs; open doors led onto a terrace, where I could see another table, terra-cotta pots; a lawn dotted with bushes and fruit trees, falling downhill toward more buildings.

I left the box of groceries on the counter and walked through a door on the right into a small study area—cramped and dark, low wooden beams, a threadbare rug—and out into the lounge. Here in the gloom, I could make out a squishy dark gray settee and two upright armchairs arranged around an enormous open fire, the brickwork blackened with soot. I unhooked the latch on the double doors, pulled them in, and then unclipped the shutters on the other side and pushed them back. The light that flooded in was lazy, warm. The picture on the wall was of a village with a hill behind it. Tiny insects were inside the glass, squashed against the mount. Poor doomed things. They must have crawled in and got stuck.

From here, I walked back through another door

directly into the hall. A passage in the opposite direction from the kitchen ended in a space for a washing machine, various stacks of towels, and some bossy notices. ("Navy towels are for the pool. On no account should the white towels leave the house.") Another door opened into a separate bathroom where a curating person had gone to a lot of trouble—pretty pictures, fancy soap, a basket for the toilet paper—to try to distract from a strong smell of urine.

In the hall I glanced up the stairs again—but decided not to push my luck. I went back outside to the front, the heat of the afternoon hitting after the coolness of the house. I shouldered my backpack and picked up the suitcase and lugged it around the side in the direction Rebecca had taken. The gravel made way in the shadow of the house to scrappy grass. The kitchen terrace was behind me, and ahead was a lawn on which blocks of shadow were advancing. In the distance, beyond some fruit trees, was a hedge with a gate in it; a glimpse of gleaming water, with, on either side, an assortment of creamy-colored stone structures—one of which had to be the *pigeonnier*.

I wheeled the suitcase down until I reached the gate. I paused. The pool beyond was in a long courtyard. Wide steps disappeared into glimmering turquoise water, giant pots filled with rosemary, a great stretch of pink stone with pale wooden beds for sunbathing.

Mother and daughters were squashed under another hedge in the last triangle of sun at the far end. Rebecca rested her book in her lap when she saw me, shielding her eyes from the low rays. "Ah, Lulu," she said. "You found us. Come and say hello."

I opened the gate and walked toward them. The two girls were lying on their fronts, arms dangling over the sides of the loungers, like people drowning. I knew very little about them; their social media privacy settings were frustratingly high. One was dark and one was fair; that was my first impression—like in a Ladybird book about two princesses.

Slowly they both turned their heads.

"Hi," the fair one said in a friendly but sleepy voice. Closer, I could see she wasn't fair at all but blue-gray. That old-lady dye that was in fashion. She hadn't yet opened her eyes, the lids coated in thick black eyeliner.

The dark one twisted all the way around and leaned back on her elbows. She had a short bob with heavy bangs and was wearing an old-fashioned satiny red swimsuit—draped around the bust like a dress for a 1950s prom. "You came," she said, patting one palm on her chest and pretending to breathe out heavily. "Thank the Lord." She pressed her hands together in prayer.

"Oh, for goodness' sake, Martha," her mother said. "I wasn't that anxious." ("Martha, 17": listed in Rebecca's first email.)

"Are you joking?" The other daughter pushed herself up. ("Iris, 15.") She was wearing a green bikini, the top asymmetrical with a single strap. "You've been stressing all afternoon."

"She's here now," Rebecca said. "That's all that matters." She spoke slowly, to underline her composure, and gave me an even-tempered smile—the display of placidity more for their benefit, I was sure, than mine. Not that either of them seemed to notice. Iris was inspecting the diamond in her navel, while Martha was still looking at me.

"Nice smock," she said. Her expression was considering, curious; already prepared to be disappointed.

"Oh, thanks. It's from . . ." I plucked at the fabric, trying to visualize the label. "Eggnog, I think."

"Oh, Eggnog!" She stretched her arms above her head, reminding me of a cat. They both did in a way; Martha angular and sleek; Iris something more feral. "To be fair, I found an Eggnog dress on Depop recently, but the girl was asking too much."

"I love Depop. Do you sell as well as buy?"

"Yeah, actually I mainly sell."

"Martha's quite the entrepreneur," Rebecca interjected. "Mind you, it's always muggins here who ends up going to the post office."

I rolled my eyes in solidarity, but then quickly, turning back to Martha, said: "I think that's so great. It's basically recycling. All this upselling is so much better for the planet."

"Yeah. I guess," she said. "I mean, I hope."

"There's a lovely vintage shop in one of the local towns," I said. (There had to be, surely.) "I'll take you one day."

"Oh goody," Rebecca said. "A girlie trip."

"Fuck's sake, Mother," Iris said. "Stop saying 'girlie.' It's demeaning."

Rebecca looked at me and raised her eyebrows. "Apparently, I must at all times refer to myself as woman." She spoke slowly as if explaining rules that were both tyrannical and imbecilic. She turned back to her younger daughter. "Or would you prefer old hag?"

I smiled sympathetically. The dynamic between them was interesting: close, but combative. Useful.

"Well, I'd better dump my stuff," I said.

Rebecca swung her feet to the ground and was putting her things—lotion, sunglasses, a Saturday supplement—into a giant pink tasselled beach bag.

"Same as last year," she said, nodding at a building, some sort of converted outhouse on the righthand side of the pool. "You should feel at home."

"Yes." I smiled, and set off toward it, wheeling the suitcase behind me.

I pushed open the door. Inside, the air smelled musty and sweet like moldy oranges. There were various pool contraptions—a gigantic sieve on a stick, a vacuum-like gadget with a hose, and a sad bundle of deflated pool floats. It wasn't a bedroom—even one intended for staff. I was already rehearsing my exit for the audience at the pool when I saw the narrow flight of steps rising steeply from the corner. I stuck with it and climbed them.

The stairs ended in a square room, with a low domed

ceiling and a small shuttered window. It was baking, this close to the roof, the air brittle, like straw. I could make out a double bed, clothed in a mosquito net, with a painting of some grapes above it, a chest of drawers alongside. A chandelier dangled from the ceiling, the fitting loose so you could see the wires disappearing like innards. Something above my head was rustling. Pigeons? Mice? To the right was a small shower room, separated by a bead-string divider.

I dropped the backpack and sank onto the bed, suddenly overwhelmed. Here I was. I'd made it. I'd gotten this far. I'd managed the journey unscathed. I'd survived the first encounter with my employer. No one downstairs as yet doubted I was Lulu. I should have felt relieved. But now the thought of dragging her suitcase up, touching her things again, *being* her—the intimacy and sadness of it—seemed more than I could cope with.

I closed my eyes and pushed Molly to the front of my mind. I pictured her and Steve sitting in the garden, in their tracksuit pants, under their bright, neat hanging baskets, their Jack Russells at their feet. They'd be drinking gin and tonic from a can. Saturday night treat. Or maybe Steve was in the kitchen, cooking his specialty Thai curry, treating her like a queen.

The longing to hear her voice was overpowering.

I heard the scrape of Rebecca's sunbed then, and the soft thud of her bare feet right beneath me, the rattle of the gate. She said something about unpacking. I moved to the window and pushed the shutters apart. It was quiet for a few minutes, and then the girls began to talk.

"Are you going to tell her?" Martha's voice.

"No."

"I mean, I thought you said you'd wait until we were here."

"I can't."

"I'm not being funny, but she'll find out, Iris. You know she will. It's better if you tell her first."

"Genuinely, she'll kill me."

Martha said something else too low for me to hear, and then springs creaked as someone shifted position, the pool hummed. A splash as one of the girls jumped in.

I waited, but there was no further conversation. Alert now and focusing, I got on with what needed doing. Scanning the room for hiding places, I took down the painting above the bed. The frame was old and wooden and I managed to secure the passport to the back of it, using the existing nails and a stray length of string. I made sure when I hung it back up that I aligned the edges with the scuff marks on the wall. I slipped Lulu's phone between the mattress and the bedframe.

Then I unwrapped the plastic package containing the money. I looked at the wads—each one a half-inch stack of fifty-euro notes secured with a paper band. So this was 30,000 euros. I counted the wads—twelve in all, including the one I'd broken into. I picked up an untouched packet and flicked through, counting each note. There were 100 notes in each wad, which I decided just about made sense. I took a couple more notes from the packet I'd already opened. I probably wouldn't need them, but it would be good to have them accessible. I unscrewed the lid of the water bottle I had bought earlier. The mouth was just wide enough to fit a packet through, if I rolled it up tightly. I began to stuff the wads into the bottle.

Wait.

I paused.

If there were 100 fifty-euro notes in each of these packets, that meant each of them contained . . . 5,000 euros. And there were twelve of them. So . . .

This wasn't 30,000 euros. This was 60,000 euros.

It didn't make sense. Where had that extra 30,000 euros come from? Sean kept most of our money in a bank account. The safe contained the earnings from the Picasso. Nicholls had given us 60,000 euros, half of that was due to the barman, Dutroix, and Sean had met with him when I was ill. I mean, there had been that argument, but Sean had said it was sorted. Had he never given him the money? Unless the guy hadn't showed, and Sean had kept it from me, or pulled some sort of fast one. Either way, *shit*.

Sean might have let me get away with 30,000. But 60,000? Sixty thousand, of which he possibly owed 30,000?

I undid the laces of Lulu's trainers and pulled them off. My feet were relieved to be free. My head was throbbing. I was unbelievably tired. I swung my legs up onto the bed and rested my head against the wall. I was wrong to have come, but it was too late now. In a minute, I'd put the rest of the money in the bottle and hide it in the toilet tank. Closing my eyes, I remembered a café in a bookshop in a shopping center I used to go to when I was fourteen, when things were getting out of control. A place within a place within a place. It was a bit the same here. I was in a room at the top of an outbuilding on the grounds of another building.

Sixty thousand euros. I couldn't hide forever. I'd known that since I was a kid. They always find you in the end.

Chapter Nine

The air was warm and dense as I walked up to the house, the edges of the sky a pale coral. I could smell fig. Cicadas ticked, and the sprinkler on the far side of the garden was spitting. From the bushes as I passed, a gray bird exploded.

In the kitchen next to the kettle I found a file with a sticker across it—"House Bible"—and flicked through the pages until I found the Wi-Fi password. I put it into my new phone, and left the file by the door to remind myself to take it back down with me. Then I got on with supper. The chickens were still more or less warm and I tipped them out of their plastic onto a large plate. I shook the mixed greens out of their plastic bag into a salad bowl, chopped the bread into chunks and arranged them in one of the many baskets. Finally, I squeezed all the mayonnaise out of its tube into a rame-kin, added a dollop of mustard, and ground in some pepper. You pick up a lot of tips sitting close to a bar.

I had laid the table on the terrace for three, but when Rebecca came down she insisted I add an extra place. She had changed into a long white kaftan with ribbons bunching up the shoulders. She had curled her hair, and her lips were pink and glossy. "Oh, *please* join us," she pleaded, fetching a bottle of wine from the fridge. "Go on. Phil's just rung to say the traffic's terrible and he won't be here until *much* later. We'll be lonely on our own."

I was laying out the glasses, and I paused to give one a little polish with a linen cloth. "Your husband doesn't like flying?"

"He'll fly for work. If he has to." She sat down at the table. "It's just when we come to France, he prefers driving. He takes it slow, stops in a couple of hotels on the way down. He likes to have a bit of time on his own after the office. He does work terribly hard."

I asked politely what he did then, although I already knew (editorial director for a major publisher). She was telling me in more detail—how he'd started at an academic imprint, and in fact how it was she, Rebecca, who'd interviewed him when he wanted to join the company—when Martha came onto the terrace.

"I mean, basically, Dad took Mum's career," she said. She looked almost sculpted in a high-necked gold blouse and tight black shorts, her thighs smooth and brown, her ankles slim. She had changed her part to the side and scooped her bangs across her forehead, so the effect was softer, less severe, and from her earlobes dangled long black earrings that looked vintage.

"She sacrificed it for us," Iris said from the doorway. She was wearing a peach corset above tracksuit bottoms and a visible G-string.

Martha brought her palms together as if in a prayer of gratitude. "We are duly obligated."

"Very funny, you two. Martha, get Lulu a plate. Sit. Sit. Sit."

I wished I'd changed then. Or at least showered. The white bits in Lulu's mirrored dress were grimy. I knew I had sweat patches under my arms. It was dark now, and yet the air was still warm as bathwater. I'd lit the candles in the glass lanterns and the light seemed to sink into their cheeks and hair and bare skin, making them glow.

I passed the food around to sighs of satisfaction. Rebecca was particularly thrilled with the salad. ("I'm a rabbit; I'm quite lost without my greens.") When she poured me a glass of wine, I pretended to sip from it. (Drinkers like you to drink with them. They feel judged if you don't.)

"*Santé*," she added, raising her glass. "Here's to a lovely relaxing holiday."

I raised mine, too, meeting her eyes, and then quietly put it down.

"It might not be so relaxing for Lulu," Iris said. "She is here to work. Maybe think before you speak?"

Rebecca had picked up a chicken wing and was

tearing at the skin with her teeth. "Lulu doesn't mind. And anyway . . ." She placed the chicken bone at the side of her plate and gave the tips of her fingers a quick lick. "Cooking isn't a chore for her. It's her 'joy'; she said so in her email."

"It's true," I said, still smiling. "I'm delighted to be here."

I was starving. I'd made a sandwich with the chicken and the bread, and I took a bite. It was delicious.

"You'll find us an easygoing crowd," Rebecca carried on. "Hopefully easier than last year. Just kitchen suppers. Lasagna. The occasional nice bit of fish. That sort of thing. Not forgetting your world-famous chicken cacciatore. Oh, and Katya mentioned in her email you do a yummy seared-tuna thing?"

I nodded.

"It sounds right up my *strada*. As I said on the phone, lunches can be cold meats, salads, Ottolenghi style. And breakfast's just a matter of a quick nip to the local *boulangerie* in the village for bread and croissants. I mean, obviously you'll need to do a big shop sooner rather than later. Actually, the Leclerc at Castels is open until midday on Sunday so you can do that in the morning. You can take the Audi."

I looked up from my sandwich. "Sure."

"It's probably simplest if I give you my credit card to use when you like—we'll find a basket for receipts."

I glanced at her, trying to figure out if she was the sort of person who threw receipts into an envelope and forgot them, or the sort of person who would go through each one individually. I thought about the way her teeth had torn at the chicken wing. The former. Definitely.

I'd find another time to ask about my wages.

"The other thing is, as I think I mentioned, we're leaving for boring reasons on the Thursday, not the Saturday as originally planned. I will honor the agreement, of course, and pay you for the full two weeks. It's up to you what you do. Obviously you can bugger off, if you like, or stay until Saturday, which is when Brigitte will come and do the turn-around. Totes up to you."

"I'll let you know," I said.

"So, who's arriving when?" Martha asked. She was only picking at her food.

"Tomorrow, I think. I mean, Clare's already in France, 'decompressing' as she puts it, before slumming it with us. My little sister," she added for my benefit. "She works for Microsoft—terribly high up. God knows what she does there. Vice president of something or other. She's always trying to tell me, but I'm afraid I switch off." She let out a tinkle of a laugh, telling me the job might be important but not *so* important it was worth remembering.

"Is she on her own?" I said. "No partner?"

"For the moment," Iris said. "But Rebecca has plans."

"Of course, she's not *incomplete* as a single woman," Rebecca said. "I'm just saying she might be happier as a person—because, let's face it, she's not easy—if she had a man in her life. And I'm not saying Rob's the answer. I've never even met him. Nor has Dad actually; they've only spoken on the phone. But I can tell Phoebe, his editor, is rather smitten."

I said, "Who are we talking about?"

"Rob Curren," Martha explained. "Our father's new author."

"He wrote a fearfully successful novel," Rebecca said. "*Wall Game*. Did you read it?"

I hadn't. But I could visualize the cover. It had been by every pool a few years before. I thought Sean had read it, and he wasn't a big reader.

"The plan," Iris said, "is to set him up with Clare."

"No, it's not." Rebecca picked up the bottle of wine. This time I put a hand over my glass. She refilled hers. "All I said was, wouldn't it be nice if they did hit it off. Honestly, you two."

She looked at me again for support.

"He's coming here, too, is he?" I said. She'd mentioned "guests" in her email but no one by name.

"Yes, yes. I was going to fill you in. And we're also expecting the Lawrences."

"Will Rob hit it off with the Lawrences?" Martha asked.

"Yes, I hope Rob'll hit it off with the Lawrences," Iris added innocently.

Martha smiled and bowed her head. Some private joke.

"Layla Lawrence is my oldest friend," Rebecca told me. "We were at Edinburgh together back in the mists of time. They've got one kid—Elliot. He's fifteen. Madly in love with Iris."

"I mean, are you joking," Iris said. "Are you actually joking? You literally make these things up."

Rebecca ignored her. "Layla's very bright, terribly capable. Knows everything about everything. She has her own GP practice, and is on hundreds of committees. I love her. But her husband Roland's a complete bore."

Iris gave her mother's arm a vicious swipe.

"Oh, I don't mean it. Not really. But you do agree, don't you? He's got no conversation if it doesn't pertain to Layla or the law."

"To be fair," Martha said, "all those sniffs. And that weird gulp."

Iris said: "It's not really a gulp, it's more like he's clearing his throat, like he started doing it because he needed to, and then it became a nervous habit."

"Like Arthur overgrooming his front paws when next door's cat's been beating him up," Martha said.

"Maybe Roland is stressed? Could Layla be beating *him* up?"

"Could we buy him some of that calming hormone thing you plug in?"

"Feliway!"

The two sisters roared then, delighted with each

other. Rebecca, encouraged, leaned forward: "He's so deeply unattractive, I've always assumed he must be very good in bed! I think they have a lot of sex."

"Oh my God, Mum. Shut up," Iris said.

"I genuinely don't understand," Martha said, "why do you always go too far?"

Rebecca looked unembarrassed. I asked her whether she was anxious about hosting this Rob Curren, someone she'd never met.

"Not really," she said. "He's a writer, you know . . ." She shrugged. "He's been staying nearby with his brother, and to be honest my husband thought it was a good opportunity. He's supposed to deliver in September, but no one has seen anything, and after all the money they've chucked at him, Phil quite fancied the opportunity to crack the whip. I used to be an editor myself," she told me. "So, I know how tricky it can be when a writer has to pay back their advance. You know, their agent still expects to keep their cut. I once worked with a writer who had a massive film deal too. They had to pay back everything, ended up bankrupt!"

She began to talk about publishing rather drearily, in the manner of someone who used to be important and now isn't, the narrative less about being entertaining and more about bolstering her sense of self. Iris and Martha were vocal about having heard the stories before, and while I wanted Rebecca to feel she could talk to me, we were all tired. At the back of my mind, I had begun to plan out the following day. (The big shop.

113

The Audi. My bloody fucking yummy seared-tuna thing.) In a gap between anecdotes, I collected up the plates and carried them through to the kitchen. Rebecca asked if she could help. "No. I'm fine," I called, keen to locate the dishwasher before anyone noticed I didn't know where it was. "Don't get up." I had checked each door in turn and was on the last one when I felt her standing above me.

"The cleaner's days are Saturdays and Wednesdays, so leave stuff for her to clear up. I'm not paying her just to flap a few bedsheets. I'm sure you can sort it out between you, who does what? Actually, you know her, of course. You'll have met her when you were here last year. Presumably that worked out OK between you?"

The last door had, luckily, concealed the dishwasher, and I had started putting the plates in one by one. I managed not to break the rhythm. Brigitte: she'd met Lulu. She knew her. This was an obstacle I hadn't anticipated.

"Yes," I said. "Last year was fine."

"You're not a rinser, then?" Iris had brought in the empty salad bowl and was standing by her mother. "I could have sworn you'd be a rinser."

I sat on a damp sunbed by the pool in the dark, the courtyard illuminated only by the light from the *pigeonnier*. Motes swirled in the doorway. No, not motes. Mosquitoes.

I was just about in control. I'd looked up most of the

guests on social media. I'd found a recipe for seared tuna, and another for chicken cacciatore—and I'd discovered from the bible that Brigitte came twice a week for two hours between 11 a.m. and 1 p.m. I was safe now until Tuesday and I'd just have to make sure I was out of the way when she came. The bible also had informed me that there was a bakery and a small Casino in the village, and that the closest big supermarket was a Leclerc, eight miles away outside Castels. The weekly market, on Thursdays, had a "lovely atmosphere, though get there early as it can be super busy." There was also a vegetable patch on the other side of the house; "Help yourself! The zucchini are particularly spectacular."

I lay back and looked up at the dark sky. I thought back over the evening. The relationship between Rebecca and her daughters was interesting; it was flipped, the girls behaving as if she were the child and they were the parents. I wondered why she let them. She was spiky about Clare, resentful even, but her unquestioning admiration of the creepily perfect Layla was odd. And then there was Iris's secret; I should find out what it was. The sister in her boutique hotel. And Phil: insisting on driving down on his own, spending so long over it; it was intriguing. There was stuff going on.

Wispy clouds trailed across the moon. An owl yelped. The air felt velvety. I shivered, hating that I'd relaxed into it, that I'd let myself forget. And with that, the thoughts surged back. Had he driven the boat out to sea and thrown her body over? Had he weighed her down with the anchor or chains? My stomach clenched. He would have done everything to ensure she didn't float. But what about tides? Fishing nets? My forehead felt stretched thin, as if the membranes were under pressure. If only we'd never spotted her. If only Sean had looked away. Or if I'd said no to him, sunbathed as I'd planned, gotten the fucking Jet Ski. But I had been too scared to stand up to him, too hungry, as always, to impress. I thought about the cooking burns on her wrists, the relish with which she had eaten those prawns. I'd lied to her, asked her about Notting Hill and Val d'Isère, pretended to be *like* her. I was the one who'd noticed her first. She'd still be alive if she hadn't met *me*.

I sat up. My head was pounding, my ribs tight. I thought about all the other people we'd conned. Our first mark, Mrs. Williams, in Jaipur: she'd cried when she talked about her dead husband; redecorating the ranch had been her attempt, she said, to "move on." I thought about a woman in Barcelona, so desperate to lose weight she'd sold her wedding ring. Jamie Nicholls, the Etonian who had run off with the "Picasso"; his father had rung once when we were with him and his hand, as he picked up the phone, had trembled.

I thought about all the violence in my life that I'd hidden from. Pete, Joy's boyfriend, used to beat her up; I'd take Molly into the closet under the stairs and sing to drown out the sickening thuds. At Fairlight House, there was screaming, pulled hair, bloodied noses. The death I'd seen before: it was an overdose, a boy called Shane. His eyes rolled back into his head; saliva frothed from his mouth. The rest of us ran. I chose not to look.

I'd known all along Sean was capable of murder. There was always menace. There was always violence. It was always there, just under the surface. I had tried to leave him once before, in Marrakech. He'd worked on me, threatened me—I'd seen too much—and then he'd switched on the charm. We were a team. "How can you break us up?"

The turret of the *pigeonnier* looked forbidding against the night sky. I thought about the money sitting up there in the tank. Sixty thousand euros.

It might be this week. It might be next. But he was going to come after me. He was going to find me. Even here.

Chapter Ten

I was unconscious as soon as my head hit the pillow, sunk like a stone, but I woke with a jolt a few hours later. Lulu's death hit me again, and I lay, after that, obsessively going over her last few hours. When sleep did creep back, it was fitful, like a fever.

I reached for my phone as soon as light crept around the edges of the window. In the search field, I put, "Body found, south of France," and I forced my eyes down the list—a missing hiker in the Dolomites, a murder-suicide in a retirement village near Rouen, an elderly casualty of a flash flood. I suppose I was relieved when there was nothing about Lulu, but it didn't feel like relief. There was so much sadness.

I listened. It was quiet outside—birds cooing, a burble from the pool. I made as little noise as possible moving around the room. I checked the money and the passport, and then I got dressed. I'd washed my shorts and T-shirt the night before and they were dry.

Downstairs, I moved the pool cleaner away from the door where I'd lodged it, and quietly lowered the latch.

The house was asleep when I got up there. The French doors had been left open, and there was an empty bottle of red wine and two dirty wineglasses on the kitchen table. A single cigarette butt was squashed into a saucer. I put the cork back in the bottle and the glasses and the ashtray in the sink.

Rebecca had left a shopping list and a credit card on the counter. Sean told me always to print in small capitals, to give the minimum away. Rebecca's hand was round and sprawling, as if she had nothing to hide—never the case. I picked up the credit card and put it in my pocket.

I emptied the dishwasher and had a quick check around. There was milk in the fridge, a tub of Lurpak, as well as an unopened pot of Bonne Maman apricot jam. In a box under the sink were two reinforced plastic bags. I took one of them and the credit card and left the house. A large black 4 x 4 was parked out at the front now. Cards on the table. I can't drive. Expensive lessons aren't exactly a priority for kids in the care system. I'd gone out once or twice with Sean, so I knew the basics, but I wasn't confident. Certainly not in anything that size. For now, I'd walk.

It was downhill at first. The light was hazy, the pale blue sky wispy with clouds. I didn't like being out in the open—I was too exposed—but at least the views were good. I could see if anyone was coming for miles. The lane scooped around and, up ahead, the fields on either side were soft and rolling, bathed in gold, striped with white and black and dark green. I passed a few stop-offs, a couple of houses, and a corrugated barn structure, then crossed the river on a short humpbacked bridge, and shortly after met the main road.

After five or ten minutes there was still no sight of the village—just an endless avenue of tall, feathery trees. The sun created a sort of strobe effect and I began to feel hot and agitated. Several cars passed, going very fast, and there wasn't a sidewalk, so every few minutes I had to step down into a ditch. The stuffing in Lulu's trainers kept slipping out of place, and my ankles felt itchy and scratched from the long grass.

I had begun to worry after all this walking that the *boulangerie* might be closed, so it was a relief, when I finally reached the village, to see a queue trailing from its front door. I joined the end and leaned my head into the brick of the building. It was crumbly and warm, the smell from the open door of the shop sweetly, saltily yeasty. It was peaceful, but after a minute or two I became aware of a conversation in English just ahead of me.

A young woman with curly blond hair was talking agitatedly to a thin man with bulbous eyes. "Les Cyprès: booked. La Bastide des Mûriers: booked. Mas Michel: this year not for rent. La Maison de Verdure: booked." She was swinging a doll-like straw basket by tiny handles, and she pressed it to her chest.

"Villa du Bois?"

"Fully booked."

"Yes, of course." The man stepped off the sidewalk into the road as if removing himself from danger.

"Quentin. You *know* that." The woman sighed aggressively.

"Yes, of course I do."

"We're running out of options." She let out a frustrated growl. "God, I could kill the Lamberts. Really. Of all the years to have a kitchen fire."

I drank all this in, instinctively intrigued despite myself.

"Fuck the budget," the woman was saying. "I'd pay *anything* as long as it's halfway decent and free for the week of the wedding."

The queue began to move, and when he reached the door, the young man, with an embarrassed hunch of his shoulders, said: "There should be bread put aside? Prepaid. Name of Trevisan." The baker came out from behind the counter with a large armful of paper-wrapped bread. And then the man—Quentin Trevisan—and the young woman walked off down the road.

"They must be hungry," the old man behind me said in French. I smiled at him.

I bought six croissants, three *pains au chocolat*, two *chaussons aux pommes*, and four baguettes. A fridge by the door only sold small cartons of orange juice, the sort children take in packed lunches, and, to the amusement of the old man, I bought ten.

———

A man in a silk paisley dressing gown was sitting at the kitchen table when I got back, looking at an iPad. I had a split second to cold-read: balding but not ashamed of it—the hair around the sides cropped short; glasses on the end of a long nose, pinched at the nostrils; slightly protuberant ears; thin hairy legs crossed, the bottom heel bouncing up and down as if a song might be playing in his head.

A grille high on the wall with Eurokill written across it let out a sudden crackle.

He looked up.

"Lulu!" he said with enthusiasm. "Up and at it already. You're amazing. I'm Phil. The husband." He stood, securing the dressing gown around his lower half, and stretched his hand over the table.

Two more staccato sizzles from the machine on the wall. "Flies," he said. "Can't stand them, can you?"

I put the bag of shopping down at my feet and shook his hand. He held it for a fraction of a second longer than I'd have expected, looking at me intently. "You OK here?" he said. "Comfortable in your quarters? Everything as it should be?"

I nodded. Unattractive, but charming; a lot of his success in life, I calculated, rested on the axis between the two.

"Marvelous." He took his hand back. "Don't let the women in my family bully you. Together they're quite a force of nature." He collected the iPad and tightened the belt of his dressing gown, making to leave. "If they start teasing you, come to me and I'll have a word. Trust me, I've had years of practice. I've got your back!"

Three nights en route; it was beyond leisurely. What had he been up to?

I smiled and said of course, and that I was fine—that everyone seemed lovely, and that anyway I could look after myself; adored my job, cooking my joy, etc., etc., lucky to be here.

I opened the fridge and reached in for the butter.

"Also, for God's sake, do use the pool," he said, at the door. "*Mi casa es su casa.*"

There was another crackle from the Eurokill.

I decanted the orange juice cartons into a carafe and put the butter and jam on little plates. The coffee machine was the type with a pot and a space in the back for water. The filters were in a cupboard and I found ground coffee in a jar.

The water was still dripping through when Rebecca came down, picked up a cup, detached the pot, and helped herself. "Oops, sorry," she said, as the machine hissed in complaint. She was wearing a bikini today—orange with scalloped edges—beneath an open white kaftan, the neckline and sleeves decorated with Moroccan tufty tassels. "Lovely, this all looks," she said, wafting out to the table. "We must get fruit and yogurt for tomorrow. Remind me to put that on the list." When I put the pitcher of milk down on the table, she said, "Are you going to join us?"

At that point Phil ambled back, dressed now in open leather sandals, salmon-colored shorts, and a tight navy T-shirt with a small logo above his left breast. His hair at the sides was slicked back, and a tiny blob of shaving foam adhered to his chin. "Let the poor girl go," he said. "She's been up since dawn."

"I'm not forcing her to stay. We're having a lovely chat that's all."

"I've told her you're a gorgon and that she shouldn't take any shit from you."

I watched Rebecca arrange her face. She opted for put-upon. "See what I have to deal with?" she said. "Be a darling," she added, "and quickly grab me some hot water, will you?" She puckered her lips, as if she'd sucked on a lemon, and flicked her tongue in and out. "Tiny bit too strong for me, this coffee."

I slipped back into the kitchen and put on the kettle, listening to the two of them bickering about whether or not to wake the girls. Phil seemed to be suggesting it was Rebecca's fault they weren't already up. "The problem with your daughters, they have no discipline."

Rebecca looked relieved to see me. "Sit!" she said. "Tuck in."

I sat, reluctantly, and let her pass me a plate.

"Rebecca tells me you need the car this morning," Phil said. "For the big shop. You OK with an automatic?"

I nodded.

"And you're insured?"

I nodded again.

"Fine. Just remember to drive on the wrong side of the road."

"Phil, honestly, she knows what she's doing. She's been in France plenty of times. Lulu—you remember how to get to Castels? And I don't need to make a list, do I? You know by now what we like. All the usual lovely yummy French things."

"Of course."

"Oh, and the girls love Petits Filous—not fruit, the plain ones you can't get at home. They're by far the nicest. Your friend Olly Wilson could make a fortune if he started importing those. Total gap in the market. Oh, and if you can get some of that lovely butter in a pat with the salt on it. I adore that, don't you? Otherwise, we're in your hands. I trust you completely. Oh, darling. We're honored! You're up!'"

Martha was standing in the doorway, wearing a black slip-dress and enormous trainers, laces trailing. She'd pulled her bob back into a short ponytail and was wearing glasses. She looked pale.

"You woke me," she said. "Talking so loudly."

"Sorry!" Rebecca said, not sounding sorry at all. "Did you sleep well?"

"No, I feel a bit off. I don't know if it's something I ate."

Pulling out a chair, she dislodged her mother's resting feet and, realizing, made a disgusted face.

"I have feet, darling," Rebecca said. "I'm so sorry they offend you."

"It's the bunions." Martha shuddered, her stomach contracting as if she were going to be sick.

"For goodness' sake. Sorry for living! Never have daughters." Rebecca seemed to be angry, but also completely not angry. "Coffee, Martha?" She moved swiftly on. "Though you'll need hot water unless you want to strip the roof of your mouth off. Sorry!" She laughed, and turned to me. "You'll have realized by now I say it as it is. It's better to be honest from the beginning rather than suffer in silence for a fortnight. I know you'd hate that. Anyway, Martha, there's delicious bread, and kind Lulu has bought *chaussons aux pommes* especially for you." She smiled at her and then at me, brightly, as one might encourage small fractious children to play nice. "*Chaussons aux pommes* in the plural—is the *s* on the *chausson* or the *pomme*? Oh, Lulu, sorry, you're not the person to ask. I still can't believe you haven't picked up any French on your travels."

"I think," Phil said, "it's on the *chausson*, and it's already on the *pommes*. So both."

Martha took a pastry and put it on a plate, which she then pushed away a few inches.

"Now pass the basket to poor Lulu. She must be starving."

I put up my hand. "I'm fine."

Phil had been back on his iPad, but he looked up. "Yes, poor Lulu. We're tormenting her. You're celiac, you told us in the email? So's my assistant. It's a nightmare. Office parties: war zone! *Everything's* cooked with flour. Even a crisp could practically kill her. I hope the bakery sold something gluten-free?"

The world stood still for a second. Yesterday I'd eaten an entire sandwich in front of Rebecca and her daughters.

A fly landed on the jam and stayed there. I felt a drip of sweat move slowly between my breasts.

I got to my feet, clearing my throat. "I should get to the shop before it closes."

"Ah, yes. The key." Phil rummaged around in his shorts pocket and handed me a fob. I looked at it. I'd have to drive now.

In the kitchen, I collected the supermarket bags and picked up Rebecca's credit card. Out on the terrace it was quiet. They could be waiting until I had left to discuss the situation. *Is she a liar? Or a hypochondriac? Did she pretend to be celiac for attention? The size of that sandwich!*

Best not to have come up with an excuse. Politeness would probably prevent them from confronting me. As time passed, maybe they would forget. Or think they'd imagined it. I'd buy gluten-free bread and eat *another* sandwich as soon as I could. Overlay the memory of the last. They wouldn't make the leap from that to thinking I wasn't Lulu at all, that I was a different person. Would they?

Chapter Eleven

Phil had parked the car at a slant, facing the house, the trunk pointing toward the gate—which I opened as far as it would go, pushing it right back into the branches of the fig tree. When I was in the driver's seat, I felt high up, as if I could peer in at the bedroom windows. I'd thought it would smell black and leathery, but the odor was of cheese, sour milk, stale clothes: like a pile of coats in an under-stair cupboard. A take-out cup, with drips of dried coffee down the side, sat in the cupholder. Next to me on the passenger seat was an empty bag of Doritos.

I put my right foot on the left-hand pedal and pressed the start button. The car began to vibrate. I moved the stick back to "R" and slowly lifted my right foot. The car jolted backward. I slammed it back down. Waited a few moments. I looked at the gate opening in the rearview mirror. It seemed to be lined up. I tried again, lifting my foot more gingerly. Another jolt, but less violent.

I put the foot back down and repeated the maneuver several times until I had hiccupped a few inches toward the gate. A bit too close on the driver's side, but I seemed to be on a straight trajectory. Just. Yes. Encouraged, I realized I had made it through the gate, but the car was now slanted across the road, the trunk up against a tree on the other side, the nose very close to the gate post. I pulled the lever down to "N" to work it out.

"Wait!"

Phil was coming out of the house toward me, his forehead furrowed. Martha was following.

He was at the driver's window, head ducked to avoid the branches of the fig, gesticulating as if rolling wool at speed around his hand. The front door was yanked open. Martha was clambering into the seat behind me. "Phew! Caught you," she said.

"Caught me?" I said.

Phil was in my face. "Just in time. Hop over," he said. "I'll drive."

No getting past him. No choice but to scramble over the cup-holders into the passenger seat.

"Thank God," he said, looking over his shoulder, easing the car back a few inches and then spinning the wheel one-handed, easing it forward—the perfect angle—and out into the open road. "I need a few things."

Phil drove blithely down the lane to the main road, not slowing for the bumps. He was animated and chatty. Martha, though, turned her face to the window and stared out, apparently preoccupied. She stayed like that all the way to the outskirts of town and, when we reached the parking lot, she was first out of the car and heading across the hot tarmac to the automatic doors.

The supermarket was cold and glassy and smelled strongly of fish. We separated at the entrance. Phil insisted on taking his own cart, "flying solo" as he put it, and Martha said she wanted to look at the makeup. I was glad to be on my own. I told myself there was no logical way Sean could have tracked me here, but still as I looped around the aisles, I scanned the face of every solitary man. There weren't that many. I was in the dairy section searching for the yogurts and salty butter Rebecca had requested when at the far end, I caught sight of Phil with his back to me, gazing up at the bottles of beer. He took a step toward me, and I realized he was holding his phone to his ear. He began to move away and saw me. "Work," he mouthed.

I stared at him for a moment. He had been smiling, talking intimately. It hadn't looked like "work" to me. Then I waved, nodded, and pushed my cart in the opposite direction.

The newspapers and magazines were in a short aisle next to the stationery. I forced myself to open *Le Monde*. A murder had taken place in a beauty spot outside Paris, and the husband had already been arrested. Eight migrants had died in the Med. There was plenty of tragedy but nothing that had any bearing on Lulu.

The security guard at the door was watching me and I put the paper back and pushed my cart toward the toiletries aisle. There was no sign of Martha, and I wandered around for a bit, looking for her, until I made my way to the row of checkouts. She was standing against the far window, her arms wrapped around herself, looking unhappy.

"You all good?" I called.

"Yeah, I'm fine." She switched on a smile.

"Did you find what you wanted?"

"Yeah." She turned to look out of the window at the parking lot, and I noticed she was clutching a small paper bag under her armpit.

Phil joined me then, hunched over his cart like a kid on one of those rides they used to have in the Arndale. It was stacked with wine, piled high with various cooked and uncooked meats and cheeses, cakes, biscuits, and what looked like three types of mustard. "Have I gone overboard?" he said. "I'm sure we can make use of it all, don't you?"

"Of course."

"*Confit!*" he cried, throwing his arms out in appeal. "A woman of your many talents—you can manage that, can't you? I adore duck confit."

I agreed managing confit was something my talents could do.

Stepping outside, it was immediately scorchingly hot. Martha walked ahead to the car, still clutching the small paper bag close to herself as if trying not to draw attention to it. I wondered what was in it. It was slim. Too small for tampons. Too big for nail varnish.

The sun hammered on our heads as we packed the trunk—not just the two bags I had bought, but four more Phil had paid for, plus two boxes we found at the end of the conveyor belt. The final bill had been more than I could ever imagine anyone spending at a supermarket. I'd been worried he'd be angry when he saw the total, but if anything it seemed to have put him in an even better mood. When we'd finished loading up, he stood back to admire the results of his generosity. "Very good," he said. "Excellent work, team."

I sat in the back on the way home. Martha and her father talked about the days ahead, and Martha asked if this year he could properly switch off from work, go email free as he had promised in the past. Phil paused and then, in a little speech about family responsibilities, rather pointedly referred to Rebecca as "she," which made it feel as if he and Martha were in allegiance against her. They talked after that about the writer who was coming, about whether he would fit in. "I think Rob's house-trained," Phil said.

A small battered blue car was parked outside the gate when we got back to the Domaine. Maybe Rob had already arrived, I thought. Or Clare, the sister. Martha opened the gate and closed it behind us as we eased in. Phil cut the engine, and we both got out. He clicked the fob to release the trunk and we began to unload. Martha and Phil went ahead with the bags and I followed, carrying one of the boxes, through the front door, along the corridor, and into the kitchen. I met them in the doorway, on their way back for a second trip. Above my head, I was aware of a grinding, as if upstairs a heavy object, maybe a suitcase, was being dragged across the floor.

I began to put the food away, the fresh items into the fridge and the dry goods into a cupboard. Martha came in with more bags, followed by Iris, who was rubbing her eyes sleepily. She was still in her pajamas: a loose tank top and baggy shorts, droopy at the crotch.

She peered into the shopping. "I'm starved," she said. "I haven't even had breakfast."

"Your fault for getting up so late." Martha put down the bags. "Anyway, it'll be lunch in a minute."

"Also, darling," Phil added mildly, arriving with the last box, "those shorts, they are really quite indecent. They leave nothing to the imagination."

"What's going on upstairs?" Martha asked her sister.

"She's sorting out sleeping arrangements. Layla and Roland's bed was set up as a twin, when she thinks they'll want a double."

"*Of course* the Lawrences will want a double," Martha said.

"The Lawrences are very much double-bed people," Iris said.

"You know the Lawrences," Martha said. She was edging back toward the door, the small package clasped closely to her side. She was clearly keen to go somewhere and I wished I could follow her, see what she was up to.

Phil sat downs at the kitchen table and, picking up his iPad, began to type quickly. Above our heads, the scraping had been replaced by a creaking and the sound of shuffling. He looked up, sliding his finger across the screen to close it down. "Mum rearranging the furniture all by herself?" he said. "Gosh. Maybe you should be helping?"

"No." Iris yawned. She had found a package of madeleines and was unwrapping one from its plastic. "She rang . . . um . . . the cleaner to get her to come and help. What's her name?" She took a bite, mopped her mouth for crumbs. She dropped her wrapper into the trash can and then she moved across the room to sit down next to her father.

The sun was pouring through the window. Flies were circling.

"Brigitte," I said.

Footsteps on the stairs then, the sound of two women talking together in French. By the time they were in the corridor, I had dropped the cheese I was holding at the door to the garden.

It was too late. They were in the kitchen.

Rebecca called—"Lulu, here's Brigitte come to say hello."

A woman with black hair carrying a pile of sheets was squinting into the light.

I didn't move, but I waved from where I was, and she

lifted one hand, unsure, and then dropped it. I made my "*bonjour*" generic, high-pitched and cheerful.

"Lovely to see you again," I called across the room. For a moment I thought she would stay where she was, but she began to walk toward me, frowning but also smiling.

I couldn't think what else to do. Before she could get too close, I twisted to face Phil and put my hand up to my forehead.

"I'm really sorry," I said. "I've just started to get a migraine. I think I should probably lie down for a bit. Do you mind if I don't do lunch? I'm so sorry . . ."

Phil looked surprised and then doubtful. "Oh," he said. "Oh. OK, well . . . Yes, of course. I mean . . . I'm sure we can manage. We got that lovely celeriac rémoulade, didn't we? And the cold meats? Is that what you had planned?"

"Yes," I said, though I thought it had been what *he* had planned.

I saw him look at Brigitte, then up at his wife, and widen his eyes slightly.

I went through the doors and walked away, feeling all three of them stare after me.

Chapter Twelve

It was hot in the room. Rustling came from the rafters, a rodent of some kind; the rattle of dislodged masonry. I sat on the bed. The way Brigitte had frowned when she saw me. I had to hope the sun had been in her eyes, that I'd looked similar enough to Lulu to have gotten away with it. All I could do was wait.

Two fat gray pigeons cooed on the ledge outside the bedroom window. I clapped my hands and one of them flapped off, landing a few feet away on the roof. The other obstinately didn't move. They'd flown up here, expecting an *-ier* all to themselves, only to find me in it. A cuckoo. A pigeon. *A sitting duck.*

The minutes ticked by. My heart rate began to settle. If she'd said something, one of them would have been straight up to confront me. I felt a trickle of relief, which became more forceful.

I stood up then and went into the shower room, climbed onto the toilet seat and checked the tank; the money was still there. *Sixty thousand euros*. I dropped the bottle back with a splash, and got down. Washing my hands, I stared at myself in the mirror. I looked drawn; my eyes wild. It made me feel sick how much I looked like her. I began to rub at my features as if, if I did it hard enough, I could change them. And I thought then the wrong person had died. My life was worth less than hers. I was the one who should be lying at the bottom of the sea. It should have been me. Fuck. It *could* have been me.

I went into the bedroom and once again checked the news sites.

Still nothing.

From down below I heard the click of the gate. Phil's and Rebecca's voices. The sound of a sunbed being dragged. "Martha was obviously just not feeling hungry," Rebecca said, and Phil grunted in agreement.

"I hope she hasn't gotten a bug," she added, sounding put out. "That would really put a blight on the holiday."

"Yup."

"And what with"—she whispered or gestured perhaps in my direction—"being ill too."

A pigeon landed on the ledge outside my window again and began to coo noisily. I listened as Iris arrived, and waited in the hope she might tell them whatever it was she was keeping from them, but when the silence persisted, I went down into the sunshine. The three of them were prone. The pool gleamed. Half a dead cicada floated by the steps. I scooped it out in my cupped palms and left it in the base of a pot, under a plant.

"Are you feeling better?" Phil asked, turning his head as I passed him.

"Much," I said. "Sorry about that."

Lazily, eyes closed, he said: "No problem."

In the kitchen, they had cleared away their lunch and stacked their dishes in the dishwasher, but they'd left the butter on the table and it had melted to liquid. I put it in the fridge. The house was silent; no sign of Brigitte or Martha.

I left the kitchen along the corridor to the hall. I took a guess then and continued along to the right, to the downstairs bathroom. I switched on the light and locked the door.

The trash can was small and stainless steel, with a lid. I pushed down the pedal and peered inside. It was empty except for a small crumpled sheet of cellophane. Nothing else, but then this wasn't a good hiding place. I tried to think what I would do if I were Martha. She wouldn't take the evidence up to her room—too dangerous. There was an outside trash can, but she might not bother to go there.

I flushed the toilet in case anyone was listening, and wandered back into the kitchen. The trash can had a black push-button, but I lifted the entire lid. I was willing to put on the rubber gloves and go deep, but she hadn't put the box very far in at all, almost as if she'd wanted it to be found. No test, just the box. Clearblue, the writing in French.

I checked that it was empty, and then poked it back, farther down this time, deep under an empty milk carton, and secured the lid.

I put the kettle on then and thought for a bit. When it had boiled, I made a pot of tea, laid a tray with three cups, a pitcher of milk, and a plate of some of the Petit Beurre biscuits Phil had bought in Leclerc. I'd take it down to the pool, earn Brownie points to make up for disappearing at lunch. But before I did that, I made a separate mug of tea and carried it up the stairs. Two of the boards creaked—the third and fifth; I made a mental note.

At the top, the corridor ran in both directions, most of the doors open. Only the one opposite was firmly shut. I knocked.

Martha's voice was muffled. "What?"

"It's me," I said, turning the handle and pushing the door open. "I've brought you a cup of tea."

The room was warm and messy, and smelled of clothes and perfume. She had been lying on one of the twin beds, staring up at the ceiling, but she quickly swung her feet around when she saw me. "Oh, thanks," she said, a little uncertainly.

"I thought perhaps you weren't feeling yourself."

"Oh, no, I'm fine." Her eyes looked puffy. She'd been crying. "Too much sun maybe."

I set the mug on a low table between the two beds. It

crossed my mind to sit down on the bed opposite, but I decided against. Instead I stayed standing, and after a few seconds, she picked up the mug and clasped it to her chest. "Are the others here?"

"Not yet."

"Oh good." She looked down at the floor and then up. "Sorry, I'm not feeling very sociable."

I let my eyes rest on her for a moment. "Just stay up here," I said. "Sometimes we all need a bit of space."

She seemed to lose control of her lower lip; and she squeezed it between her finger and thumb.

"Poor Martha," I said. "What can I do?"

"Don't worry." She managed a smile. "I'll live."

After I'd left her, I took the tea tray down to the others by the pool and then retreated to my room. I lay back on the bed. No proof—no actual stick—but the evidence pointed to the test having been positive. The father: who was he? I wondered what she was going to do. Seventeen; a year older than Joy when she had me. I was used to thinking of my mother as a grown-up, angry, damaged, out of control, like some of the bully girls at school. But the way Martha had tried to control her lower lip just now: how young she was. Just a child.

My mother would be in her forties now. I'd lost touch, though I knew Molly was in contact. She was living down on the south coast, doing something with crystals. I hoped she was happy. That yearning to speak to Molly came again. If she and Steven had a baby, would she let me know? The last time we'd met things hadn't gone well. I'd found the atmosphere in their house claustrophobic. She told me I was a mess. We'd argued bitterly. I'd said things I shouldn't have. When I'd spoken to her on the phone later, she'd told me to stay away.

To distract myself, I got out my phone and looked up "Quentin Trevisan," the man outside the bakery. It didn't take long to create a profile. He was a wine dealer specializing in "rare grapes," and he was engaged to Sophia Bartlett, a content designer. The wedding was at the end of August. They had posted pictures of themselves on Facebook, tasting cakes. She had a hefty social media presence—proud of her holidays, her sporting prowess, her clubs.

I put down the phone. My head had begun to ache. It was really very hot. I closed my eyes and tried to shut everything out.

I must have fallen asleep because I was aware of my face feeling hot on one side. Noises were rising in drifts—peals of laughter, guffaws, shouts. There were new people outside, several conversations going on at once. A man was talking about his flight: the lack of overhead bin space, the bumpy landing at Marseille, the "criminal" queue at the kiosk for the car. Roland Lawrence, it must be. (LinkedIn: "Private Equity practice, PE houses and M&A, leveraged buyouts, joint ventures, equity capital markets.) "The whole car rental system is basically a scam."

"Phil—you drove the whole way!" Another female voice—with a slight accent, clipped consonants. "Did you stop en route? We love Orléans."

"No. I stopped at Le Mans."

"I mean, what a shame. Orléans is the perfect place to stop. We know a wonderful little *chambre d'hôte*. We could have given you the details."

"Oh, Phil, you should have asked the Lawrences!" Rebecca called.

"Yes, Dad." Iris's voice now. "The Lawrences always know the best *chambres d'hôtes*."

I smiled even though no one was there to see.

I went down for a swim as soon as they'd gone. The sunbeds were all at different angles, with cushions bunched. There were pages of newspaper scattered around, a glass on its side. A pair of red swimming trunks dangled from the struts of an umbrella. In the pool, an acid-green pool float rested, motionless.

The water was blood-warm and tasted slightly metallic, salty. The tiles were a blue so pale they were almost white; the grouting between them rough under your toes. I swam ten lengths and then lay on my back, listening to the hum of the filter, aware of a breeze ruffling the water, cooling the bits of my skin that were exposed to the air. The sky was still a piercing blue. An airplane crossing looked like a fish.

I closed my eyes, feeling the liquid move beneath me. My eyelids were a kaleidoscope of orange shapes. I tried to clear my mind, but images flickered, one overlaid by another. The bikini top I was wearing merging into another bikini top. The buckle at the back in the shape of an *S*. A blurred strip of white beneath the strap, the strings around her neck skewing as she fell. The silence of it. Her chest moving. The white marks his hand left on her sunburnt skin. Her body limp in his arms.

I spluttered upright, swam to the side of the pool, heaved myself out, and made blindly for the *pigeonnier*. I pushed the door open and stood in the doorway, with my hand on the wall, steadying myself. It was dark, out of the bright sun, the storeroom bulky with shadows and shapes; the air rancid. It seemed to me the smell had shifted—not rotting oranges now, but old clothes and illness, stale breath and sweat.

I felt the surface of my skin tingle—that instinctive prickling that comes when you know you are not alone.

My eyes began to adjust. In the corner, against the wall, knees pushed forward, shoulders pressed back, a figure crouched.

I could have run. But, somehow, I wasn't scared. It was anger that surged through me as I lunged for the switch. And that anger stayed lodged inside when the light came on, and I was staring at Lulu's suitcase and a pile of flaccid inflatables, a shrunken lounger with armrests, an abandoned pair of goggles.

Chapter Thirteen

I didn't want to touch any more of Lulu's things, but I couldn't go up to dinner in shorts, and the long mirrored smock was dirty. Unzipping her bag carefully, I took out a flowery dress from the top. I tried not to think about her buying it, wearing it. I tried to disassociate, to tell myself the clothes had been in the *pigeonnier* when I got here. They'd been bought for me, like the emergency shopping that used to happen when I was moved on unexpectedly as a kid and found myself in Tesco with a woman I'd never met throwing pajamas into a cart.

The kitchen was empty when I got up to the house, and I took comfort from the sounds of the others getting ready: more shouting and laughter, creaking footsteps, the occasional thump. "Phil," Rebecca yelled at one point, "where are you? For God's sake, bring me a drink!"

The recipe I'd found said the tuna would take twenty minutes to prepare and "two to three seconds" to cook.

It took much longer and was quite a lot trickier in practice, involving a lot of chopping—ginger, scallions, chiles—and some chaotic frying.

When finally I'd "seared" all the bits of tuna and roughly arranged them on a platter, I took a basket and went in search of the vegetable patch. At the front of the house, the big Audi had been joined by a shiny medium-sized Citroën. The main gate, I noticed, was slightly open and, as I walked between the cars and the fig tree, I sensed movement in the lane. I stood still to listen, picking up a quiet murmur. Two people were out there, talking quietly—whispering really. One of them took a step and I saw colors through the greenery: a flash of pink and navy, a flicker of grayish blue. I waited for a bit; I couldn't hear anything else.

A gap in the wall beyond the fig tree led into a small walled area, about the size of a small community garden. It was pleasant in there, warm and peaceful. You got the impression you were cut off from the house. Bees buzzed; insects twirled in shafts of sun. In a corner there was a small conservatory, with broken windows, a deck chair leaning against the wall. There were several beds, one apparently untended, full of thick tangled fronds and crazy leaves, another containing raspberries and tomato plants, long escaped from their canes, and the third a row of sluggy lettuces, two of which I managed to tear out. I collected a few tomatoes and a handful of raspberries and set off back toward the house, noticing as I passed that the gate to the lane was now closed.

In the kitchen, a petite blond woman, in what was definitely a grayish blue dress, was picking at the tuna. "Ah," she said. "Caught in the act." She held her hands away from herself and swept over to the sink to wash them. "So," she said over her shoulder, "you're Lulu?"

"I am." I put the basket down on the counter. She was pretty, ten or so years younger than Rebecca, but with the same piercing denim eyes, the same snub nose. "And you must be Clare?"

"Yes, the naughty little sister." She was drying her hands on a tea towel. "Though actually I always think I'm the sensible one. Becks thinks I'm out of control because I occasionally meet a man on Tinder." She rolled her eyes, as if irritated, though if that was the case it was unnecessary to have mentioned it.

I laughed companionably. "Have you tried Bumble? I've heard that's good."

She hung the tea towel over the side of the stove, and then leaned back into it. "Actually, I am also on Bumble. Are you?"

"I keep meaning to be." I wrinkled my nose. "Is it better? I mean, God, not that I'm looking for anything long term."

She crossed her arms, beginning to feel at home in my company. "Girl after my own heart."

Then she asked me where I lived. "Phil says it's somewhere near me. Where are you exactly?"

I didn't hesitate. Lulu's luggage label was immediately in my head. "Stanley Terrace, 11a."

"So which end's that? Holland Park Avenue end, or the other end?"

I took a lettuce out of the basket and then a tomato. The tilt of her head implied the answer was important. "Holland Park Avenue," I said.

"Oh, perfect."

She pushed herself away from the stove and said, "So, I've been charged with the job of rustling up some refreshments. Do we have anything stronger than wine? I was thinking I could whip up a cocktail."

I told her I thought there was only rosé, but that, if she made a list, I'd get everything tomorrow and, her head emerging from the fridge, she blew me a kiss. "You're an angel."

"I hope you're thinking mojitos," I said. "I love mojitos."

She was at the door, arms clasping a bottle and two glasses, but she let out an appreciative harrumph. "I hear ya, girl," she said in American twang. "I hear ya."

Tuna done. Salsa done. Salad in a bowl. Olive oil. Squeeze of lemon. I was putting the bread in the basket when Martha came into the kitchen. Her eyes were lined with kohl, and she was wearing a high-necked sleeveless top with a heavy gold cross around her neck, a skirt made of layered net, and lots of chunky rings, including one on her thumb in the shape of a skull.

"Hello," I said. "How are you feeling?"

"Yeah, OK," she said blandly.

"Sit. Keep me company. I'm intimidated by all these new people."

She hesitated, rubbing the skull on her thumb, but then she sat down. I didn't speak at first. I was aware she was watching me and, after a moment, she said, "So you can touch bread? It's not going to seep into your pores and kill you or anything?"

"It's only eating that's a problem. Touching is fine."

"That's lucky. In your job."

I glanced up at her. "Yup."

"Do you like being a cook?"

"Yes."

"Is it what you always wanted to be?"

"No. I wanted to be an actor. I still do. It's just life doesn't always work out the way you want it. You're going along one path and there's a . . . I don't know . . . a rockfall. But then another path presents itself, and sometimes it ends up being better."

She was looking at the table now, following a grain in the wood with her finger.

I was shaking snacks into a bowl. "What do you think *you* want to do?"

She didn't look up. "I've got one more year of A levels, and then . . ." She breathed in sharply. "I was thinking an art foundation—St. Martin's or Kingston—before doing my degree and my MA. I want to go into fashion eventually."

My degree, my MA. How easily it all came to these kids. My sister, Molly—how hard she'd had to work for a simple diploma.

"That sounds like a plan." I spoke softly, and she looked up then. Our eyes met.

Footsteps on the stairs. Voices in the lounge.

She stood up abruptly. "Mum sent me down to lay the table. So I suppose I'd better."

She pulled open a drawer and started collecting knives and forks, her rings clinking against the silver. "Is the tuna a starter?" she said. "Do we need two sets?"

"Er . . . One set will do," I said.

"Is Rob Curren here in time for supper?"

"I don't know. Maybe lay a place for him in case."

"You're wearing Granny's gold necklace!" Rebecca was standing accusingly in the doorway to the study, wearing a short orange shift dress and a pair of embroidered slingbacks with kitten heels. She bustled over to the counter and tried to reach for the chain around Martha's neck. "I told you to leave it at home. If you lose it, you'll be in big trouble."

"OK," Martha said, pulling away. "I'm not a child."

"I'm just saying be careful. It's very valuable. Solid gold. Now, Layla." Her tone changed as she turned to the woman who had followed her in. "Come and meet Lulu."

I got to my feet as the newcomer, a slim woman with shoulder-length dark hair, took a few steps toward me, her strong forearm extended. She looked at me intently as she shook my hand. My internet search had provided a list of her achievements: managing partner at Woodbridge Road Surgery, on the board of various charities, a regular runner of marathons, half and full. In person, everything about her was neat, from her short dark bob to her perfectly creased ankle-length black trousers.

Her grip as she took my hand was firm. "I know you're working fearfully hard," she said, nodding encouragingly. "But I hope you're also managing to have a lovely time?"

"I am," I said brightly. It wouldn't have done to disagree.

Still holding tightly on to my hand, she searched my face for a moment, as if *making sure,* before finally dropping it. Behind my back, I gave my wrist a surreptitious rub.

"Are we being bitten?" Rebecca said, to no one in particular. "I feel maybe we are."

"I've got a very good spray," Layla said, turning, "I get it online. It's the only one that works."

She unclipped her bag and brought out a small canister that looked pretty ordinary to me, but Rebecca took it as if it was some sort of magic potion. "You are brilliant," she said.

The kitchen was filling up now. Phil was over by the fridge, inspecting wine labels in the company of a man I assumed to be Roland, though no one actually introduced us. He was tall and stooped, with a slightly hangdog face; heavy dark brows, a large nose, small mouth. "Very good, very good," he said to something Phil had said but it sounded practiced as if he wasn't really listening. It wasn't just that he was much less attractive than his wife, for all his size, he was also much less present as if he perhaps he went through life wishing he could disappear.

He moved away from Phil toward the garden and I heard a noise, almost a sniff, almost a clearing of the throat, which I realized was his famous *gulp*.

Clare swished back into the room then, wearing a fresh layer of red lipstick. More talk broke out about the necklace. Clare hadn't realized it had gone to Martha. "First granddaughter. Mum said that before she died," Rebecca insisted. "You remember. You were there."

Clare didn't.

"Well, you got her engagement ring. And the Spode, so . . ."

"I was always going to get the Spode."

"Girls, girls," Phil said, moving away from the fridge with a bottle of wine in each hand. He stretched his arms out wide as if to coax them physically together.

He had showered and shaved since the pool, his face fresh and shiny. He had also changed, and was wearing navy shorts and a short-sleeved linen shirt. Raspberry, I think you'd call the color. Anyway, pink. Undeniably pink.

Iris arrived from the garden with a pale, etiolated boy, whom she introduced as Elliot. Blushing, he rubbed the back of his neck as if he would disappear into himself if he could, as if his very body was an embarrassment. I felt sorry for him for just existing. I mean, I wouldn't be a fifteen-year-old boy for anything.

They began to drift outside then and Rebecca corralled her guests into their seats. She took the head of the table and directed Phil to the foot as if they were presiding over a formal dinner. She mentioned to several different people how Martha had been responsible for laying it. "I've always made sure my kids do chores," she said as she passed down the tuna. "It's really important they don't take anything for granted."

When I brought out the bread and the salad, she was still going on about it.

"I want them to learn a proper work ethic, to realize how privileged their upbringing is, not to think of themselves as special, you know?"

"I understand where you're coming from," Layla said. "It's an issue I like to discuss in the parenting class I teach. Although, of course, when it comes to work ethic . . ." She tilted her head and smiled patronizingly. "Not everyone has a choice."

Rebecca looked mortified. "Yes, no, of course."

Noticing that I was hovering, she said, "You will join us, won't you?" She didn't sound particularly enthusiastic, but there was an empty chair next to her and, unable to think of an excuse, I pulled it out and sat down. The sky had darkened to a deep satin blue. Martha had lit candles, and a moth was fluttering at the edges of the umbrella. The white daisies she had put in a jar looked like stars. "This looks quite delicious," she said, beginning to eat.

"Isn't it funny how 'quite' is both an intensifier and a qualifier," Clare said.

"I hope in this case the former," I said.

"Very good," Roland said—a comment on the conversation, I think, rather than the food, though it was hard to tell with him.

I should have made more, or something else, too, because although they ate the tuna happily, it didn't take them very long.

Rebecca leaned across. "We've always got cheese," she said in a loud whisper, "if there are any holes that need filling."

"We'll always have cheese," I whispered back romantically, pressing my hand to my heart.

She laughed then, and we exchanged a look that made me feel better.

The conversation drifted about in a jolly but rather aimless fashion. They talked more about their journeys and expressed delight at "finally getting away." The British weather came under review as did the inability of *some people* (Phil, Roland) to appreciate how much work was involved in getting ready for a holiday. They talked at length about their pets. The Ottys were cat people, while the Lawrences had always had dogs, currently a cockapoo who wasn't at all food oriented, unlike labradoodles. Clare was also thinking about getting a dog—just a small one—though she realized she'd need someone to walk it.

"Oh, we have an absolutely wonderful man," said Layla. "Don't we, Roland?"

"Yes, we do."

"He picks dogs up from all over London and takes them to run around a big field in Surrey. He's very much in demand, but tell him the Lawrences put you in touch and he'll bump you to the top of his list."

"That's a good idea," Rebecca said. "If you are set on getting a dog, you should definitely use Layla's dog walker."

The Lawrence joke between the girls—it sprang, I guessed, from Rebecca's almost pathological deference to Layla. What was that about? Layla's confidence, or Rebecca's insecurity?

Martha had eaten a small plate of food, but she was still quiet. She noticed me looking in her direction and gave a small smile.

Clare was keen to engage the teenagers. "How are my lovely nieces?" she asked. "Tell me everything. Still working your little socks off at St. Agnes? Oxbridge in your sights?"

The girls looked embarrassed, but Rebecca said: "Yes, there is a lovely course at Cambridge—Natural Sciences—that would suit Iris, we think. Obviously, it's a way off."

"STEM," Clare said approvingly. "We're very keen on STEM at Microsoft."

"Now," Rebecca said, "what *is* STEM? I keep hearing about it."

"Honestly, Becks." Phil laughed, but he raised his voice in the way of a parent admonishing a child for the benefit of the people listening. "Science, Technology, Engineering, Math. How can you not know that?"

I breathed in sharply. But Clare was still focused on the youth: "I hope you're also having a bit of fun. Boyfriends? Come on . . . What about this mystery boy Martha's seeing?"

"Rebecca," Phil said, "what have you been saying?"

"Nothing. Nothing. For God's sake, I'm allowed to speculate about my own children with my own sister."

Clare moved on to drugs then—chummily, the groovy aunt getting down with the kids. Did young people still smoke marijuana, like in her day, or was it all ketamine and tramadol like she read about in the papers? Iris and Elliot stared at their plates and Martha said not really, and Rebecca, looking across at Layla, said how glad she was that neither of her girls were "remotely interested"; their heads, she added, were "far too tightly screwed on."

"Good thing, too," Phil said. "Or they'd be out on their arses. Zero tolerance *chez nous*."

"I quite agree," Layla said, clasping her hands in front of her on the table. "No drugs. It's the absolute number one rule in our house because of my brother." She didn't expand, but it explained the recent half-marathon run on behalf of DrugFab, which, according to her JustGiving page, was "a charity close to my heart."

"But, you know, we never have to worry with Elliot." She turned to her son, who slumped back in his chair. "Do we, sweetie?" She smiled tightly and then turned to address the whole table. "Sports are so important to him, his water polo and his lacrosse. We know he wouldn't do anything to compromise his commitment. Do you understand what I'm saying?"

She had a verbal tic that forced whoever she was with to actively shore up whatever it was she'd just said. I thought that if I were to spend much time in her company, I'd begin to find that, among other things, quite annoying.

"Yes. Yes." Rebecca was enthusiastic, and also earnest, in her agreement.

I got up to clear the plates and when I came back out with the cheese, the subject had changed. Clare was talking about a TV drama she'd recently watched. Based on a true story, it was about a con artist who murdered travelers in the Far East. Rebecca hadn't seen it, and didn't want to either. "I mean, isn't that exploitative?" she asked. "Using the victims' suffering and the grief of their parents—many of whom I assume are still alive—for entertainment?"

"No, not at all." Clare sounded irritated. "They did it very well."

"It was quite gripping," Layla said. "I'm sure I told

you to watch it. The guy is creepy, but so clever. You should find it on-demand."

"It's sensitively done, darling," Phil added. "They don't glamorize him."

"So you've seen it too?" Rebecca said. "When did you do that?"

There was a very tiny pause before, collecting himself, he said smoothly, "One of those many nights you went to bed early." He rolled his eyes and added, for the sake of the gallery, "One of the *many* nights." I thought then about the clandestine conversation in the lane, the man in pink and the woman in grayish blue.

"What about the girlfriend?" Layla said. "She was almost as bad as he was."

"It was very hard to have any sympathy for her," Clare agreed.

I stood up and, after collecting a few rumpled napkins, walked quietly into the kitchen. I didn't want to listen to this.

Behind me, Phil said, "Wasn't she also a victim?"

"You could argue she was an accessory to murder," Layla said. "By turning a blind eye, she colluded in his crimes."

I started on the oven. The stovetop was oily from all the frying, covered in grease and blackened sesame seeds. I scrubbed hard, my face blazing hot. I wasn't sure I could bear any more of this.

I heard Phil say: "I felt sorry for her."

"I didn't," Clare said. "I think she deserved everything she got."

I had begun to scrape scratches in the stainless steel. I threw the scourer into the sink and walked out of the kitchen, along the corridor to the hall. I opened the front door and pulled it shut behind me.

It was dark and still at the front of the house, the moonless sky navy-black, speckled with stars. I crunched across the gravel past the sleeping cars, my footsteps loud in my ears, and unhooked the gate. I felt an intense need to get away from the house, away from these people. On either side of the road were pools of even deeper shadow, the limbs of the trees stretching up into the sky, the bank on the left disappearing steeply into the unknown.

I walked fast, trying to breathe steadily and regain my composure. What would they think if they knew that, like that girl in the TV show, I had also colluded in a murderer's crimes? What would they think I deserved? Everything I got?

The surface below my feet was uneven, scattered with twigs and small jagged stones, and I stumbled a couple of times. I passed the outer walls of the vegetable patch and then a grove of vines, its rows disappearing into the darkness. The lane rose and fell and eventually petered out in a small open area of rough grass. Ahead of me hulked several pieces of farm machinery and what looked like a disused barn—two intact walls, but otherwise a pile of stones and rubble, the splintered wreckage of a roof.

Suddenly afraid, I turned to go back to the house.

And then I froze.

Was that a car? I could hear a sound in the distance, down below, but getting nearer, rising up from the valley toward me. It seemed to be going extremely slow. A cone of light from its headlights came and went above the trees as it crawled its way up the lane. Still it came, the engine growing louder. If it continued to the top, it would only be a matter of seconds, surely, before it rounded the bend and trapped me in its headlights.

The car's engine stopped. The lights died, and then, a short while after, a door slammed.

I stood still, listening intently. In the silence now, the night seemed thick with small noises. Tiny rasps. A branch rustling. A distant burst of voices, presumably from the house. And then—much closer to—a loud crackle above my head. I instinctively gasped and dropped to my haunches. An owl flew from a tree, the beat of its wings almost preternaturally loud as it curled away toward the shadows of the ruined barn.

At this point, all I wanted was to be back in the safety of my room. But I didn't want to go back the way I'd come—down the dark funnel of the narrow lane, toward that now parked and still unexplained car. Better, surely, to leave the path altogether and work my way back over the open fields and find a way into the grounds from the bottom of the garden. At least in the open fields, I could spot someone approaching and would have time to run if I needed to.

I crossed the patch of ground opposite the farm machinery. My flip-flops sucked quietly against the rough grass and the full skirt of Lulu's dress shivered as I moved. Avoiding the ruined barn, I lowered myself into a deep but mercifully dry ditch and then scrambled up the other side, my hands hauling at the grass, and pushed my way through a low, thin hedge. I was now in a wide field. Beneath my feet were rows of messy, stunted plants between heaps of earth. It was very dark, but at the distant boundary on the far right was a slope, and through a bank of tall trees, I could see lights from the Domaine.

I headed toward their orangey warmth. The ground was churned and lumpy, with great tufts of weeds, and I made my way along one edge of a deep furrow, keeping my eyes down in my effort not to slide and trip. At the far end of the field was a deep ditch, the ground knobbly with large white stones and pine cones. I clambered down and up, catching the fabric of the dress on bits of spiky grass, flip-flops slipping, using my hands to gain purchase. At the brow, in scrubby ground under the pines, was a new kind of layered blackness. But a hundred yards ahead of me was the thick garden hedge, and beyond it the soft gray turret of the *pigeonnier*.

I squeezed through the hedge at the boundary, feeling it scratch at my arms and at my legs through the skirt. Now below my feet was spongy lawn. Sounds from the house grew clearer as I approached. I heard clinks, the rumble of conversation, occasional booms of laughter, a squeal from—I think—Clare. Of course! Those signs of increased animation . . . They were almost certainly welcoming the new arrival, Rob Curren, Phil's novelist. Which would account for the car in the lane. I felt overwhelmingly relieved, and then immediately sheepish—out in the dark, all scratched and breathless, earth under my fingernails. As I crossed the last patch of black grass toward the low hedging that bordered the pool area, I took a few breaths and gave myself a talking to. This had been a doubly stupid excursion. I'd been stupid to leave the house in the night, and then stupid to take fright, giving in to pure paranoia. It was weak of me.

But it was over, and I was still safe. I could relax.

On the other side of the hedging, the pool was an inky rectangle, the furniture around it in a random, abandoned arrangement. The red swimming trunks still dangled from the struts of the umbrella.

I made my way toward my room. The cicadas had quieted down to a low rattle, but the scents were intensified. I could smell warm stone and thyme and resin. My thoughts drifted longingly to bed.

It was just a small sound at first—just a ripple. But then, very quickly, the ripple became an eruption from the water, and then, beside and below me, a shape rose up over the edge of the pool, dark and sleek and morphing.

"Fuck!" I said, staggering back as the shape grew and lengthened in front of me and turned into a man.

A broad chest with an arrowhead of dark hairs.

"Fuck!"

"Sorry!"

The man, fully standing now, held out his hands, palms open, water dripping from all of his limbs. "I'm so sorry!"

"You frightened the life out of me." My hands were clamped to my chest. It was heaving.

"Sorry! Sorry! I thought you'd seen me."

He rubbed his head. More droplets.

"Fuck," I said again.

I reached out to touch the wall, and the stone was warm beneath my hand; some dust fell, a tiny cascade.

"I was just having a quick swim. I've just arrived, and Rebecca said it was OK."

"Of course." I laughed then, in a strained way, trying to make light of it. *Fuck*.

His accent was gently northern—a slightly buried Manchester—an accent people use when they actively want to establish trust, when they want to manipulate you. I've done it myself. Not necessarily reassuring.

"I'm Rob." He put out a wet hand, and I pushed myself away from the wall and took it, feeling the moisture slide against my palm. His hand was large and cold. He was wearing baggy black trunks, with a drawstring at the waist. His physical presence was disarming.

"And you must be . . . Lulu? Whose wonderful cooking I've been hearing about."

My breathing had more or less settled now. "Yes. I am."

He was looking at me oddly. He had dimples, and his mouth turned up at the edges even when he stopped smiling. "We've met before, haven't we?"

"No. I don't think so."

We hadn't met before. If his face wasn't *un*familiar, it was because I'd looked him up online. There had been several photos, but all were variations on the same theme, moody and dark, his features semi-obscured. If *I* looked familiar to *him*, it was because I often had that effect. I reminded people of someone else. It was what Sean had considered a gift.

"I've just got one of those faces," I said.

He narrowed his eyes. "I'm sure we have." He was staring at me, not smiling. And this time I felt a cold edge of danger.

"It'll come to me," he said. "I've got a very good memory. I'll remember."

Chapter Fourteen

I slept badly, head full of dread, and I woke, early and disoriented, to the sound of a light rasping, like a washing machine early in its cycle or a cat slurping milk.

I looked down from the window to see a body in the pool—Rob Curren swimming laps. His stroke was strong, but slow, his head turning in time with his arms. When he hit the end, he let out a small spluttering groan before twisting clumsily and starting back.

I took a shower, face up to the water, letting it stream into my eyes and ears. When I emerged into the sun, Rob was out of the pool and sitting hunched forward over a laptop, large knees springing out of his faded black trunks, a white towel draped around his shoulders.

"Have you been to bed?" I said. "Or have you been standing guard all night?"

He laughed. "Just doing a bit of work." His fingers

fluttered in the air. "Literally on the last pages. Nearly done."

"Oh, good. I get the impression Phil will be relieved."

"I hope so. Now." He snapped the laptop shut and clasped his hands together with a small clap. "I think I've worked it out."

I let a beat pass. "What have you worked out?"

He grinned. "Where I've seen you before."

I crossed my arms. A swallow swept down to the surface of the pool and quickly away. I let a smile play about my lips, as if I were humoring him, and said what I should have said straightaway: "You may have seen me on the telly. I'm an actor. The Argos ad?"

"No. No. It's not that. The Argos ad, really?" He laughed. "I'm not sure I know it."

"It was a while ago."

"No. I recognize you from the beach."

"The beach?"

"Yes. Last week. On the Côte d'Azur. You must have been there too. Coincidence! I was puttering up the coast, doing a few last bits of research. And I saw you; I can't quite remember where? Nice, was it? Maybe?"

There's a trick you can do. Clench and unclench your fists quickly several times, you can divert the heat from your face, stop yourself from going red. That's the theory anyway. I kept my expression steady. Quizzical perhaps. Baffled maybe. But terrified? No, not terrified.

"I don't think so," I said, lightly amused at the thought.

He frowned. "I'm sure I recognize you. Your face . . . I've just got a sense . . ."

"No! Not me. I wish." I rolled a shoulder forward. *When? Where had he seen me?* "I'd love a little spell at the sea."

"Oh. Really?"

Out on the boat? At the café on the island? At Raoul's? At the hotel?

"As I said, a doppelgänger. Not me."

"Oh, OK." For a moment he looked doubtful, unconvinced, but then he shook his head, as if to clear it. "As you say, you must have one of those faces."

He lowered his eyes, drumming his fingers on the lid of the Mac, and then looked up again.

I decided to keep it light. "You'll be in trouble. Wrong towel."

"What?" He picked up the edge of the one around his neck and peered at it. "It was in my room."

"The white towels are for baths; the navy are for the pool."

"Where do you find the navy towels?"

"There's a pile in the downstairs cloakroom."

"Jesus fucking Christ. Can't take me anywhere. They'll send me home if I'm not careful."

I was sure Rebecca, or Brigitte, would have left a navy towel in his room. He was hamming up his hopelessness for my benefit, still distracted maybe by his insistence at having met me before. *Even if he had, he had no proof. Denial. Denial. Denial.*

"Anyway, enough of this chitchat," I said. "I'm off to the *boulangerie* to get your breakfast."

I headed past him toward the gate, but I heard the clatter of the sunbed and when I turned he was on his feet and elbowing on a large gray T-shirt.

"I'll come," he said, his head emerging. The T-shirt had a white spidery pattern on the front and the words "Fleetwood Mac Rumours."

"I need to move the car anyway," he added. "In case it's in the way of farm machinery. I was in a bit of a rush when I parked. But the road is narrow, isn't it? Just my luck to be crashed into by a combine harvester."

I said, "I'm not sure fields around here are growing the sort of crops a combine harvester would need to combine."

"You're right." He stuffed his feet into his Birkenstocks. "As I am sure you're right in everything."

I gave him a suspicious look, but he smiled blithely, as if he'd meant nothing by it.

As we crossed the grass, he asked me if it was something I often did, "cook for house parties"?

"Yes. But not always in the summer. I'm generally busier in the ski season. I tend to be away then for half the year. Lucky me."

He made a polite encouraging noise at the back of his throat, and, as we rounded the house, I asked him if he skied too.

"No; would it be wanky to say I'm ideologically opposed to it?"

I laughed before I could stop myself.

When we reached the gate, he pushed it open and then held it for me to go through first. "I'm sure it's different if you've been doing it since you were a child," he said. "But skiing wasn't big on the Salford estate where I grew up."

The Salford estate—it was my cue to change the subject, but, still feeling the pressure to convince him I was who I said I was, I told him how much I loved Val d'Isère: "France has the best snow. People say Italy or Switzerland, but you don't get the range of runs."

He unlocked the Fiat with a button on his key and got into the driver's seat. He leaned over to stuff a pile of papers on the seat into the glove compartment. "Hop in," he said, opening the passenger door.

I don't usually care what people think of me. Disassociation is part of the job. But as I got in, I realized I wanted him to like me, which was confusing. I had to force myself to continue. "Obviously, the French Alps are expensive, but you get what you pay for."

"I'll remember that," he said as he put on his seat belt.

"Unfortunately, the language is a problem—I don't speak a word of French."

"Not a word?"

I was beginning to weary of this lie, but on I went. "Well, maybe *bonjour*, but not much else."

He started the engine and gingerly pulled the car away from the hedgerow. There was a tearing sound, a scratching along the door on one side as he completed his three-point turn.

I tried to think of something else trivial on which to have a strong opinion. I took a deep breath. "But French food is really the only food you want to eat when you've been out on the slopes all day. I mean, fondue—frankly! I don't know what the Swiss are thinking. Ugh."

He glanced over at me, smiled briefly, and returned his eyes to the road. He drove surprisingly slowly, his hands held at a careful 10–2 position. "I quite like a cheese fondue." He nudged his stomach with his elbow, made a rueful grimace. "Probably where I've gone wrong."

I rolled down my window. The sky was streaked with thin clouds, the light still low, hazy across the fields, the shadows of the sunflowers long. The air smelled like Lulu's shower gel. In other circumstances, it would have been pleasant. He was good company, funny, attractive— maybe even more attractive than I was comfortable with. I just had to get through this. I let out an involuntary sigh.

"It's lovely here, isn't it?" Rob said. "Much prettier than where my brother lives."

"Your brother lives in France?"

"Yes."

I swallowed. "Down south, on the coast near Nice?"

"No, that was me taking a couple of days for myself. No—Marc's a bit further north and west. It's less hilly around there, more agricultural. Cheaper though, which is, I guess, the point."

"What does he do?"

"He's an artist. Struggling." He laughed as if to signal that he knew perfectly well this was a cliché. "He's got a few personal problems."

"Money? Love? Booze?"

"All of the above."

"Oh dear."

"Yeah." He glanced at me and away. The subject upset him. I'd been watching his mouth; the lips were soft and full, like a child's, and they flattened now at the corners. "He's actually not a real brother."

"Oh?"

"Yeah. I'm the youngest of four, but my parents were social workers and when we got a bit older they took in damaged kids."

"You mean they fostered?"

I had tried to keep the shock out of my voice, but he looked at me quickly again.

"Exactly, yes. Usually kids who were proving hard to place. Mostly it was just for a few weeks or so, but a few stuck around. A couple of them, like Marc, are still in our lives. Marc and I were quite close, and I have a sense of responsibility. But life hasn't been easy for him. He can be challenging at times."

I turned my head away. Both the altruism and the

confidence of the natural offspring were familiar to me from all the failed placements early on. There were the ones who couldn't bear to have anything to do with you, and there were the ones, generally wanting to feel better about themselves, who did.

I felt a surge of spite. "This was oop North, was it?" I said, mockingly overenunciating my vowels to match his.

He pulled his shoulders back down and his mouth arranged itself into a mild smile. "Has my accent betrayed me? And I try so hard to assimilate into polite society. Yes, Greater Manchester. Not your stomping ground, then?" He darted his eyes toward me and away.

"Notting Hill these days, but I traveled a lot as a child," I said.

"Siblings?"

"Only child. My parents live in Dubai now."

"Influencers?"

I laughed. "Tax. My father's in oil."

He nodded as if he understood. He'd placed me. Fuck him. Good.

We bumped over the little humpbacked bridge and then idled at a junction with the main road to let a tractor pass. The indicator clicked and he pulled out. The avenue of tall, thin pale green trees strobed alongside us.

"What kind of books do you write?" I said, to change the subject, though I already knew. I'd found reviews online, and one interview in which he talked almost exclusively about his writing habits—elaborate timescales and detailed Post-it notes. (The wall in his flat, he said, looked like "one of those crazy boards TV detectives compile when they're chasing a murderer.")

His grip on the steering wheel tightened. "Um." He let out a noise from the back of his throat and a short laugh as if to recognize his answer was not very satisfactory. "Um," he said again. A vein in his forehead seemed to have become more prominent. His eyes flicked up and to the right.

We had reached the village and were entering the main square. "Don't worry. You don't have to tell me if you don't want to," I said.

He was moving his head from side to side, looking for somewhere to park. "Thrillers. Cold War. East Berlin. Spies. Double-crossings. Honey-traps." A space, marked with diagonal white lines, became free, and he nosed the car in and cut the engine. A moment passed before he looked at me. "People pretending to be things they're not."

I felt a surge of genuine fear then. When I opened the door, I was hoping he would stay behind, but he followed me out and across the road, and stood next to me at the end of the queue. The old man I'd talked to a bit the previous day leaned out to say he hoped the orange juice I'd bought yesterday had sufficed, that there had been enough. He laughed, expecting me to join in. I felt my stomach lurch.

I looked at Rob and shrugged one shoulder, pulling down the corners of my mouth. "What's he saying?" I asked. Rob smiled at the old man. "She doesn't understand," he called to him in French. "English!" Luckily the queue moved fast. The puzzled, slightly hurt expression on the nice old man's face put a squeeze on my heart.

In the shop, the woman behind the counter asked if I wanted the same as yesterday and I looked at Rob to translate. Outside the shop, he broke off the crusty top of one of the baguettes and handed it to me. "Cook's treat," he said, and I remembered to explain about being celiac. Turns out he also knew someone who suffered—the daughter of a friend— and he understood how serious it could be. He asked questions about when I was diagnosed, and I made up a story about being ill as a teenager—loads of tests, nearly died, etc., etc. "No wonder you don't like fondue," he said, brushing his fingers of crumbs. "It's about cheese, but it's also pretty majorly about bread."

"Oh, yeah, sure. That's what it is." I'd seen pictures of fondue and I took a guess. "Nothing to do with the fact that it tastes like vomit."

He reared back theatrically. "Rude!"

He noticed the Casino on the opposite side of the

square, and, skewing his chin sideways and rubbing it, said he was going to nip in and get some razors.

Heat was beginning to draw into the day, so I sat on a bench under the trees to wait. Sparrows were fussing over Rob's crumbs. The sun was glittering through the branches and I put my face up and closed my eyes. Maybe Rob had caught sight of me in Sainte-Cécile. Maybe even—worst case—he had seen me with Lulu and Sean. But he had no proof. If he continued to raise the matter, I'd continue to deny it. And eventually he'd lose faith in his own memory. Kaleidoscopes of color flickered across the back of my eyelids. The smell of fresh bread. Breakfast. Then lunch. I'd make a salad today. Ottolenghi style. I'd google it when we got back. And then supper. What would I do? I'd have to think about it.

I didn't immediately open my eyes when I heard someone calling. I felt no rush of adrenaline. When you take an alias, there's a reason you should choose a name similar to your own. Ali/Ellie. Sean/John. You need something, when you're distracted, for your brain to hook on to. The voice got louder, and when it pene-trated my synapses, when I realized the person being called was *me*, I scrambled in a panic to my feet. A man was ambling across the square toward me.

"Lulu! Salut! Lulu!"

He had a familiar wispy beard and a flop of hair.

"Pascal," I said. "Hello."

As he pumped my hand up and down, I checked the
entrance to the Casino over his shoulder. He asked me
a few questions in French; I answered in English. Was
I happy at the Domaine? Was everything all right with
the job? Yes, absolutely. I was with one of the guests
now. He was in the shop, but he'd be back any minute.
It was lovely to see him.

I took a step toward the Fiat, grasping the handle. I
could see through to the checkout where Rob was paying. "Lovely to see you," I repeated.

But still he didn't get the hint. He just stood there as
if he had something else on his mind and he was trying to think of the words. Finally, his hands making
small turning movements, he asked if everything was
all right? Only a man had arrived in Pugot, after we'd
left, asking people in the square if anyone had seen a
blond woman getting off the bus. He spoke to Antoine,
who felt it better to say nothing, but said if by any
chance he ran into me, I should let you know—in case
it was someone I wasn't avoiding, but actually wanted
to see.

Rob was coming out of the Casino, taking a moment
to check his receipt. He looked up, saw me with Pascal,
smiled, and began walking toward us.

Quickly, I said: "The man. What did he look like?"

"In his thirties." He made circular motions with his
hands. "Handsome."

"Was he French? English?"

175

"I'll find out."

Rob was close now, holding in one hand a can of Avène shaving foam and in the other a glass jar of Nutella. He smiled again, at Pascal, and then at me. "Hi," he said.

Pascal backed away, with a sort of servile dip of his head. "If you want to get in touch," he said in French, "I live down there." He pointed to a narrow road at the opposite corner to the Casino. "Blue door. Last house before the river." He waved and turned and began walking in that direction.

Rob said, "If you needed that translating, the man was telling you where he lived in case you wanted to meet up."

"Thanks."

"Down that road there—"

"Thanks," I repeated. "I'm good."

He opened the car door, threw his purchases onto the back seat, and got in. "Are you sure?" he added, when I was in the passenger seat. "Because I think you might have scored." He was already reversing out of the space, but he threw me a glance, widening his eyes suggestively.

I managed an artificial laugh, too high and giggly to be my own. "You think?"

The village passed by my window. Shopfronts. Two women talking. A small white dog barking. A red van reversing. I was trying to breathe quietly, but I felt claustrophobic. I would get out, if I could think of a reason. I wanted to get out of sight, to slink down in my seat. Had Sean traced me to the square where I'd gotten off the bus? Or was it someone else looking for someone altogether different? I should have asked more questions. Did he have a car? Had he asked for the woman by name?

I pressed my face to the glass. We had crossed over the bridge and were on the hill up to the house. In the side-view mirror, the heat trembled.

It was busy in the kitchen, the milling guests waiting, like zoo penguins, to be fed.

"At last!" Rebecca said, seeing us. "We thought you two had snuck off for the day."

Rob held up the jar of Nutella, brandishing it like a police badge. "I've saved breakfast."

"Oh my God, not Nutella," Rebecca cried. "You'll have the girls on you like a ton of bricks."

Iris looked up from her phone and started laying into him about palm oil and deforestation, the decimation of the orangutan's natural habitat. He made all the signs of contrition, raising his arms to protect himself from her onslaught—"I'm sorry, I'm sorry"—but the way he was laughing suggested he enjoyed the attention. I opened the fridge. "Oops, we're in the way," Rebecca said. She and Layla shifted toward the counter. Layla went back to showing Rebecca a website on her phone, which she was urging her to subscribe to. "Honestly, Adriene's an absolute miracle worker. One of her thirty-day journeys will literally change your life."

Rebecca said, with a sort of hopeful defensiveness: "I *do* do Pilates."

"Pilates is all very well," Layla said, striking the elbows-out, one-shoulder-forward pose of someone really quite proud of their physique. "But I'm telling you, you'd be so much better off doing yoga."

I took what I could—the yogurt and the fruit, the butter and the jam—out to the garden table, where Clare and Phil were looking at his iPad, and came back for the basket of bread. Rob helped by bringing the cutlery, and Rebecca, still chatting with Layla, moved out of the way so I could collect plates.

"Where's Martha?" I asked her.

"Floating around somewhere. Not feeling well. Again." She rolled her eyes. "Could you pop on another pot of coffee, that would be marvelous," she said. "Bless you."

"It's such a pain eating outside," Phil said, not looking up. "All the fetching and carrying. So sorry." He pulled his chair in slightly so I could more easily get past.

"Is there any herbal tea?" Clare asked as I put down the bread. She handed me her used mug. "Anything will do. I'm not fussy. Chamomile?" She shifted closer to Phil and his iPad, not expecting a response. "Or verveine?"

"I've done a terrible thing." Rob was standing in the doorway to the kitchen, holding out the Nutella. He'd raised his voice to get Phil's and Clare's attention, almost as if he wanted to distract them from whatever it was that was separating them from the rest of the group. "I've personally contributed to the extinction of the orangutan."

"It's not a joke," Iris said behind him.

"I know." He turned slightly, and sounded genuine. "I know."

"Oh no, that's awful!" Clare looked up from the iPad.

"I know. And it's so delicious too."

"No." She spun a wrist in the air, limply gesturing to the iPad. "Her body. They've found her body."

"The poor English girl," Phil added, eyes still on the screen.

I didn't feel the mug drop, just heard the crack of it on the tiles. I think I cried out; they were looking up at me, not down at the ground. I could see the alarm on their faces.

The shards crunched as I stepped back. Chairs scraped. I was aware I needed to get breath into my lungs, and when I did, it felt like a spasm.

I managed to get into the kitchen for a dustpan and brush. I was on my hands and knees, my face concealed, as someone asked, "What poor English girl?" and Phil dragged his attention back to the story.

"The one who was hiking in the Dolomites. They've been looking for her for weeks. Sounds like she fell into

a crevasse. Another hiker spotted her backpack yesterday and alerted the authorities."

"That's so sad. She was so young. Such a waste,"
Clare said.

"The poor parents," Rebecca said.

"At least they know now," Layla added. "I always
think *not* knowing must be worse."

Nobody noticed me leave.

Chapter Fifteen

I had taken the passage to the hall, and I stood there for a moment wishing I'd gone the other way to my room, but it was too late. I opened the front door and was out in the open. I unlatched the gate and headed up the hill toward the ruined barn. When I got there, I crouched behind a wall, in a patch of long, rough grass, opened my mouth, and let out a silent scream.

In those few seconds when I'd thought the body they'd found was Lulu's, I'd felt the world shift. I'd been thinking about her death as a solid object, a terrible thing Sean had done, but for the people who loved her it was a hole, waiting for them. The enormity of their loss opened up, gaped. Her friends. Her parents. They didn't yet know she was dead. The fact that I knew and they didn't was unbearable.

I made up my mind. They had to know. It didn't matter what happened to me. I fumbled for my phone, pressed the icon for the receiver, and then for the keypad. My fingers hovered. How did you ring the police in France? What was the equivalent of 999? I tried to open Google, but I didn't have Wi-Fi or even a signal. I'd have to return to the house. The bible—the information would be in there. Or I could ask someone. Rebecca might know.

I felt my resolve weaken. I put my head in my hands. Would the police believe me? Would they find her body with the information I could give? You heard about lakes being dredged, and rivers. But you needed coordinates for seas. And for that you'd need Sean's cooperation.

Anger rose up inside me like something big, a force. I had done lots of bad things. But I hadn't killed her. When this job was over, I would track him down, drag him to the police, expose him myself.

Most of the guests had dispersed when I got back to the house, only Phil and Clare were still at the breakfast table. I could hear Layla's and Rebecca's voices in the sitting room. And I could see Rob in the garden. He'd taken out a chair and was working in the shade next to the boules court. Iris's voice and that of another girl—it sounded like a FaceTime call—drifted down from her bedroom. Someone had cleared the table and stacked the plates and cups on the counter, so I filled the dishwasher and wiped the surfaces.

I decided to go in search of Martha.

I checked the vegetable garden first—empty—and then went out through a small gap in the wall and down to the far end of the garden: an area of untended shrubs and wild grasses that edged into a vineyard. The plants were bent and gnarled, shoulder-high, the grapes that dangled in tight clumps hard and green. It was a private spot, hidden from the house and the garden, and I found her at the farthest reach of a row, at the top of the escarpment, sitting on a log.

Her eyes were red and her face had the strained, washed-out look of someone who had been crying. She was wearing tracksuit pants and a tank top.

"I was worried," I said, sitting down next to her. "You weren't at breakfast."

"No. I'm still not feeling that great," she said, trying to smile.

A flock of small birds flew low across the field. On the far hillside, a tractor crawled.

Our hands were resting on the log, our little fingers were almost touching. A wood louse crept close and I flicked it off.

"Do you want to talk about it?" I said eventually.

At first she didn't answer, and then she said, almost angrily: "Why are you being so nice to me?"

"I'm not sure." I laughed, because it was true.

But she had started crying. "I know you know," she said, eventually.

I put my arm around her then. "How far gone are you?"

"I don't know. Five weeks? Six? I missed my period, I realized, and then . . ."

"You've got options," I said.

Her head was bowed and I had to ask her to repeat what she said.

She lifted it. "How can I fucking . . . My mother, I mean . . . I'm here in fucking France. In the middle of nowhere. He's not even taking my calls." She was angry now through her tears.

I said several things. I said I could see how upset she was, and how she would be feeling out of control and also isolated, and that it was frightening being in a position where she had choices that were maybe not the ones she was expecting. And, I said, I knew she was a brave and wise and sensible girl who would make whatever decision was right for her, and that her parents loved her—unconditionally—and that I was sure they would support her, whatever happened.

She didn't respond immediately, but I could feel my words working. The tension began to ease out of her shoulders, and there was a little bit less tension in them now. She leaned sideways into me, and I used the opportunity to ask who the boy was and whether she had told him.

A long silence.

"I've left messages," she said. "But he hasn't rung back."

"Boys your age can be very immature."

She raised her head again. "Thing is, he's not my age. At all. He's . . ." She stopped talking, as if she had said something she regretted.

184

"He's what?"

"He's a bit older."

"How much older?"

She shrugged.

"Oh, Martha." I waited as long as I could. The tractor on the hillside was making a lumbering turn. Someone shouted to someone else, in the distance—miles away. Sound traveled. Important to remember that. "Is it complicated?"

She didn't speak, but she nodded.

"Is he married?"

She shook her head vigorously.

I thought carefully what to ask next. What would give me the most information for the smallest outlay? Finally, I said, tenderly: "How did you meet?"

She swept her hands down her thighs and then clasped her knees. "Just sort of around."

"At a party?"

"No."

She was shifting slightly in her seat; her breathing had become more irregular.

"At school?"

"Kinda . . ."

And gradually, and then in a flood, it came out. He was a teacher, but only part-time, drama, and he didn't teach her, so he wasn't technically her teacher at all. They'd actually met *out* of school, at the station, after she'd stayed late to finish some art. And, anyway, he was only thirty-two, which wasn't that much older than her, and she was mature for her age. Everyone always told her that. It had started in the Easter term and they'd kept it secret. He owned his own house in Peckham, and he had lodgers, but she never went when anyone else was there. He'd been hard to get hold of since they'd broken up for the summer. He'd been traveling in Greece and first he didn't have Wi-Fi and then his phone was acting up, but . . . She started sobbing properly again then.

She was in my arms and I was holding her and stroking her hair and repeating what I had said earlier, only using different words, but all the time I was thinking, *You bastard.* She'd said she couldn't tell me his name, but it would be easy to track him down. I knew the name of her school, his subject, his age.

"Does Iris know?" I said.

"No." She rubbed her eyes. "She's busy with her own tiny little 'problems.' She failed some exams. It's like the world is ending. The school's dropped her from triple science and she hasn't told Mum and Dad. I mean, I just haven't got the energy to deal with it."

"Oh, I see."

"I don't know what to do," she said.

She had bitten a strip off her lower lip—the skin was raw. Her eyes were red from crying. I could take her under my wing, control the situation, use it to my advantage.

I felt a tugging high in my chest. "You should tell your mother," I said.

"I can't. It's the holiday. The *Lawrences* are here."

"Oh, no. Not the *Lawrences*," I repeated, and she managed a small smile.

Chapter Sixteen

A name being called—but distantly, quietly, through water, smoke, fog, in another room. Children playing on a beach.

I opened my eyes. I'd slumped sideways, my book on the ground by my dangling hand. A fly crawled across my face. My fingers had pins and needles.

"Lulu! Lulu!" The voice was loud, insistent. "Lu-lu." Softer now, farther away, but it licked into my brain like something I should attend to.

I struggled to my feet, the deck chair twisting sideways, snagged by ivy. The sunlight was dazzling, the scenery bleached white. It took me a moment to get my bearings. I was in the vegetable garden; I'd taken refuge, thinking I had an hour to myself. I must have fallen asleep.

Blood rushed to my head as I made for the gap in the wall. What time was it? The heat was intense, blocking out anything else.

In the hall I could hear voices from the kitchen. The squelch of the fridge door. The bash of plates.

"It really doesn't matter," Rebecca said, seeing me standing in the doorway. "We were just a bit hungry, that's all, and didn't want to wade in without asking you. I just thought you would be preparing lunch. It's absolutely fine, though." She let out a tense laugh. "Where were you? We've been looking everywhere."

"I'm sorry," I said. "I had a bad night. I fell asleep. I did have plans for lunch. I was going to make a salad."

"You and your disappearing acts! Luckily Rob has stepped into the breach."

The body at the stove—Rob—turned and grinned at me. "I'm frying the lardons. And boiling potatoes. Bacon and potatoes always improve anything salad-related."

Rebecca was pulling things out of the fridge: leftover rémoulade and olives, rewrapped packages of ham and cheese. She let out a heavy sigh. Layla, who was painstakingly cutting up bread, clicked her tongue against the roof of her mouth. She gave me one of her patronizing smiles. "Oh, dear," she said, either in amusement or rebuke.

My limbs and head still felt heavy, as if I'd been drugged.

Rob scraped the bits of bacon onto a plate. The frying pan hissed as he put it under the tap. "Lulu and I have got this," he said to Rebecca and Layla. "Go on, grab some wine and sit down. We won't be long."

I joined him at the sink and started washing the pan, keeping my eyes down. The two women, wiping their hands resentfully on a tea towel, found a fresh bottle of rosé and some glasses and took them outside. I heard Rebecca calling to Martha and Iris to lay the table. It was very hot in the kitchen. A strong smell of ripe cheese swept out of the open fridge. Flies looped in circles. Someone had switched on the Eurokill again and it crackled every few seconds.

"If we hard-boiled a couple of eggs," Rob said, "we could make a sort of *paysanne* salad with a nice garlicky, mustardy dressing. That should keep them happy."

"Is that Ottolenghi-y?" I said.

He laughed. "Maybe not. But hey—let's live danger-ously." He smiled. "-y," he added.

I washed up the colander and various mugs and some stray cutlery, aware of Rob moving competently behind me, opening cupboards, chopping, putting eggs on to boil. "You like cooking, do you?" I said.

"Yes, I do," he said, in a way that made it sound as if he were himself surprised.

"Where did you learn?" I asked.

"I taught myself. No incentive quite like greed." He sighed to suggest he was a lost cause. "I did quite a lot of the cooking growing up. Being an only child, you've been saved from this. But in a big family like mine, if you express an interest in anything—it becomes the solution to every birthday or Christmas present dilemma. My mum likes dogs. Literally, everything she ever gets is dog themed. For me, it's kitchen utensils and cookbooks." He stretched his hands apart, miming an expanding bookshelf. "What about you?"

"You mean, was cooking my childhood dream?"

"No. But you know." He lifted one shoulder. "Did you watch *Bake Off* and *MasterChef*, and practice your roux and think, 'That could be me?'"

I wondered why I never had thought of being a cook. Food was such a preoccupation growing up. Some homes had one kind of meal, some had others. Your clothes would smell of fried mince, or ackee and salt fish, or pizza. You learned to adjust. Also, the bigger the household, the hungrier you are. Fact.

I smiled perkily. "My mother was a good cook and we used to spend the weekend baking cakes together. She taught me how to make . . ." My mind went blank. "Um—chicken cacciatore, and things like that. I was at boarding school, but on the weekends, holidays, we were always together in the kitchen." I smiled at him. "Throwing together a roux."

He had handed me a cucumber to slice and I was concentrating on not cutting myself. "Though my childhood dream was to be an actor, which I also am."

"Of course. Rebecca mentioned you were in *Downton Abbey*—my mum loves that. Which season? Presumably I can find you on on-demand."

The others were gathering at the table. "Four," I said.

191

"I'll search it out," he said, scooping the cucumber slices from under me and adding them to a gigantic white bowl that I'd noticed in a cupboard and marveled at.

"Do we need tomatoes?" I said. "There are loads in the veg patch."

"We could make a separate tomato salad? But can we be bothered? Do they deserve it?"

I watched him carefully, then shook my head. "Nah."

When he had finished, he lowered the huge bowl into my hands and, going ahead of me, slipped into a chair between Elliot and Martha. The conversation lulled when I laid the salad down on the table in the space in front of Phil. He looked as if he had had too much sun. He was wearing a straw hat; his white T-shirt was wet across the shoulders; the bridge of his nose pink. "Oh, is this one of your specialties?" he said, mixing it up with the serving spoons. "Looks delish."

I was standing behind Martha and I rested my hands on her shoulders. I was aware of Rob's eyes on me, his quietly amused smile. I made a noise, a bit like a laugh—noncommittal, but not denying it.

"You saved the day," Rebecca said, stretching one arm out as if to hug me, though I was too far away to reach. "You going to join us?"

She was trying to make up for being cross with me earlier. Or maybe she genuinely did think I'd pulled it together. Confirmation bias.

"Actually, I've got supper to get on with," I said.

The mustard in the dressing, Layla told me, made all the difference. She always put mustard in her dressings. Seedy, actually. Next time I should give that a try.

Chapter Seventeen

They were noisy at the table—guffaws of laughter, shrieks, clinking glasses, scrapings of chairs—and then gradually quieter as the heat and the food began to get to them. Phil said something about "an excursion," and how the afternoon was "ripe" for one. He carried on repeating the word "excursion" as if he thought it was funny, which I didn't really understand. If the idea of an excursion was ridiculous, why go on one? He came into the kitchen for the house bible and stood in the doorway, flipping through the pages. How about Pugot Cathedral? Had I been? I was looking my recipe up on my phone and I shook my head.

"Who's on for a cathedral in the Southern Gothic French style?" he proclaimed to the terrace. "Bit of a drive, but lovely and cool inside."

Various others expressed interest, and then largely changed their minds. I was aware of people coming in and dribbling away, but I was preoccupied. The recipe was telling me I should have marinated the chicken overnight. Too late for that now. I also needed various herbs, which I had found in the supermarket on Sunday, only Phil had taken them out of the cart, telling me he'd seen plenty in the garden. Finding rosemary was easy enough—there were great pots of it on the terrace—but I had to google "bay tree" to be sure I wasn't picking laurel (apparently toxic). Frying the chicken was also tricky. The pieces browned unevenly—some bits blackened; others were pallid. The oil spat so badly I had to drape my arms with tea towels.

Once I'd reached the final stage—which involved throwing "the marinade" on top of the chicken, plus a jar of black olives and a tin of anchovies, and then putting the whole thing in the oven at 150 degrees Celsius—I drank a long glass of water to recover and set about cleaning the kitchen. The dishwasher had finished its cycle so I emptied that, sprayed bleach on all the surfaces, and mopped the floor. It was a relief to be on safer ground. Cleaning is something I can do. Been on enough residential duties.

The quietness of the house settled around me when I stripped off the rubber gloves. I walked out onto the terrace and sat on a chair in the shade. Heat sank into my pores. The cicadas droned. Butterflies flitted between plants. On the table, two wasps crawled in something sticky.

I tried to work out where everyone was. Who in the end had gone to the cathedral? Maybe just Phil and

Clare. Layla and Roland had crept past me at one point, going upstairs, they said for "a sleep" (as we knew, "very much double-bed people"). I'd heard Rebecca's voice and the sound of Rob typing in the study; more recently, I'd seen him, towel slung over one shoulder, lumber down to the pool. The teenagers were around, too, somewhere. One or another of them had come in for a snack—a biscuit or a yogurt—and I'd noticed Martha wandering around down by the fruit trees. She wasn't there now. I should check on her again soon.

I got out my phone. What was the name of her school? Clare had mentioned it at dinner. St. Agnes, that was it. I went on the website. It didn't take long. There was only one male teacher listed in the drama department: he was called Liam Merchant. I found a photograph of him on a trip to the National Theatre. He had a goatee beneath a soft mouth, and eyes that sloped down at the corners. In the picture, he was standing between two pretty girls with a smirk on his face. He was wearing a pair of white Gucci trainers. Private income. He wouldn't have bought those on a teacher's salary.

The gate at the pool clicked and I looked up to see Elliot, hands in pockets, walking toward the house from the pool. Halfway along the slope, he veered away, heading toward the far side of the garden. His shoulders were rounded, and there was something both furtive and determined about his pace that caught my interest, so I waited for a moment or two and then began to stroll in that direction, holding my phone out as if I were searching for a signal. Ahead of me, he reached the fruit trees and plunged into the vineyard behind.

Small yellow plums were scattered all over the grass and I bent my head, as if I were searching the ground for good ones. When I reached the spot where he had disappeared, I crouched to collect a handful and, through the vegetation, a couple of rows over, made out a glint of white T-shirt, the gleam of bare skin.

I crept closer, still low on my haunches, to get a better sight line. I could hear voices now. I angled my head to see under the first row of vines. I could see then that he was with Iris, both of them sitting on the ground, cross-legged. He was unzipping a brown pouch, like a makeup bag, and he withdrew a small thin stick. Iris handed him a lighter and he thumbed it a few times until he got a spark and then lit the end. When he finally inhaled, he tipped his head back, his neck pale, then opened his mouth to puff out a smoke ring.

Dark horse; that was my first thought. This quiet studious boy with his water polo and his lacrosse, his easy blushes. Not just smoking but smoking weed, and smoking weed *here*, on holiday, around all these zero-tolerance parents. Where had his stash come from? Had he bought it in France? Or had he smuggled it in with him? High risk either way.

He handed the joint to Iris, who took a puff and handed it back. Another smoke ring.

Shane, one of the boys at Fairlight House, came into my head then. He used to shape his cheeks and lips as if he were sucking on a lollipop, and then open his mouth and hold the smoke, his tongue white with vapor, before releasing it, clicking his lower jaw forward in a silent cough, once, twice, three times. He practiced until he could do tricks, pushing the rings away with the flat of his palm.

I visualized Shane's scrawny face, the hairs on his upper lip that had ambitions to be a mustache, and remembered that he was dead, and I felt suddenly sick of these kids, with their privilege, their chances, and I went back up to the house.

The sitting-room doors were open and, as I went through them, it struck me again how strongly it smelled of woodsmoke, how blackened the hearth was. A mug and a wineglass with lipstick on the rim were discarded on the coffee table. The corner of the rug was flipped over, and some of the seat cushions were dented to show two people had recently been sitting there. I thought, as I walked through and into the study, how many previous lives a room held, how many secrets.

Rob's MacBook Air was sitting on the small table, and as I passed it, my foot caught on the cable, the laptop moved slightly and the screen came to life.

It was open on a bright green square, cards laid out in a pattern. A game of solitaire.

The brown leather notebook was next to it. He'd mentioned it in one of the interviews: how it was where

he wrote down all his ideas, where he plotted everything out.

I touched it with the tips of my fingers. I had sold
notebooks in my "shop"; I'd loved choosing the hides
and the colors, the rough irregular paper inside. I picked
it up and brought it to my nose. Moroccan leather smells
of cow and the tannery. This smelled of men's after-
shave. I felt a stab of curiosity, a desire to know about
him. I was about to open it, to look at his mind maps, his
crazy TV detective serial-killer boards, but a floorboard
creaked above my head and I put it back.

The cicadas had died down and the light was salmon-
pink when I heard a car purr through the gate.

Rebecca must have heard it, too, because she came
into the kitchen. She had dressed for dinner in a sleeveless pleated dress with a high neck that looked tight
and uncomfortable under the arms. But her face looked
pinched, the corners of her eyes bloodshot.

"So, your lovely *pollo alla cacciatora* for sups?" she
said, looking toward the corridor.

I nodded.

"With cannellini?"

"Maybe," I said, trying to sound enigmatic. "Or
mashed potatoes."

The sound of the front door opening and closing.
Phil's voice in the hall.

"Lovely." She touched my shoulder, squeezing her
lips together. Her nostrils were raw, as if she'd been

blowing her nose. "I don't know what I would do without you."

They'd had a nightmare, Phil explained loudly as he strode into the room. One thing after another. Pugot, the town with the cathedral, was farther away than they'd thought. They'd had to queue for a space in a parking lot at the bottom of a hill and then hike up. On the way home, "positively parched," they'd stopped for a drink, but then they'd taken the wrong turning and gotten lost. "Drove round and round in bloody circles." He had been addressing his wife, but his explanations sounded more like a series of public declarations. He took off his straw hat; his forehead gleamed.

Rebecca was smiling now. "Did you find somewhere for a swim? It's been so hot. I was hoping you had passed a river and had a lovely dip."

"That would have been a good idea." Phil threw his hat on to the counter. "But we didn't."

"Next time we'll take our swimming things." Clare was standing, barefoot, in the doorway. She seemed wary of coming in. "Just in case."

"We bought wine, though," Phil said. "And chocolate. Some delicious chocolate." He put his arm around Rebecca's shoulders, squeezing the flesh on her upper arm. "I know you love your chocolate." He kissed the top of her head as if she were a child.

They both went upstairs for showers, but Rebecca continued to hover, fiddling with some paper napkins, lining them up more neatly on top of each other. I asked her if she had seen Martha, watching her response carefully. I wanted to know if they'd had "the talk."

Her response suggested they hadn't.

"God knows where that girl has gotten to," she said. "She's slunk around in the shadows all day, says she's had too much sun. I mean, honestly." She let out an unconvincing tinkle of laughter. She picked up Phil's straw hat, smoothed it with her fingers, and put it back where it had been. "You spend a huge amount of money on a family holiday and all your children do is avoid you."

I was carrying a pitcher of water out to the table, and I spoke lightly, throwing my words casually over my shoulder: "You're such a wonderful mother. She clearly adores you."

I didn't want to make too big a thing of it; I would sound more genuine that way.

It was the right call. When I came back in, she threw one arm around my shoulders and pulled me toward her. "I know it's only been a few days, but you're one of us now, aren't you?"

She kissed the side of my head with an audible *mwah*, and then released me so suddenly I almost fell. "What a treasure you are."

When I'd finished bringing out the food, there was a space left for me between Rebecca and Martha. Iris and Elliot were this end, too, giggling about something to do with the table leg. Martha was smiling as though she were part of the joke, and when I murmured "OK?" she nodded. She had her armor on again: eyeliner, a central part, and a black Victorian lace blouse. Rob was opposite and looked up. He was wearing a green linen shirt, the sleeves rolled up above the elbows. "Survive the great poultry fry-up?" he said softly. "It looked like it was getting quite hairy in there."

"I did. Thank you. What about you? Productive day?"

"Yes, thank you. Very."

"Good."

I felt like we were talking in code.

I'd lit candles and the light bounced off glasses and the tops of arms and cheeks. The temperature had dropped a little. I lifted my head to look up beyond the umbrella. The sky was popping with a million prying stars. The Milky Way looked like phosphorescence. I wished I could think of something witty to add, maybe mention the solitaire, but I felt awkward.

The food was being passed along to general murmurs of appreciation. I hadn't done cannellini beans but mashed potatoes, only the ones I'd bought in the supermarket had been fiddly to peel and didn't mash very successfully; small bits stuck between the prongs of the fork no matter how hard I worked at them. Helping himself to a dollop, Rob said, "Oh, smashed new potatoes; how delicious. Do you ever do that Nigel Slater recipe with watercress?"

"Sometimes," I told him.

"Very good with salmon."

He had cut the chicken conventionally with his knife and fork, but he laid the knife down and crossed the fork to his right hand to eat.

Layla, farther down the table, had taken her first mouthful. She put her head on one side. She seemed to be considering something. "Interesting flavor," she said questioningly.

"There's a secret ingredient," I said. I'd meant the anchovies. I'd never heard of having chicken with canned fish.

Layla was still frowning, lightly smacking her lips together and apart. "Is it . . . Is it lavender?"

I took a quick taste of the sauce myself. She was right. There was something odd about it, almost medicinal. Rob caught my eye. "Such an underrated herb, lavender," he said. "I added some to the parmesan biscuits the other day. And they were corking."

He smiled, looking down into his lap, which is something I'd noticed he did when he was genuinely amused.

At the other end of the table, Clare was complaining about the plumbing. She was wearing a low-cut red dress and her hair was up in a loose bun. "It's gross. Every time you run water for any length of time, there's a really strong smell."

"I hadn't noticed," Rebecca said. "Layla?"

"It does smell *a bit* off," Layla admitted. "A bit like drains."

Rebecca turned to me. "Did anyone complain about it last year?"

I said I didn't think so.

"I'll ask Brigitte when she comes. I really am terribly sorry." She looked at Layla and then Clare and then back again. "I hope it isn't ruining your holiday." Her smile was brittle.

"No of course it isn't," Clare said. She lifted her hands to adjust her hair and one of the tiny straps slipped off her shoulder. "Honestly, Becks. You always take everything so personally."

Rob leaned forward then to ask Phil about the cathedral. Despite the hike, had it been worth it? Yes, very much so. Particularly magnificent was the 250-foot bell tower and the fresco of Christ's last journey. Clare agreed. She'd been struck by the contrast between the military exterior and the elaborately decorated interior. There had been an entire leaflet in the house bible. Anyone would think they'd read it cover to cover.

"I hope you lit a candle," Rebecca said.

"Of course," Phil said, with a small courtly bow. "We lit one for each of you. Wishing happiness for all."

Layla asked if there had been any shops worth visiting.

"Everything was closed," Clare said languidly, "because it's Monday."

"I thought everything in Pugot was closed on Wednesdays?" Rebecca interjected.

Clare laid her arm along the back of Phil's seat. A

muscle at the corner of her lip twitched. "Then it's Mondays and Wednesdays. Everything must be closed in Pugot on Mondays *and* Wednesdays."

Phil said: "When it comes to the work-life balance, the French certainly have their priorities right." He lifted his arms and caught his hands behind his neck, leaning into them like a hammock. Clare laughed, and as she did so, her breath or the wind caught the wick of one of the candles and blew the flame out.

Tension had stiffened the muscles in Rebecca's cheeks. The skin of her neck stretched as she lifted her chin. Her knife and fork clattered on the surface of the plate.

I wanted to change the subject, but I couldn't think of what to say. I caught Rob's eye, and something passed between us. He swallowed hard and said loudly, "So, here's a weird and wonderful thing. It turns out Lulu here has a doppelgänger!"

"A doppelgänger?" Rebecca said.

"Yes." He was hamming up his amazement. "There is someone out there who looks just like her. I saw her with my own eyes."

"Where?" Martha asked.

Rob picked up his glass, swirled the wine, and then put the glass down. "A few days ago. Down on the coast. At first, I thought it had been in Nice, but it came to me today." He lifted his eyes to mine. "It was the next day at a small place called Sainte-Cécile-sur-Mer."

He was smiling. Sainte-Cécile-sur-Mer. Under the

table, I was digging my nails into my palms as I smiled back. So, he *had* seen me. I had to hope I'd at least been on my own and not with Sean. Or, worse, Lulu. What if he'd heard me use her name? Or, God, spotted me that terrible afternoon when I was running back from the boat?

"Maybe it *was* Lulu," Layla said.

"It wasn't." I managed to laugh.

"So, you weren't at Sainte-Cécile-sur-Mer?"

"I've never even heard of the place. I don't even know where it is."

"With eight billion people on the planet," Roland said pedantically, "it's not entirely without reason to think that we all might have a nonbiological look-alike."

"Or maybe it's just how we process faces," I said. "Something to do with psychology."

"We should ask our resident scientist," Clare cried. "Iris?"

"What?" Iris hadn't been listening.

Clare began to explain, and as the conversation drifted into genetics and became more general, I was aware of Rob's silence. He carefully removed a moth that had fluttered too close to a candle and fallen in the melted wax. A curl of hair had loosened down onto his forehead. Was he telling me he was on to me? I felt a shiver of fear.

Phil insisted on making the coffee—"No, sit down. Sit. I insist! Girls. Come and help me."

206

He carried the tray, elbows at an angle, hamming up the heaviness. "There," he said, plonking it down on the table. He sat and passed the cups down.

"Oh, damn," he said. "The chocolate! I forgot the chocolate. Did you see it in the kitchen? Or did I leave it in the car?"

He had fired the question down the table to me and I realized that was my cue. "I'll go and look," I said, relieved to get up.

"You angel. Key's on the side."

It was dark and quiet at the front. An owl hooted. I opened the boot first, but all it contained was a box of wine and some empty bags. Nothing on the back seat either. I opened the passenger door. The seat was pushed down at a low angle, but there was nothing obvious in the footwell. I looked in the glove compartment and then felt in the pocket in the door. A package: three large bars of Crunch milk chocolate in a small paper bag.

I looked again at the passenger seat. Really, it was very low. You could almost say *reclined*. The footwell had a black mat and, thinking I'd dislodged it, I put my hand down to put it back in place and touched something soft. It felt like a garment of clothing. I fished it out. A bikini top? No, a bra.

I dropped it back where it was.

Chapter Eighteen

I woke in the night with a raging thirst. The room was pitch-black and I lay there, heart pounding, too scared to get up, as if all I had to worry about was the dark space under the bed.

In the shower room, I drank from the tap, and then wiped my face on the towel. I remembered how fussy Sean was with "his toilet," as he called it, and how he liked a particular styling balm for his hair. In the darkness, I began to imagine I could smell that wax, the combination of almond and sweet orange. I was being paranoid, I told myself; it was the soap on the side of the basin. I lifted it to my nostrils and breathed in. Then I went back to bed and slept fitfully for the rest of the night.

My intention had been to steer clear of Rob, but early the next morning, I heard the creak of a sunbed, and when I looked out of the window he was already down there, legs up, laptop propped against his thighs, his bath towel laid out to dry on the ground like a white flag.

I threw on my clothes.

"So, are you writing or pretending to write?" I asked him from the doorway.

He looked up. "Pretending to write."

"I thought if you were a proper writer it was supposed to pour out of you."

He blinked slowly. "Yes, but then I'm not a proper writer."

"So, it's all a big con?"

Another beat. "Something like that."

The sky was blue and he was wearing a blue collarless shirt. Dandelion fluff floated in the air. His hair was slicked back and his legs were still wet, glistening. He was looking at me with a small smile, and I felt confused, not sure how to behave, but there was a click, and we both turned our heads to see Clare unhitching the gate.

"Hi," she said. "Great minds think alike. I thought I'd have a quick dip before breakfast. But first I just . . ." She cast her eyes around. "I just . . ." she said again. She began to look about herself, stooping to look under the pool furniture.

"Have you lost something?" Rob asked.

"I'm sure it's in my room somewhere." She sat down on the edge of a sunbed. "But, yes, I've lost . . ." She pulled off her T-shirt, revealing a swimsuit, navy with a white band below the bust. ". . . a black . . .

er . . . You know, a black . . . thingy. It doesn't matter. I just don't know what can have happened to it, that's all."

Rob moved his computer off his lap and spun his legs to the ground. "Can we help you look?"

She didn't answer immediately, just sat there, frowning thoughtfully. And after a few seconds, she stood up again and checked behind the pots. "Don't worry. I thought maybe I dropped it when I changed down here yesterday. But, um, I'm sure it'll turn up."

I was adjusting to how I'd felt when he said *we*—my stomach had swooped—but I pulled myself together and asked what sort of black thing?

She walked to the edge of the pool, dipped her toe in the water, and then brought it out again. "A black . . ." She rolled her hands around near the top of her swimsuit to illustrate her general chest area.

I realized what was happening then. "Oh," I said. "A black *bikini* top. I think I've seen one somewhere." I tapped my forehead, as if racking my brain.

"Yes." She looked relieved at the suggestion. "That's it. A black *bikini* top."

I clicked my fingers. "The Audi. When I got the chocolate, I saw something under the passenger seat. Now that you mention it, it might have been the top half of a bikini."

Clare's teeth were raking her lip.

"You must have taken it with you," I said. "When

you and Phil went to Pugot. It must have fallen out of your towel."

That's not what happened, of course. *Next time, we'll take our swimming things.* Which one of them had said that?

"Yes. Yes." She nodded. "Exactly, yes." She started pulling her T-shirt back over her head. "I'll go and retrieve it before . . . before . . ."

"One of your nieces swipes it."

Shaking her head free, she laughed gratefully. "One of my nieces. Yes. Can't be too careful." And then, happier now, we had settled on a story that made sense of her missing bra: "It's Heidi Klein."

Rob was quiet in the car on the way down to get the bread, and when we reached the village he asked if it would be really annoying if he cooked that night, only there was this lamb dish he was longing to try. I said, as long as Rebecca didn't think I was shirking, it was fine by me. He said he'd checked and she was cool. Was I sure?

"Yeah." I shrugged casually, thinking, *Fuck, yes.*

He disappeared into the Casino while I was in the bakery and emerged some time later carrying a large paper bag. "A few necessities," he said over the top of it. "And some extras just in case."

As we belted ourselves into the car, he said he hoped I didn't think he was interfering.

I said, "I mean, if it brings you pleasure, interfere away."

He looked at me for a moment and then laughed, relieved. "OK, good."

A few minutes later, driving back, he said, "I can see why you do what you do. You get a lot of freedom, get to stay in lovely places. Summers in Provence, winters in the Alps . . ."

"Living the dream," I said.

"I can also see it's quite exhausting, slotting into other people's lives, being part of the family and yet also being paid." He laughed awkwardly. "I mean, I assume you *are* being paid?"

"I hope so." I laughed, too, though I realized I still hadn't checked how that worked.

"Anyway, you're managing that tightrope very well. They seem to all love you."

"Thank you."

He was pulling into the space opposite the gate and I hoped that was it. He switched off the engine, undid his seat belt, and opened the car door. I was standing next to him at the gate when he added coolly: "Unless you're just a really good actor."

"I'm obviously not that good an actor," I said. "Or I would be in the West End and not doing this."

"Good point."

Martha was coming down the stairs as we went into the house. Rob went straight into the kitchen, but I hung back to ask how she was.

She was ready for the day—in a green-and-white-checked sundress—but she was pale, with dark circles under her eyes. I mouthed hello and she stood for a moment, listening, and then gestured for me to follow her along the corridor into the laundry room.

I closed the door and she hoisted herself up onto the washing machine.

"I still can't get through to him," she said mournfully. "I think he must have lost his phone."

I asked if he could ring her from someone else's phone.

"I don't know if he knows my number by heart."

"Could he get it from the school?"

"He couldn't ask *them*."

"No, of course not."

I asked if she had gotten any closer to telling her mother, and she became more agitated.

"I can't. She'll ask questions. She'll want to know who he is and what I'm going to do. And I can't answer any of those questions until I've spoken to Lia—to him."

It was touching, her attempt to protect Liam Merchant's identity.

"Will he be supportive?" I asked carefully.

"He's got loads of money. His family's loaded. I mean, he owns his own house."

"I meant in other ways."

"I don't know."

She looked suddenly lost and I gave her a hug.

"I'm here," I said, "if you need me."

———

Over breakfast, Layla raved about a self-help book she'd just read—"you know, it really forces you to think, what *is it* that makes me happy?"—after which Roland, at her urging, told everyone about his recent diet: large quantities of red meat interspersed with periods of fasting. "It's worked very well," he said. And then made a couple of little gulping sounds as if he regretted having put himself out there.

"I don't know." Rob patted his stomach, somewhere inside his T-shirt, and then breathed in sharply. "I might be a lost cause." He rocked back on his chair, one arm stretched out behind Clare's. "Or maybe when I've finished this book, I'll take myself in hand."

Phil said, "Sooner rather than later, I hope."

Rob groaned. "Is my body in need of such urgent attention?"

Phil laughed. "I was referring to the book."

When I brought out a fresh pot of coffee, they were still talking about the new novel. Layla asked what it was called and Clare wanted to know what it was about.

Rob glanced back at Phil and then tapped his finger against his nose. "Need to know only, I'm afraid."

Roland lowered his head and winced: "We're going to have to watch ourselves or we'll be in it!"

Rob laughed awkwardly. "Don't worry. It's too late for that. At this stage, I'm just fine-tuning."

Layla leaned forward, her expression earnest. "Tell me, how do you come up with your ideas? Where do you get your inspiration?"

Rob shifted uncomfortably in his seat. "I start with, um, a character."

Layla pressed on, oblivious. "And how does that work?"

Rob was looking increasingly ill at ease. He picked up the remains of a croissant that had been resting on his plate and began tearing it into little pieces. "You, um, start, I guess, with basic features—gender, age, height, facial structure. And that, um, once you have them in your head, you work out what that character feels, what drives, what motivates them."

Layla was nodding as if weighing up the relevance of his contribution. "You're like a puppetmaster," she said.

"I guess. Kind of."

I went back into the kitchen then. I hadn't disliked watching *him* being under interrogation, but I realized, with a slight panic, I hadn't yet thought about lunch. I looked in the fridge. Someone had put back the wrappers for the ham and the salami, but they were empty, and only a few gnarled scraps were left of the cheese. I'd finished the potatoes. Rob's concoction had used up the eggs and bacon, as well as the lettuce and cucumber. Even that celeriac-mayonnaise thing seemed to have gone. I felt a kind of sinking despair. *Another* meal; did meals never end? No. I suppose they didn't. That was sort of the point.

Rob came into the kitchen. "I bought some lentils and some walnuts in the Casino," he said. "Just in case anyone fancied that salad—you know the one with goat cheese?"

"There's not much left."

A beat. Was he testing me? And then he nodded. "We only need a little bit."

"In which case, good idea," I said, closing the fridge.

After breakfast, Rob went to a butcher in a nearby village for the lamb and, when he came back, he and Phil had what Phil called "a quick confab" in the study. I heard Rob murmur assurances, there'd be "something to read very soon."

"Exciting." Phil clapped his hands and said loudly: "I'm on a knife-edge of anticipation."

Phil wandered back to the pool, and Rob stayed in the study. I heard vigorous tapping at the computer.

A lentil and walnut salad was easier to make than it sounded. The hard thing about meals, it turns out, is not reading a recipe but the thinking and the planning. I was roasting the walnuts when I noticed the tapping in the study had stopped.

When I looked up, Rob was standing in the doorway. He looked hot, his hair damp at the temples; his blue shirt was loose.

He let out a long sigh and leaned into the doorjamb.

My stomach flipped. "Everything all right?" I said.

He just stood there, gazing at me, and I found myself gazing back. I thought how broad his chest was, how comforting it would be to take a few steps toward him, to rest my head on his shoulder, to feel his arms wrap around me.

He opened his mouth to speak, closed it, and then opened it again, but all he said was, "Lulu." And then, again, "Lulu."

I said quietly, "Yes?"

Another pause and then he said, "You need any help?"

"I'm OK."

"OK then."

He pushed himself out of the doorway and turned back. I heard his laptop creak open and the tapping resumed.

Chapter Nineteen

Lunch that day turned into what Layla referred to as "self-service" and Rebecca called "Liberty Hall." They came to the table, in dribs and drabs. Phil took a long work call, and Clare, who wasn't feeling well, went for a lie-down. Elliot, Martha, and Iris were allowed to take their plates down to the pool.

I had cleared the table and was putting away the bread when Rob joined me in the kitchen. He unwrapped his leg of lamb, slung it in a baking tray, and began rubbing it with olive oil, garlic, and a mixture of the spices he'd bought in the Casino, slashing the skin and massaging it into the cracks. He was humming to himself, and when I asked if there was anything I could do to help, he said, "Ooh, yes," as if the prospect brought pleasure to both of us. He gave me some tomatoes to peel while he chopped some onions, and I sat at the table with a board and a thin knife. I was making a bit of a mess, and after a few minutes, he said: "Do you know, I reckon those skins will come off more easily if you leave them for a few minutes in a bowl of boiling water. My fault. I probably bought the wrong kind of tomatoes. Sorry."

He rolled his eyes at his own stupidity, but I had that feeling again that I'd been skirting a precipice and walked too close to the edge.

He found Spotify on his phone and music filled the room—Billie Holiday or someone, a throaty voice singing sweet songs of love and longing. At first, as we worked at the table, he talked about tomatoes— how they always taste more delicious if they've been left to ripen in the sun. He'd once had some nice ones from the Isle of Wight, where they also, he said, grew a lot of garlic. It was easy enough to make the right noises, to suggest I got what he meant. I began to relax—to feel dangerously drawn in. He moved on to his own love of cooking, and then he asked me about acting—where had I trained (Central); did I have a good agent (Yes). The tomato skins slid easily from my fingers. He mentioned my upbringing: had it been unsettling moving so many times? I was still thinking about Lulu, and maybe it was subconscious, but, in my head, my own experience began to merge with hers. Yes, it was, I said. I'd been to eleven different schools. They all had different exam boards, so you tended to zone out. And friendships were hard— you learned to be self-sufficient, never fully to commit.

He'd handed me a knife and motioned at me to chop up the tomatoes I'd peeled.

I moved the bowl of water out of the way and started to cut. "I guess I got in the habit, too, of never sticking at things. If anything ever goes wrong, or the pressure gets to me, I run away. I never stay and face the music. I just don't know how to. It's not in my nature."

"Natures aren't always fixed in stone. People can change."

He was looking at me with a gentle expression on his face. I let out a noise from the back of my throat.

After a minute, he asked if I was close to my parents.

I said no and then almost immediately thought: Lulu *is* close to her parents. She mentioned them a lot. Her confidence, the way she breezed through life, it came from being loved and loving back. I put down the knife. She *had* been close. She *had* breezed through life. The table suddenly came up to meet me. I shut my eyes as I tried to settle myself.

It was quiet then, and Rob started talking about his own parents. They had worked hard and had really wanted to make a difference. Sometimes, in his opinion, they had taken on too much. At one point there were nine kids in the house. And it wasn't a big house. He had shared a room with Marc, and two younger boys. Bunk beds. Two sets. He kept talking, and after a bit, to prove I'd been listening, I said: "So nine of you. Your three siblings and . . . ?"

"Yes. Us four, plus five foster kids. All different ages, but quite a handful."

"So the council was paying them—what? I don't know what the going rate is these days, but you know five cared for kids, that'll have added up."

He swept the onions he'd chopped into a pan and then glanced back at me, with a slight frown. "I don't know how much the council gave them. I don't think it was about the money for them. I really don't. They had a mission to help." He shrugged. "It was hard for me and my siblings. We didn't get much attention. They expected us just to get on with it. And I often resented sharing them."

I'd been looking closely at him. I had never thought what it was like to be one of the natural kids in a foster family. I'd been jealous of them. Us and them. I'd thought they were the wanted ones, that we were the unwanted appendages. But I could see it was more complicated—that being "unwanted" might actually be a state of mind rather than a reality.

"Does that sound awful?" he said.

"It doesn't sound awful," I said.

He had stood up and had taken the pan to the stove now, bending his head to light the burner. He began to volunteer more information—mainly about Marc, the brother he'd just been staying with, how it wasn't an easy relationship, but they'd always gotten on. He was "one of the ones that had worked."

An image came into my head: Molly tucked up on that horrible velvet sofa with Mrs. Ormorod.

I saw myself standing watching her in the doorway.

"What about the ones that didn't work?" I asked.

He thought for a while and then said it was a bit of a blur, really, but he thought the ones that didn't work had been brought to the house when they were older, that they tended to have "anger issues"; that they were more "damaged."

He turned to get something from the fridge. I thought about how people used to say I had "anger issues," and that they hadn't said it about Molly. And I thought maybe it wasn't just that she'd been younger when we were taken from the flat, but that wherever we were after that, at school, in interim care, she'd always been protected from the situations that were most frightening, the situations that could bring out your anger issues if you had them, and that the thing that had protected her was me.

I looked up and realized Rob had come back from the fridge and was watching me.

He wasn't smiling, but his mouth was at a tilt, and there were crinkles around his eyes. A lock of hair had fallen forward again. I felt another lurch, a strong pull of attraction, as if my insides were leaping toward him.

Eventually, he said: "Those tomatoes done?"

"Yup."

I carried the board carefully over to the stove, and he

scraped them into the pan and stirred them into the melting onions.

The smell that rose was delicious, both sweet and savory. I watched him sprinkle in a little bit of salt.

"What can I do to help now?" I said.

"Um." He seemed distracted, still stirring. Then he looked up and said casually, "By the way, are you actually celiac?"

"What?"

"It's just I just noticed you picking at a bit of bread earlier."

A split second of hesitation before I took a gamble and said, "No, I'm not. I'm gluten intolerant, but I say celiac because it sounds better. It makes people take the issue more seriously."

"OK." He smiled briefly. "I see."

The onions at the edge of the pan were beginning to catch. "You're quite the detective," I said.

"I'm perennially curious. It's my downfall."

"I'll have to be more careful."

He laughed then. "You've got nothing to worry about. You're doing really well, keeping it all together."

"Keeping it together?"

He nodded, and then, bending down to lower the heat, said, "I'm the only one who's even begun to guess."

A piece of onion spat from the pan onto the floor.

I found a cloth and wiped it up. Begun to guess what? That I was lying about being celiac? Or something else?

I returned the cloth to the sink. "Any other jobs, or do you mind if I go?" I said, coming back.

His eyes moved around my face. I felt myself flush. But then he rested the wooden spoon against the side of the pan and turned away. He gave a little bow. "Consider yourself relieved of your duties."

In the safety of my room, I realized it was already 4 p.m. Most of the afternoon had gone, and I hadn't noticed. I'd been swept up by—what had I been swept up by? I was sitting on the bed and I found I was crossing and uncrossing my arms, like I was coming unpinned. I felt as if I'd been worked on. I went back over the conversation. Had I slipped up? I'd known how much the council gave you to foster a child, and there was a moment when I'd been peeling the tomatoes when I was thinking about Molly, and I couldn't remember if I'd said anything out loud. But I'd done well with the celiac confession; that had been the right move. I imagined Lulu was the kind of person who *might* pretend to be celiac. Otherwise it was tiny things—like the bread, the tomatoes. I was all over the place.

Was I *falling* for him? Was this what it felt like? There had been a boy once at Fairlight House. I'd found myself wanting to be near him; was painfully self-conscious when he spoke to me, had no control over the pitch of my voice, the loudness of my laugh. I'd cried bitterly when he got a placement elsewhere. I had so little to go on—but I knew these things happened on holiday. Time was more intense, emotions got confused. I couldn't afford to let them, that was the thing. This wasn't a moment for weakness. I had to be sharp, to be on my game.

Chapter Twenty

It was still very hot as I walked up to dinner that evening. The sky was overcast, tight bubbles of cloud trapped across it.

I was late, having taken a long time getting ready. I'd washed my hair and found a blow-dryer in the cupboard under the basin. There was a stain on the flowery dress, but it wouldn't budge, so in the end, I went back to Lulu's suitcase. I wished I didn't care what I wore. It seemed terrible to be choosing from her dresses, to be using her stuff for anything as trivial as to make myself look nice. I picked out a green one.

Rob was in the kitchen, and the remaining five adult guests were milling about the terrace, in the process of sitting down. Phil and Roland, who were sorting the wine, were both wearing patterned shirts and knee-length shorts, and Clare made a joke about not having "got the memo." I should have gone into the kitchen to help, but wanting to avoid Rob for as long as I could, I lingered in an empty chair next to Rebecca. She turned to bring me into a conversation she was having with Layla about family holidays, "the best kind and the worst." They were both wearing black, Layla looking stern and headmistressy in a high-necked top, Rebecca more bohemian with a lot of dangly necklaces. Layla said their favorite holiday ever had been a windsurfing trip to Portugal. "We loved it, didn't we?" she called down to Roland.

"Yes, darling," he replied. "We loved it."

Clare was at the head of the table, looking younger and more casual than the other two women, in a denim jumpsuit. "I don't care where I go on holiday," she said. "It can be anywhere. All that matters is that I'm in a lovely hotel, with someone attending to my every need."

"Oh." Rebecca made a face, as if to say *Get you*.

"Which is not to say I'm not enjoying myself here," Clare said. She shrugged, caught Phil's eye, and laughed. "It's just a different thing."

"You have expensive tastes," Phil said blandly. "Nothing to be ashamed of."

The teenagers arrived as Rob was bringing out a large platter of food. Iris and Elliot, disheveled and out of breath, had "been for a walk." Martha had come straight from the shower. She sidled into the empty seat to my right. Her hair was still wet and she was wearing her grandmother's gold cross over a voluminous white dress. She looked a bit like a novice nun— only one with God *and* fashion on her side—though, of course, under the circumstances, also *not*. I asked her in a whisper if she was OK, and whether he'd rung? She lowered her eyes, shaking her head very slightly.

Rob had stayed standing, at the other end of the table, to serve up. His blue linen shirt was crumpled and he looked hot and a bit tense. "There's far too much," he said. He pushed his hair back from his face as he sat down. "I always overdo it."

"We're all very grateful," Rebecca said. "Especially Lulu, I'm sure."

"You bet," I said, looking at the plate that had arrived in front of me: a slice of lamb, next to a pile of roasted vegetables, a swirl of tomato sauce, a mound of fragrant, nut-studded rice. "I hope it's not too good. I wouldn't want to be outdone."

"Trust me. You won't be." Rob caught my eye and grinned.

It was airless under the umbrella and Roland closed it at Layla's urging. But that meant it became an obstruction, furled in the middle of the table, so he put it back up again. Everyone told Rob how delicious the lamb was—me included. Layla said that thing people often say about how much nicer food always tastes outside, and Clare started talking about some garden furniture she'd recently had installed on her roof terrace—a modular L-shaped sofa and lounge chair, in an all-weather weave. "I just thought I'd splurge, what with everything. In the end I went with Indian Ocean—well worth it."

She was so boring, with her luxury goods. I didn't

know what the attraction was for Phil. I felt a tug of loyalty toward Rebecca and I asked her about a book—a bestseller in its time—that I'd "heard" (knew from googling) she'd edited when she was in publishing. Her expression lifted, as she told me about discovering it in the slush pile and how gratifying it had been when it had started winning awards.

The rest of the table had tuned in.

"I didn't know that was one of yours," Layla said. "Gosh."

"Trust me." Rebecca had gone pink with pleasure. "I was quite the talent-spotter in my time. Wasn't I, Phil?"

"You were." Her husband nodded. "You were a force of nature. I was in awe of you."

"Shame I gave it all up for this ungrateful lot."

"Nice," Iris said.

Clare was smiling, her head on one side. "Thing is, it was your choice," she said. "And I'm sure you don't really regret it. We all have our priorities."

I'd wanted Rebecca to feel better about herself, and for her to associate that feeling with me. If it had the collateral effect of pissing Clare off in the process . . . well, that was a bonus.

"I wouldn't have said you gave anything *up*," I said to Rebecca. "Isn't it more that you channeled all that intellectual vibrancy into being a good parent? And it works both ways. Those skills you've picked up as a mother—well, I suppose they're also valuable if you did want to go back to work."

It's never about lying, Sean used to say. It's about telling people what they want to hear.

I could see Rebecca considering. She breathed in sharply through her nose. "Yes," she said, nodding. "You're right. Thanks, Lulu."

I sat back. At the other end of the table, Phil was telling a story about a mutual friend, a former "rugby blue," who had given him a lift to a cricket match in Surrey. "Honestly, I wished I'd gone by train. This powerful Lexus, and we crawled along in the inside lane. I don't think I've ever been driven so slowly. I had a take-out cup of coffee in my hand. Didn't spill a drop!"

"He can't have been as slow as Mum," Martha said. "She is genuinely the slowest driver in the world."

"That is true," Phil conceded.

"Not gonna lie," Iris agreed.

Rebecca began laughingly to protest. "Now come on. I'm not that slow. I'm cautious."

"That's one word for it," Clare said, rolling her eyes.

Rebecca looked marginally less amused. "Come on, guys," she said.

"Actually, I have to admit," Layla said, "if ever Rebecca and I are going to the same place and she suggests traveling together, I make sure I volunteer to drive before she can!"

"Layla!" Rebecca said, in reproach.

Her friend raised her hands, as if to ward off objections. "It's true."

Rebecca leaned back in her chair. "Yes, well, at least I'm not always getting speeding tickets."

Layla laughed and then tucked her hair behind her ears. "I'm not 'always' getting speeding tickets!"

Rebecca left her mouth hanging open, to demonstrate stunned indignation. "Ahem," she said.

Roland gulped a couple of times. He had gone red. "Shall we change the subject?"

Rebecca glanced across at him. "Er . . . I don't think you should get involved. Didn't you take some points for Layla last year?" She was speaking in a sort of jolly-along sing-song. "Otherwise weren't we about to lose our license?"

"I'm a GP," Layla said, raising her hands. "I have to be able to drive in case I'm called out on an emergency."

"Oh, don't worry." Rebecca was still smiling. "None of us will tell on you. You're among friends here."

Layla laughed—more nervously this time. "Well, as I say, it's not something I'm proud of."

I felt a rush of adrenaline. So Layla and Roland had broken the law: interesting. I stood up to collect the plates. Layla pushed her chair back, too, but although she followed me into the kitchen, she crossed the room and left it through the door that led to the corridor. I wondered if she was upset. No, she was probably just going to the bathroom. She wouldn't think Rebecca's revelation was that big a deal. She thought she was "among friends."

It was dark in the room, but I kept the lights off so as

231

not to attract mosquitoes. I stacked the dishwasher and had started on the washing-up—the sink was piled with pots and trays and saucepans, all greasy, caked with gunk—when Layla came back into the room. She strode straight out through the double doors to the terrace and, bending behind Rebecca, whispered in her ear. Rebecca stood up and the two of them came back into the kitchen. They conferred quietly for a moment. And then Rebecca said, "You have got to be fucking kidding me," and spun around. Bending her index finger, she said, "Girls. Quick chat, please."

"Elliot. You too." Layla sounded more cautious.

Phil said, "What's going on?"

Roland had clumsily got to his feet, and Clare pushed back her chair for a better view.

The teenagers funneled through into the kitchen and stood in a line just inside the door. Iris was laughing, but Martha looked as if she was about to cry.

"I'm assuming this belongs to one of you three." Layla was holding out her hand. "I've just found it on the floor of the downstairs toilet. Would one of you like to tell me where it came from?"

The three kids had looked down at the object in her palm, fleetingly, and then immediately away as if to leave their eyes on it too long was an admission of guilt. All three were now staring blankly at Layla.

I took a step closer. She was holding a small brown object I recognized. Soft and leather, the size of a makeup pouch.

Elliot's stash.

Rebecca said: "In that nobody has had a chance to meet up with a local dealer, I can only assume one of you smuggled this into the country—through two sets of customs. I mean, do you have *any idea* how stupid that is?"

Elliot lifted one foot, scratched his other calf with it, and then lowered it again. A giveaway—if Layla or Rebecca had noticed.

"It will be much simpler if you own up now." Layla looked pointedly at Iris. Clearly, she had her down as the culprit.

"Come on." Rebecca sounded more impatient now. "It belongs to one of you."

Elliot was knitting and unknitting his fingers. Martha was standing still, very pale. Iris had stuffed her hands into her pockets and was staring up at the ceiling.

There was a long, agonizing silence.

I stepped forward out of the gloom.

"Oh my God. I'm so embarrassed," I said. "I'm really sorry, but that's mine."

As I crossed the room, the two women seemed to reel backward. Layla looked at the pouch in her hand and then back at me. "It's *yours*? This belongs to *you*?"

I was aware of the others outside at the table, at their silent, staring faces.

"Yes." I took the pouch from her, clutched it between both hands, pressing hard as if I thought I might be able to make it disappear. "It was a present from

someone. Here in France. No smuggling involved. I
don't even . . . I mean, weed isn't really my thing."

"It's *yours*?" Rebecca sounded stunned.

I turned to her and said apologetically, "I had no intention of smoking it. I've just been carrying it with
me. On the sort of off chance, I suppose. Earlier, before supper when I went to the toilet, it must have fallen
out of my bag."

"Goodness." Layla's empty hands fluttered. "Maybe
don't leave it lying around."

"As I say, I'm so sorry. Stupid."

I turned and walked back toward the washing-up. I
put the pouch down behind the sink next to the bottle
of detergent. The counter was damp—the brown
leather was already darkening.

"And maybe," Rebecca said behind me, "save it for
when the job's over, for when you're not being paid to
keep your wits about you?"

"Yes, of course."

I began to busy myself with the coffee machine. I
filled the pot with water and replaced the filter. The
teenagers melted away into the house, and Layla and
Rebecca walked back out to join the others at the
table.

I saw Rob get to his feet and watched him walk
through the door. He crossed the kitchen and came to
stand next to me. I could feel the warmth of his arm
against mine, smell the laundered scent of his clothing.

"So," he said.

"So." I spooned coffee into the filter and snapped the lid shut.

"That was a bit of drama."

"Yes."

He swallowed hard and his lips parted like he was about to say something.

"Anyway," I said, flicking the switch on the machine.

"I have a feeling you have just thrown yourself on your sword."

"My sword?"

I turned to lean backward into the counter. I looked at him, my eyes slightly narrowed.

He started rubbing his chest hard, where his heart was. "I hope they're grateful, the little sods."

I laughed, but he was biting the corner of his lip, not laughing. "It was very kind of you."

Outside, Rebecca was asking if anyone knew any parlor games, and Phil was telling her to calm down. "No one wants to play parlor games."

The coffee had started dripping through. I reached across and jostled the glass pot for something to do with my hands.

Rob said, "I'm beginning to suspect you might be a nice person."

He put his hand on my hand. He meant just to still it, but his fingers stayed on my wrist, his thumb against my wrist bone. We both looked down, as if shocked, and then we both looked up. I felt a pressure in the center of my ribs, something physical that seemed to trap my breath. His skin was warm. I could feel the pad of his thumb against my pulse. We were both standing very still. I moved the tips of my fingers so they were curled around to touch his hand too. We stood like that for what seemed like several minutes, his thumb stroking the underside of my wrist, and then he took his other hand out of the front pocket of his trousers and brought it up and looped it behind my neck, and once it was firmly there he gently drew me toward him. I didn't look, but I could hear the chatter outside, the voices that didn't falter, as I lifted my chin and pressed my mouth to his.

A peal of laughter outside. We broke apart.

Rob's arm had slipped to my shoulder. He smiled down at me. "Are they watching?"

I looked past him, out to the table. Shook my head. "It's too dark. They can't see."

"Do you mind if I ask you one question," he said. "Before we go any further?"

"What?" I was looking up at him, defenseless, just waiting.

"What's your real name?" He asked with only a small amount of curiosity, as one might say, "Have you finished?" when clearing a plate.

"What?" I said again.

He was still smiling. "Because I know you're not actually Lulu."

"What do you mean?"

"I only ask . . ." He reached toward me. ". . . because I think I should know who I'm kissing . . ." He took a handful of silk dress, bunching it, so as to draw me closer. ". . . if I'm going to do it again."

He didn't really need an answer—the intensity in his eyes had nothing to do with the question. But I was suddenly cold. I wasn't Lulu *because Lulu was dead.* How could I have even begun to forget? Nothing I could do would ever make amends for that.

I pulled back, swiping my hands down to loosen his grip on the dress. "The coffee's ready," I said, turning away. "They're waiting." I disengaged the pot and put it next to the cups and the milk on the tray and handed it to him. "Could you take it out?" I forced myself to meet his eye.

He looked at me quizzically for a moment before taking the tray and walking out onto the terrace.

"At last!" I heard Rebecca say when he got there. "What were you doing? Grinding the beans by hand?"

I filled the kettle, and when it boiled, I poured the water over a tea bag in a mug. I carried this out and placed it on the table next to Clare. Rob had sat down in Martha's chair. He smiled at me, his expression hopeful. His feet were resting on the bars under my chair, and he pushed it out to make room for me.

"Sit!" Rebecca cried, with a forced smile, awkward after the recent scene in the kitchen. "We're just talking about September and how it always feels like a new start, more of a new year than New Year, how we should all have September resolutions. I'm going to say yes to more things. You know, like when people ask if you'd like to go to the theater, and your heart sinks and you desperately try to think of a reason not to. Well, I'm not going to do that anymore. Lulu—what are you *not* going to do?"

I heard Clare say, "Apart from not smoke weed."

I was gripping the back of the chair. I looked around, unsure, vaguely panicked. "I'm not sure. I think I'm going to turn in actually."

I stepped around the table and scurried down the grass toward the pool. As I reached the gate, the murmur of their voices resumed, and by the time I was through the door of the *pigeonnier*, I convinced myself I could hear laughter.

Chapter Twenty-One

I had gotten used to thinking every day would be like the one before—the same blue sky, the same sun, the same heat. But the following morning, it was overcast, the sky crosshatched with a strangely formal pattern of high clouds. The area around the pool looked flat without the contrast of sun and shade. The blue paint on the shutters was peeling in strips. Thrusting my feet into my flip-flops, I noticed speckles of black in the corners of the square stone slabs, which I realized was mold.

Rob was already in the kitchen, squeezing oranges into a big glass pitcher. He was wearing a pale T-shirt and off-white trousers made of a loose thin cotton. Both were splashed: damp patches dotted with orange pith. "I'm so sorry," he said, sucking the juice off the heel of his hand. "I waited, but when you didn't emerge, I bulldozed in. I'd understand if you hated me." He scooped the fruit carcasses from the counter into the trash and carried the pitcher out to the table, which was already laid—crockery, cutlery, basket of bakery goods, the lot.

"Of course I don't hate you," I said.

"It was busy in the village this morning," he continued, as he came back in. "*Very* long queue at the *boulangerie*." He was telling me as if the whole experience was something we usually shared, like it was *our thing*. It was a good tactic: pretend nothing was wrong. But my face felt very hot, my mouth tight with embarrassment. I went to the sink and began washing up.

In the continuing silence, the pressure rose to say something, anything. "This is interesting," I said, holding a bulbous wooden contraption with a ridged head under the tap.

Laughing, he took it from me and dried it with a tea towel. "There's an electric squeezer in the cupboard, but I thought it would be quicker by hand." He looked ruefully down at his T-shirt. "Might have made less mess."

"Oh, I see, for the oranges."

He looked at me for a moment, and a troubled expression crossed his face. And then he shook his head, as if clearing his ears. "But of course. What other use might you have for this tool?" He pursed his mouth when he said "tool" and twirled it in the air before returning it to a stoneware pot. He cleared his throat, flushing slightly as if he had embarrassed himself. He opened the dishwasher and lined the clean glasses up on the counter above. I ferried them over to the cupboard and put them away, glad he couldn't see my face.

"By the way, I have a message for you from your friend in the village," he said. His tone was different now, a bit more formal. "He was having a smoke in the square as I parked. Anyway"—he closed the dishwasher and straightened up—"he said you should pop by and see him next time you're shopping. He's got a bit more information?"

I put away the glasses. When I closed the cupboard door, he was still standing there, waiting for me to say something.

"OK. Thanks," I said.

Rebecca and Layla bustled into the kitchen and headed straight for the terrace. "Amazing!" Layla called. "What a wonderful spread, you two. You make quite a team."

Rob hesitated, then, turning as if to address them, said, "Any time."

He walked out to join them. He had a tell—one hand in his pocket, juggling invisible change—which he did when he felt awkward. He was doing it now. He pulled out a chair this side of the table and sat down with his back to me.

I felt breathless suddenly, as if breathing itself was hard. I didn't know if it was fear or lust. I'd felt an intense longing to push myself against him, to feel his tongue in my mouth. I had churned it over obsessively in the night and in the morning as I'd stayed in bed listening to him swim outside my room. How had I let myself kiss him? Get that close? I'd forgotten the danger. I should have steered clear. I'd made it worse for myself. Dispositionally, he made a bad mark. He paid attention to the things that didn't fit the pattern; he didn't rationalize them away like Rebecca. He'd noticed things the others hadn't, like the lavender, the business with the tomatoes. He knew too much, he was *toying* with me. And yet I seemed powerless to resist.

Out on the terrace, they were discussing the weather like it was a conundrum that needed solving. Rebecca called for me to "run and find" the house bible, and they began looking through the loose leaflets in the plastic wallet. The coast was considered too far, as was a vineyard where you could taste wine. A zipline was mentioned, and dismissed, along with "a tree-climbing center." Shopping in Castels was out as they'd be going there the following day for the market. It's such a shame, Rebecca said, that Phil and Clare had nabbed the cathedral on Monday, as today would have been a much better option. "Let's go again," Clare said. "I don't mind seeing it twice, or even staying home."

"I'm happy with that," said Phil, ambiguously.

"It's fine," Rebecca said. "You were both desperate to go on Monday and you did."

Rob hadn't said much. At one point, he mentioned perhaps needing to stay behind and do some work on his novel, but Phil said, "You're in control, aren't you?"

"Yes. Yes."

"Good. So how about I give you the day off. What do you say?"

A voice hissed: "Lulu!"

Martha and Iris were standing at the door to the study, beckoning me. They stepped back into the room when I got close, and when we were out of sight of the terrace, Iris said, "I'm not being funny, but you literally saved our lives." She gripped my shoulders and gave me an awkward hug. "We owe you."

Martha put her hands out. "Nothing to do with me, by the way. It was just these idiots."

"I have to say, smuggling weed: quite ballsy," I said. "Maybe don't do it again?"

"Trust me," Iris said. "We won't."

She wandered back into the house and I asked Martha if she was feeling OK. "Yeah, bit less off. I dunno. It's like it hasn't properly hit me yet." She cupped her hands over her stomach. "I spoke to Liam's lodger and he said he was back from Greece tomorrow, so I should hear from him then."

She bit her lip.

By the time I got back into the kitchen, the adults had settled on something—a trip to a river where you could walk and swim and hire canoes.

"An excursion!" I said.

Rebecca didn't smile. She was being offhand with me. Her manner when she'd asked me to get the house file had been bossier than the day before, as if she felt let down and was putting me in my place.

"We're taking the Citroën and the Fiat and leaving you the Audi so you can do another big shop," she told me.

"Who's going?" I said.

"All of us. Rob—if you can spare him—is one of our designated drivers. I'm not sure how long we'll be, so really don't worry about supper. We'll grab something light, or I don't know. We'll sort it. Either way, you'll have a bit of peace." She flashed a smile.

Clare came into the kitchen: "Could you ask the cleaner when she comes about the drainage? It's really no better."

"Oh, dear," Rebecca said. "We're not very 'boutique,' are we? So yes, Lulu, if you could talk to Brigitte about it. Ask her to organize a plumber if necessary. Let's hope there isn't a dead body in there."

As soon as the cars were out of sight, I left the house on foot—no way was I risking the huge Audi. It was even hotter than usual, airless under the web of clouds. I felt damp at the back of my hair and under my bra strap. Myriad tiny insects followed, getting in my hair and sticking to my lips. I had the feeling I was being bitten.

Along with my other worries, I was anxious Brigitte would pass me on the lane up to the house and stop for a chat, but I reached the safety of the main road and then the town itself without seeing her.

The Casino was diagonally opposite the bakery, and there was a small turning just beyond it, narrow enough for a single car. I crossed over and walked along the side of the supermarket and past a row of garages and a concrete area set aside for recycling bins, and then a couple of angular houses, front porches busy with hanging baskets and kids' toys. A dog barked and strained against its chain.

The road widened ahead of me, dropping downhill toward the river and open countryside. There was one house left, red brick and single story, with a steep pitched roof. I peered through the gate to make sure. But yes. Front door: blue. And also I recognized Pascal's battered white car in the forecourt.

An elderly man in a red tracksuit, his face wrinkled like an old apple, came when I knocked, and then shuffled away as Pascal swung down the stairs to see me. I could smell the caramel of his vape on his clothes.

"You had information for me?" I said, leaning into the doorframe. "The man asking about me at the café; did you find out any more?"

Pascal ran his hand over his goatee. His eyes were bloodshot. "Yes, yes. I asked Antoine for more details. The man spoke French, he said, but he might not have *been* French. He was big, bulky." Pascal shrugged up his shoulders to illustrate and then kept them there. "Brown hair. Glasses."

"Did he say anything else?"

"Only that you had left without leaving a note. He

was agitated, apparently, very keen to catch up with you."

He offered me a coffee, but I told him I didn't have time, and I backed away, down the steps toward the road. When I reached the square, I sat under a plane tree and tried to think straight. Sean didn't have brown hair, but he could have dyed it. The glasses could be a prop. He wasn't bulky, but he knew how to throw his body, to shapeshift. He was good at creating a legend. In Marrakech, as a "property dealer," he'd used layers and a wide-legged walk to bulk up. In Barcelona, dressed all in black, he was slim, narrow-hipped, the king of weight loss. So what had I learned? The man in Castels might have been him. Or it might not. But who else, if not him?

I wondered where Sean was, that minute? I felt an itching inside, a hungry, restless desire to know.

Swifts were flying high across the square, their screams thin and frantic. I pushed my head against the tree. The trunk was cracked and split, the fissures filled with crumbling sap. If I survived until next Thursday, when the job ended, what would happen next? I could get to the UK on Lulu's passport. And then, with advice from Molly's husband, go to the police. It wouldn't be easy. I'd be prosecuted myself, as an accessory or for obstructing justice. Not to mention all those other crimes. I'd serve time. I didn't know for how long, but I'd be put away. Not that I didn't deserve it, and anyway, at least I was alive.

In front of me, between two larger buildings, was an old house, ocher-washed, with faded blue shutters. The door opened and a woman stood holding a baby in her arms. She called to a man coming toward her down the street, and when he reached her, they kissed over the baby's head and then they both went into the house.

That's what I want: I thought suddenly. A house with blue shutters and a man to kiss me over a baby's head. Could that happen way ahead in the future for someone like me? Was it unrealistic to dream?

I stood up then, sick of myself, and headed into the Casino. Cool and empty, it smelled of cured meat and disinfectant and old ice. The freezer department was full of unexpected gifts: not just duck confit, but turkey cutlets, potatoes *boulangères*, asparagus risotto, quiche Lorraine, a "tartiflette," raspberry roulades. I also bought ham, salami, cheese, coffee, and lettuce, enough for several lunches and at least two suppers, as well as a pair of large oval-shaped sunglasses with heavy black rims. I used Rebecca's card and kept the receipt, though I knew enough about her by now to know she wouldn't ask to see it.

The bags were heavy, the handles cutting into my fingers, and I put them down at the door to readjust my hold. Someone was waiting politely for me to clear the way, and when I stood up, I recognized her as the woman outside the bakery. I quickly recalled the details—getting married at the end of the month; on an emergency hunt for a house to accommodate her parents. I scanned my memory for everything I'd gleaned from the internet. It was like a buzz, an electrical charge.

"Sophia!" I said. "Sophia Bartlett?"

"Yes!" She stopped, surprised.

I felt my body language shift. Sometimes when you create a legend, particularly on the spot, it's as if you're mining your own soul. *Newly married, one kid, small house in Fulham.* After my moment of weakness in the square it felt good, like wish fulfillment.

"You don't recognize me. Don't worry. It's been a long time. We used to play tennis together at the Hurlingham?"

"Oh my God. Amazing," she said, her eyes widening. "Wow! Yes. Hello."

Her Facebook page made much of her Oxford education. Underestimated fact: the smarter you are, the more likely you are to trust.

Her face broke into a smile. "I haven't seen you . . . for ages."

"Oh God. I'm sorry." I rested the bags on the ground again with a defeated shrug. "I know I promised to come back after I'd had the baby, but it's been so full on. Maybe when he's a bit older."

She asked what he was called then—Frank, I said, eighteen months now, a little scamp. He was loving the pool at the French house. We were out for the whole summer. My grandmother had recently died and we were doing the house up, preparing it for rental.

Sophia was powerless in the face of her want for the house, her *need*. She didn't even bother with condolences. "Oh my God," she said. "Is it free next month? You could be the answer to my dreams."

"Oh, I'm sorry, no." I was apologetic but polite as I prepared for departure. "We'll still be here then."

"Is there nothing we can do to persuade you?"

She started gushing then, telling me all about her forthcoming marriage to Quentin Trevisan, "you remember him?" and the nightmare they'd had with the rental for her parents. I gave the tiniest hint that I could be swayed, but then shook my head. Probably not, I said.

Oh, but please.

In the end, reluctantly, I took her number and, as we parted, told her I would talk to my husband. She didn't even ask my name. "You'll never guess who I bumped into," I imagined her telling Quentin. "Oh damn, I can't remember. But *she has a house. And it might be free*."

The clouds started breaking up as I left the main road and it was properly hot as I walked along the lane. In the whorls of sun, the world was rich with new textures, the landscape on either side patched with green and gold. Far away, in a long sloping field on a hillside, a tractor silently moved. I was completely alone. If Sean was looking for me, he hadn't *found* me. Sophia Bartlett's card, like an insurance policy, nestled in my back pocket. I might use it. I might not. But I felt stronger now I had it—more *myself*.

Chapter Twenty-Two

The smell had shifted: something human and sharp now above the scent of leathery wood. I stood motionless, listening for Brigitte. I thought I'd timed it right, but was she still here? Upstairs a faucet dripped. I stepped quietly through to the kitchen. I let my breath out. She'd been and gone. The floor was wet, and she had written a scribbled note under the one I'd left her, saying that she had poured *entretien de canalisations* down the drains in the upstairs bathrooms. If that didn't work, she would arrange a visit from the plumber. I scrunched the note into the trash, and then I buried the frozen meals on the bottom shelf of the freezer. They'd be safe for now. None of them looked beyond the ice tray.

I felt self-conscious walking down the grass to the pool; I wasn't used to having the place to myself. The gate clattered. The door to the *pigeonnier* opened with a grinding scrape. It was hot. I'd left the bed unmade, and little curled scraps of what looked like hay had dropped from the beams onto the sheets. I shook them off, pulled the sheet tight, and plumped the pillows. I convinced myself again I could smell Sean's body odor, that gel he used on his hair. I remembered a time I had gone out without permission and he had been waiting for me in my room. Maybe I was being overcautious, but I checked the passport behind the picture and the money in the toilet tank; both were undisturbed.

I swam after that, and then read, holding the book up against the sun, the deep blue of the sky hard against the white of the pages. I had only a chapter left, and when I finished, I tried to lie there with my arms by my side, eyes closed. The courtyard was very still, as if suspended in jelly, the air thick and sultry, hissing with cicadas. I opened my eyes. I'd heard a noise, I was sure, a snap of twigs, from the rough area beyond the hedge. I got to my feet, put on my T-shirt, and moved to the gap between the hedge and the wall. In the rough grass beyond was a grid of gnarled fruit trees, their trunks sun-bleached white. A ripened plum detaching from its stem, rustled through the branches, landing on the grass with a quiet thud.

I tiptoed through the clearing into the cover of the trees. It was cooler here and smelled sharply of pine and maybe manure. I looked down across the field, the sweep of yellow and green, an explosion of white cloud like a volcano on the horizon. I had a sense of distance and emptiness.

I was being stupid, I told myself; paranoid.

I walked back up to the house, feeling the guests' absence in a series of objects: Iris's sunglasses on the table, a scrunched tissue under a chair, a pair of swimming trunks dangling from the catch of an upstairs shutter. I wondered how they were getting on, how Martha was. She wouldn't be able to confide in her mother today, not with everyone else around. What *was* going on between Phil and Clare? I tried to imagine the course of their relationship. Was it a relationship, in fact, or something more fluid? How had it started? A grope, I decided, at a drunken gathering. Did it mean anything? I thought probably not. They were both selfish, out for the thrill of the moment. Poor Rebecca. Was it better if she knew, or if she didn't? Either way, it was humiliating for her.

I passed through the kitchen and along the corridor on the other side, and then into the hall. Looking up the steep flight of stairs, I could see a segment of wooden floor and a half-open door. A faucet still dripped, not regularly like a heartbeat, but irregularly, like the tapping of fingers. Somewhere a fly was bumping its head against a window.

At the top of the stairs was a long passage running most of the length of the house. The air smelled musty, of sleep and old pillows, with a tang of drain disinfectant.

I headed to the far end, starting with the door on the left. It opened into what was obviously the master bedroom, a large bright space, with three large shuttered windows, a stone fireplace, and a canopy bed with a padded headboard. A tatty flesh-colored cotton nightie was folded on the pillow closest to me, and on the bedside table were earplugs, an eye mask, and a paperback book.

The table on the other side was piled with newspapers, a copy of *The Week*, and several hardbacks. Phil's glasses rested on top next to a packet of Imodium Instant Melts and a tub of probiotics for "Gut Health."

The next bedroom along clearly belonged to Layla and Roland—a double, with windows facing to the front, as tidy as expected, the bed tightly made. On a chest of drawers squatted two jars of expensive-looking face cream (one night, one day), and a hard, plastic case containing a dental retainer, and some legal books. An en suite bathroom linked through to a single room next door. Elliot hadn't unpacked, and T-shirts and boxers spilled from a carry-on suitcase. Two enormous trainers sprawled under the bed. Across the corridor was another bathroom, and next to that the girls' room, which I'd already been into. Beyond was a small double that was clearly occupied by Clare. Dresses with designer labels lined the wardrobe, and the counter next to the basin was heaped with expensive makeup. The bed was made, and her nightdress—a black and oyster-pink slip with a diamanté trim—had been arranged on the pillow. The contrast between this oyster pink and her sister's overwashed beige was painfully poignant.

A leather bag leaned against her bedside table and in an inner pocket I found a credit card—both sides of which I photographed—and a thick plastic envelope of euros, several hundred by the weight of it. I put them back, and flicked through her copy of *Condé Nast Traveler*. She had folded down one corner to mark an article on "the best wellness hotels in the world." They were far-flung, mainly in South Africa or Australia, but one of the retreats was in France. Maison Ila: "a five-bedroom sanctuary filled with Indian antiques, hand-painted tableware and pale wood . . . a natural pathway to revitalization." It was in the Aude, in the southwest, and had a famous chef.

In the bag's outside pocket were some pieces of neatly folded paper. I unwrapped them: money-off vouchers, one for Liberty (£10), several for Waitrose, and a couple of Boots receipts, promising thirty percent discount on the next purchase.

Clare had expensive tastes, but she was also thrifty. It was worth remembering.

The last room was, by a process of elimination, Rob's. It was dim in here, the shutters only half open, his black swimming trunks dangling from the central catch. The bed was unmade and there was an unfolded suit bag on the floor, containing trousers and shirts, layered up over an internal hanger. No sign of his laptop. I sat on the edge of the bed and breathed in deeply, and then an urge came over me to put my head on his pillow, and I flicked my legs up and slid sideways so that I was staring up at the ceiling. My hair was still damp. I could smell laundry and shampoo. I imagined him lying where I was, and I felt a series of small leaps beneath my rib cage.

What was the matter with me? I was supposed to be in control.

There was something hard under the pillow, I drew out not the paperback I'd been expecting, but Rob's leather notebook. I rubbed the cover with my finger-tips and then sat up still holding it. It felt solid and thick. I remembered how he had described his working method in the newspaper article as being like the board of a TV detective. I wondered if he had written any-thing about *me*.

I slipped my index finger inside the front cover and flipped it back.

What was I expecting? An insight into his mind. At the very least diagrams, maps, character studies, sketches.

But the first page was blank.

I flipped again. Blank.

And again.

Blank. Blank. Blank.

Closing the notebook, I stroked it thoughtfully with my thumb. Was this a second notebook, a spare? Why would he be keeping it under his pillow if so? Why would he hide an empty book?

I stood up, and noticed next to the bed a battered paperback: *The Scapegoat* by Daphne du Maurier. I turned it over to look at the back cover. There was a mug stain that had dragged away some of the words, but I read enough to see it was about a man who took on another man's identity. ". . . his face and voice were known to me too well. I was looking at myself."

It was just a coincidence, I told myself, as I put it back.

But I left the room unsettled.

There was only one place left to explore. The corridor ended in an open-plan space, described in the bible as "the snug," which contained a sofa, a small desk with a basic computer, a printer and a stack of paper, some of it letterhead (useful), and a row of bookshelves. I did a quick scan—John le Carré, *Sapiens*, *One Hundred Years of Solitude*, Marian Keyes . . . But then, halfway along the top shelf, was a familiar black and red cover—I'd seen it around a lot at one point: *Wall Game*.

It was hardback, with a loose jacket, frayed at the edges.

I pulled it out.

The blurb read: "A secret state, a mysterious woman, a terrible crime. A breathless Cold War thriller, unputdownable, about the lies we tell others, and the lies we tell ourselves."

I studied the picture on the back flap.

The subject's face was thinner, and his hair was longer, floppier over his forehead, dark lamb's curls around his ears. It wasn't a studio shot, just a holiday pic, and his face was turned slightly away, his farthest cheek and eye in shadow.

It looked nothing like Rob. I stared at it. *Was* it Rob?

Of course it was. Author photographs, I was sure, often looked nothing like the person themselves. Vanity got in the way, or a publisher's desire to create a certain mood. I looked at the date on the inside cover. It was published five years ago and the photo would have been taken maybe even the year before that—so it was six years old. It was a younger Rob Curren was all.

I turned to the biography on the opening page.

"Rob Curren grew up in Oldham, Manchester, and qualified as a teacher. He lives in Dalston with a Maine Coon and his girlfriend, the political lobbyist Cara Burton."

I sat down on the couch. I felt as if I might be sick. My face felt hot. A *girlfriend*. A political lobbyist—real and committed, and properly engaged in the mechanics of the world. She'd have A levels and a degree, and a Caffè Nero loyalty card. She probably belonged to a gym where she did those classes on bikes, and when Amnesty International knocked at her front door asking for donations, she'd listen carefully before revealing her bank details.

The perfect mark. I could con her in a heartbeat.

They lived together. They had a cat.

What was he playing at, flirting with me? He had made me feel understood, *seen*. All the tricks I used, he'd used on me.

Who even *was* he?

Chapter Twenty-Three

I was jealous, I realized as soon as I was back in my room. Intensely jealous; agonizingly jealous. It wasn't just that I didn't want him to have a girlfriend, I didn't want him to have *had* one. Even if the relationship was over, it was evidence somehow that he was out of my league, from a different world. I felt both desperate yearning, a numb kind of disappointment.

I thought back to the previous evening, to how close to him I'd felt at the coffee machine. Not just the kiss. Before that. He knew I'd taken the rap for the kids and he assumed I'd done it not to get on their right side, not as the buildup to a con, but out of kindness. And I realized, with a shock, that he was right.

I heard his words again in my ears.

I'm beginning to suspect you're a nice person.

I sat up, feeling something loosen inside, a sort of lifting. I'd lived my life on the edge. I'd allowed myself to be sucked into Sean's world. But I had gotten away.

I was *here*. I was making different decisions now. I was *already* moving on.

The rest of the afternoon, waiting for them to return, passed quickly. I opened Rob's book out of curiosity and was immediately absorbed. The story was about an East German woman called Astrid who is sent to West Berlin by the Stasi to infiltrate the life of an American academic unhappily married to a CIA operative. Astrid is uptight and rule-bound, and he isn't, but there's a sense of genuine sexual tension between them, and I was willing the relationship on, though I knew it would be a disaster for him if anything did happen . . .

A sound. I put the book down. The click of the gate, followed by the scrape of a sunbed being moved. Iris's voice, low and conspiratorial; she was talking on the phone. "I've told them I'm at Phoebe's for the weekend. They never check." She talked about collecting sleeping bags and decanting vodka into water bottles. Later, she said: "I don't know what their problem is. Reading Festival's a rite of passage. They just don't get it."

I thought how everybody has secrets. Rob. Iris. Martha . . . Everyone at some point pretends to be something they're not. I wasn't the only one in that house who was selective about what they revealed.

She ended her call and shortly after there were new voices. Rebecca's and Martha's. I returned to my book, vaguely aware of soft splashes and the sound of water lapping at the side of the pool. I should probably go down, I told myself, check that they didn't want any help at supper. I'd just finish this chapter . . .

"Lulu!"

Rebecca's voice was actually *in* the *pigeonnier*. I slipped *Wall Game* under my leg as she appeared at the top of the stairs. "Sorry to bother you," she hissed in a stage whisper, as if that made her less intrusive. Her hair was wet, and mascara was smudged under her eyes. "I just wanted to find out if you wanted to join us for supper tonight?"

She was holding a flimsy leaflet across which "Pizza de Minuit" was written in jagged red writing. She thrashed the air with it. "We thought we'd get pizza— there's a place that does takeout in the next village. But as there are so many of us, we have to get our order in early." Her hair was flat across her scalp. "I've missed you today. We'd love you to join us."

She was wearing her swimsuit with the anchors on; it was darker in stripes across the stomach where the bunched fabric was still damp; you could see the shadow of her navel.

She was smiling at me, and I felt she was trying to make amends for having been short in the morning.

"Yes, that would be nice," I said.

"Don't worry; they do gluten-free crusts. God knows what they use instead." She grimaced, handing me the menu. "Spelt? Cauliflower?"

I moved my legs to make room for her on the bed, but I could see she didn't want to sit down because of the wetness of the swimsuit. She looked about herself. "Well, it's OK up here," she said, persuading herself. "Cosy."

"Yup."

"Is it hot at night?" She looked anguished when she said this, her face contorted, and I realized I didn't want her to feel bad.

"Not at all," I lied. "There's always a breeze."

"Oh, good." She gave me a quick smile. "Now—what are you going to have? I thought eggplant and zucchini sounded nice. You know me, I love my veggies. Of course, the boys all want sausage. What is it with men and meat?"

"You know me," that verbal tic of hers, sounded different to my ears now. I thought about the way she talked about "boys" and "girlies," making the world safe and cosy. And I wondered again if she did know about Phil and Clare and, if so, how much effort and anguish it must be taking to keep it together. I thought how nice it would be to make life smoother for her and how Clare would be easy enough to work on. I thought about that article in the magazine, the one about the posh hotels, and how she'd folded down the corner of the page. A plan began to form in my head.

"I'll have the same as you," I said, handing the menu back, hoping to prove allegiance.

"You're reading Rob's book," she said.

I glanced down. I hadn't been quick enough to hide it after all.

"Yes," I said. "I was interested, seeing as I've met him."

"Any good?"

I laughed, surprised. "You haven't read it?"

She shook her head. "Should I?"

"Yes. It's exciting. I'm only halfway through, but . . ." I picked it up and studied the cover.

"The two of you have been spending quite a lot of time together."

I shrugged. "I suppose so. Though I think he's got a girlfriend."

She considered me a moment longer. "I don't disapprove," she said. "You're probably a better fit for him than Clare." She sighed. "I don't know what I was thinking with that one." She glanced away, flicking her eyes around the room—at the fan, the window, the chest of drawers, where I had left Elliot's leather pouch. Her eyes settled on it and then moved away. With her toe, she prodded at a knot in the wood.

She looked up at me then and said, her tone vulnerable: "Do you think everyone's having a nice time?"

"Yes. Definitely. And I hope you are too?"

She crossed her arms like someone holding their ground, but when she spoke she sounded wistful. "I just always feel so inadequate. Clare's so successful and glamorous. And Layla . . . she's so organized. She just knows how to do everything. I just . . ." She seemed to be about to say something else, but then to change her mind. Her shoulders collapsed in a bit. "I just want to make sure they all have a nice time."

She sounded so deflated that all I wanted was to cheer her up. "Well, if that's your mission, I think you're definitely succeeding."

"Do you?"

She brought her fingers to her lower lip as if stilling it. I wondered if she might be about to cry.

"Yes. Hundred percent."

She tucked a piece of hair behind her ear. "I don't know what to do," she said. "Apart from just muddle on."

"Sounds like a good policy," I said.

She turned away finally and took a step toward the stairs. At the top, she hesitated, and then, breathing in sharply, tapped the menu against her bare thigh. She lifted her chin. "By the way," she said. "Rob doesn't have a girlfriend. She left him for a Labour MP. Tooting, was it? Or Totteridge? One or the other. Anyway, he likes you. I can tell."

She smiled, either gratified or amused by whatever was happening on my face.

If I think back to how I felt in that hour when I was getting ready, I remember butterflies, a feeling of intense agitation, like the sensation you get when you stand somewhere very high and you don't trust yourself not to jump. It was both dark and exhilarating, like the adrenaline rush before a con.

I felt Rob's eyes on me as I walked up the lawn. He was standing with his elbow resting on the big urn of what I now knew to be lavender. The light was so clear, the colors seemed to move. I was barefoot, and each step prickled between my toes. My eyelids felt heavy, my lips full. I smiled at him, held his gaze. He seemed to be alone. The pressure on my sternum was almost suffocating. I was so nervous; I wasn't sure I could even speak.

I had nearly reached him when Phil came up behind and handed him a glass, and at the last minute I veered away, heading for the table. Iris and Martha were sitting together, their heads bent. Iris was painting Martha's nails a purply gold. Martha looked up, holding out the hand that was already done. "You like?" she said. Her eyelids were a vivid red, which matched the thin scarf she had tied around her neck like a choker. Iris was wearing shorts and a waistcoat; she'd painted freckles on her cheeks. These two girls: they were magnificent.

"I like," I said.

"Me next," Elliot said, scooting into the chair on the other side of Iris.

"Lulu!" Rebecca said the name like a trill. "You're here! You came!" She held out her hand to grab mine and squeezed it, before pulling me into the kitchen. "You look lovely in that dress—were you wearing it yesterday? Yes, I thought so. That super-dark lipstick—very Eastern European. Now, a drink! Us girls are making mojitos! Will you have one? I'm already on my second. They're delish."

Layla and Clare were leaning against the counter. Clare was laughing at something, her glass tipping sideways. She was wearing a long, floaty thing that looked like a nightie. "Oops," she said as a shot of wet mint leaves slopped onto the floor. She moved to one side so as not to step in it. I went to get a cloth. Neither of them acknowledged me.

"Leave that. Leave that." Rebecca lifted the cloth out of my hands and threw it sloppily back into the sink. "We'll do it later."

"The floor will be sticky. People will step in it."

"Oh God." She thrust a glass at me. "Doesn't matter. Relax."

Her hand movements were exaggerated, her eyes unfocused. "I'd kill for a ciggy," she said, bending forward a little too close to whisper. "I don't suppose you've got some tobacco in your stash?"

I told her I thought I probably did; should I fetch it?

She giggled. "Oh, never mind. Maybe later!"

"Becks," Layla called. "What's the name of that TV show I told you to watch?"

Rebecca turned to reply. "*Call My Agent*? You've recommended so many shows."

"No. Not that one. The one set in Israel."

"*Fauda*?"

"No."

The two of them swayed toward the terrace, continuing to run through the TV listings, and Clare and I found ourselves alone. It was probably my best chance.

I picked up the jug and refilled her glass. "Here you go," I said. "Don't get left behind."

"I know." She clinked her glass with mine. "Might as well get drunk. Few other excitements around here. *Pizza night*." She made a face.

"Oh, dear. Not your thing? I guess the kids like it."

"It's OK. It's just I don't get much holiday." She smiled wanly. "Maybe I sound spoiled."

"Yes. No. I'm sure. Did you at least have a nice lunch?"

"It was fine." She shrugged.

I began to see a way in.

"It's surprisingly hard to find really good food in France," I said. "I mean they do the basics really well, obviously, but you have to dig around for anything interesting."

"Yeah. I guess." I hadn't yet engaged her. She was looking bored.

"Though, God, it can be amazing when they get it right. I've got this friend who's just taken over as head chef at this beautiful hotel in Nice. He's all about fusion and seasonality and flavors. The hotel's new. It's called Maison d'Anglais. I don't know if you've heard of it."

She put her head on one side, frowning slightly as she considered. "It rings a bell."

That was the plan. Maison Ila was the place in France listed in the magazine. I'd searched for somewhere closer with a similar name.

I took a sip from my glass. "Actually, funnily enough, I've got a table and a room booked for this weekend. I won it as a special package in a charity raffle and then this job came up. I must let them know I can't make it."

I watched as the information began to register with her, and then, hearing the front door, I turned away. "Sounds like Roland's back with the pizzas."

I crossed the kitchen with my back to her, moving away as casually as I could.

A beat, and then her voice, slightly raised, behind me. "If you don't go, does the special package just go to waste?"

"Vouchers," I said airily, only half turning my head. "I'm sure they'll let me use them another time."

Roland walked in with the pizzas, a great tower of boxes, and I followed him out through the French doors, feeling almost disturbed about how simple it had been. Most people had sat down, but Rob was still standing by the urn. I met his eyes and smiled, waited until he smiled back. Behind him the shadows on the lawn had lengthened. Laughter erupted at the table. I pushed the ice down with my finger, and took another sip. I looked up at him again and this time there was something questioning in his eyes.

Roland had lowered the pizzas to the table and Phil

was peeling back the lids and calling out the contents. "Zucchini? Someone? Anyone?"

I sat down next to Elliot. "Me," I said.

A chair scraped back and I heard and felt Rob sit down next to me. I'd known he would, and the knowing and then it taking place set something ticking inside. He poured me a glass of water from the jug, passing it across without speaking. He smelled of citrus and fresh herbs. His leg was close to mine, not touching.

"I do like that dress," he said quietly. "Green's my favorite color."

He was wearing a fresh shirt, still collarless, but white this time. He'd done the buttons to the top as if he were trying to be smart. The sleeves were rolled up, his forearms strong and brown. His hair was still damp from the shower.

"It's my favorite color too," I said, though I couldn't remember if it was true for me, or true for Lulu, or whether it was something I'd just read in his book.

"Oh my God!" Rebecca had opened her box. "I've got the gluten-free. Lulu—stop eating. Swap. Swap."

Her box was passed down the table, and I passed mine up.

Rob cut a piece of his pizza; then passed me the knife. He laid his arm along the back of my chair. I didn't know whether to lean backward or keep forward. I was highly aware of every movement of his body.

"This is the most delicious thing I've ever eaten," Rebecca said.

"That's brutal," Iris said. "After all the meals Lulu's cooked."

"I'm sorry. Are we literally the worst clients you've ever had?" Rebecca asked.

"Oh, Mum, fuck's sake." Iris rolled her eyes. "Don't fish. Honestly, Lulu, ignore her."

I don't remember much about the meal. I know they talked about their day—what fun the canoeing had been and how pretty the river had looked once the sun had come out. They had stopped at a vineyard on the way back and tasted the wines, while Iris and Martha had played with the most adorable Jack Russell puppies.

Rob had caught the sun; freckles were scattered across his nose. He had a fresh scratch on his upper arm.

"Never get a Jack Russell," Layla said. "They look harmless, but they're actually vicious. People forget they're fighting dogs."

"We're not getting a dog," Phil said, in the tone of one who'd said this several times already. "We've already got enough animals."

"Poor Arthur the cat," I said. "You'd ruin his life. You'd have to up the Feliway."

Iris and Martha laughed and Rebecca said, "Oh, Lulu, you are a hoot."

It was over quickly enough. The three teenagers wandered off to play boules. The table was a mess of brown cardboard, smeared tomato, and abandoned crusts, and I stood up and went into the kitchen to fetch a trash bag and begin collecting it all up. The world was fuzzy at the edges, tilting a little. I'd drunk a glass of wine on top of the mojito, which was a mistake.

"So, who's on for the market tomorrow?" Rebecca cried. "Rob? Everyone loves a French market."

"Yes. Probably." He made a little drum roll on the table with the fingers of both hands. "I tell you what, though. I'm longing for a swim. Would it be OK if I slipped off? I just feel after being in the car all day . . ."

"Of course. That's absolutely fine!" Rebecca threw her arms out. "It's your holiday. Liberty Hall."

I was standing across from him, but he kept his eyes averted as he stood up. "Anyone else want to join me?"

I put the last two boxes into the trash bag, folding them in half and pushing them down deep.

"Go, go." Phil made a shooing gesture at Rob with both hands.

Rob moved his chair back, picked his bag up from the floor, passed behind me, and shambled, shoulders self-consciously hunched, down the grass toward the pool.

I took the trash bag into the kitchen, secured the handles, and rested it against a cupboard.

It was just bottles of wine and glasses on the table now—all still in use. I asked if they were ready for coffee, but they decided they weren't. When I said I might turn in early, Rebecca blew me a kiss. "*Bonne nuit!*"

Beyond the gate, the pool gleamed like silver.

Rob was already in the water. I unzipped the green dress and, in my underwear, stepped quietly down the steps into the shallow end.

He was in the middle of the pool, motionless but for a gentle stirring of his hands, and I moved toward him, feet on the bottom, pushing the water away with my hands. I could hear my breathing, the pulse of my heart. The water felt like blood. The sky was high and black; it was like moving through ink. A few more steps and I could rest my hands on his shoulders, or wrap them around his chest, cling to him. It was in the air between us, waiting to happen.

His eyes were dark, and he was just standing there, expecting me, but at the last minute, I plunged my head under the water, and swam away to the far end of the pool. I swam three lengths, overwhelmed suddenly by the anticipation. When I surfaced in the center of the pool, toes just touching the bottom, he had moved and was sitting in the shallow end on one of the steps, watching me, his arms crossed, his legs outstretched.

I lay on my back and floated, with my eyes closed. I felt a shudder through my whole body. It was pure and real, unadulterated for a few seconds, long enough to register, and then I remembered Lulu. She was dead. And I shouldn't be carrying on with my life. I had no right to be happy. And that might have stopped me if his arms weren't already holding me up, if his lips hadn't already touched mine, if it hadn't already been too late.

Chapter Twenty-Four

He was gone when I woke early the next morning, but my bed held the memory of him—the bulk and safety of his body. I rolled facedown into the hollow where he'd slept, buried my nose in the pillow, and breathed him in: salt, dampness, pepper, and cloves, sweat. I didn't have much to go on—a drunken experiment at Fairlight House; that single occasion with Sean. But it had been good, I knew enough to know that.

Out of the window, I could see him in the pool—up and down, rest, up and down. I watched him for a while. I wondered if he knew I was watching, if the knowledge affected his strokes. I felt a flutter in my stomach.

I was there, dabbling my feet in the water, as he got out. I was hoping he'd suggest we go back to bed, but he pulled on a T-shirt and shorts, stuffed his feet into his Birkenstocks, and said we should go up to the house, for the market. He held my hand until we were on the other side of the gate. I could feel the calluses on his palm, relived the touch of them on the rest of my skin. He asked if I'd slept well and I said I had, for the first time since I'd gotten there. He looked at me once, and when our eyes met, I felt, I don't know, out of my depth. Like the ground wasn't solid, that I couldn't trust it to hold me. I'd never felt like this before. I didn't know what to do with it.

He walked ahead of me when we reached the terrace. People were already in the kitchen, milling. For a moment I was scared that that was it, he was going to ignore me, but when I stood near him, I felt his fingers brush my leg and, for a second or two, hold tight to the hem of my shorts.

We took all three cars to the market—for the sake of "flexibility." A few of the guests—Layla and Roland, Rob—didn't seem that keen to go. But to have broken ranks in the face of Rebecca's enthusiasm would have been tantamount to telling her the holiday was shit. As I wasn't actually *on* holiday, I might have been able to escape, but so much was made of my insider knowledge—the best jewelry stall, the secret vintage shop—it would have been impossible to say no. I was powerless anyway. Where Rob went, I went. So in the end, it was, as Rebecca kept saying, "a house trip." The Lawrences took their own car. Phil drove Rebecca and Clare. Iris, Martha, and I went with Rob.

The two sisters sat in the back, leaning forward to

ask questions. Was the bracelet stall really good? Necklaces *and* bracelets? And was I sure the vintage shop was open, only sometimes ordinary shops closed on market days? They were like small children, their problems—failed exams, teenage pregnancy— forgotten. We rolled down the windows and I flipped through the radio channels until I found an Amy Winehouse song we all knew the words to. The sky above the sunflowers was a supernatural blue, an ex- plosion of white clouds like volcanoes on the hori- zon. The air smelled of lavender and thyme, and as Rob sang "did you get a good lawyer?" hiccupping out the last syllable of "lawyer" in a way that made fun of himself, and the two girls clicked their fingers to the chorus, I felt what it must be like to belong somewhere, to feel part of something. I looked across at Rob and he looked back at me, and in my chest, I felt my heart expand.

Castels wasn't one of those French medieval hill towns that spiral tightly up into a high center, but was laid flatly on each side of a river. It had suburbs and sprawl. We circled several small roundabouts and passed a succession of supermarkets, including the Leclerc. The traffic was heavy, and after we'd watched a set of lights change twice without moving, it became hot and airless in the car. I switched off the radio. Rob closed the windows and flicked on the AC. The girls slipped back into the corners of the car, faces slumped. Martha looked queasy. I hoped she wasn't going to be sick.

It was hard to find anywhere to park. Rob looked serious, and it began to seem, as I was supposed to have been here before, that it was all my fault. When a car pulled out of a space just in front of us, and we managed to nab it, I felt almost high with relief.

Out on the pavement, you could see the town center ahead—a church tower slightly higher to the left, and in the distance, a sense of bustle and clatter, a throng of people, multicolored awnings fluttering beneath tall plane trees.

Rob pointed at a *boulangerie*. "Coffee, breakfast," he said. "No discussion."

The table closest to the door came free, and he took Iris's and Martha's orders—hot chocolate and *chaussons aux pommes*. When he turned to me, I heard myself say, "Let me do this."

"You sure?" he said, surprised. "Thanks."

There was a queue in the bakery and I joined the end of it, breathing in the smell of vanilla and spun sugar. The assistants seemed hassled, and when it was my turn, my server, an older woman with sloping shoulders, gave me a tight, impatient smile as if to hurry me along. I ordered the coffees and the hot chocolates, and the apple turnovers, and a croissant. In the fridge under the counter, the only item that was obviously gluten-free was a giant meringue, dusted with something pink, so I got one of those too.

The total was twenty-two euros forty cents, and I handed over a fifty-euro note. The cash drawer was open and the shop assistant rested the fifty-euro note on the top of it. She lifted the metal bar and removed a twenty-euro note.

I asked her to confirm the meringue didn't contain flour and explained that I couldn't eat gluten.

"Yes, no. No flour," she said, looking up. "Just sugar and egg."

I told her I was glad and that everything looked delicious. Was it made on the premises? She didn't answer immediately, busy counting out my change. Finally, as she put the twenty-euro note on a little metal tray, dropped the coins on top, and placed the tray on the counter, she said, yes, everything was.

The coffee machine was grinding and whooshing; the younger assistant was banging down a pitcher of milk to settle the froth. A small boy who had recently pushed forward from behind had started licking the glass. "Hang on," I said. "I'm being stupid." Scooping up the change, I produced a twenty-euro note from my wallet and a two-euro coin, plus forty cents from the change she had given me. I handed it to her and held my wallet open, smiling expectantly, as I pointed at the original fifty-euro note.

She paused, momentarily confused.

"It all looks delicious anyway," I said, smiling, and she reached then for the fifty-euro note and handed it back, her face already turned to the next customer, the mother of the small boy.

"Thanks."

I moved to one side to wait for the hot drinks.

It's another version of "Change Raising," subsection: "the short count." I'd been given change for fifty euros and then the fifty euros back. I had paid nothing for breakfast and was twenty-eight euros up. It was an instinctive play. And yet, leaning against the wall, watching the two women in their hairnets cope with market-day trade, I felt this thing creep up from my toes, a horrible dirty feeling.

When the younger woman beckoned me forward for my cardboard tray of coffee and hot chocolate, I held out the fifty-euro note in my hand. I pointed to the other assistant and told her she had given it to me by mistake, that we'd gotten in a muddle with the change.

Her eyes glanced over to the older woman. And she stuck out her lower lip to express doubt. Maybe even irritation. She looked harassed; she had more customers to serve, more coffees to make. But she took it from me anyway.

It was packed in the market, hot and airless. Motorbikes revved, dogs barked, babies cried, and the smell of garlic and olives, cheese and ripe fruit was almost overwhelming. We stood in the vibrations of a big white truck selling raw meat to gain our bearings.

"Right," Rob said, "if it's all right with you, I might find a café to work in. Would you feel abandoned?" He looked at me, and I grinned and said I wouldn't. He lifted his arm as if he were about to hug me, but then

278

he glanced at Martha and he dropped it. "OK. So, see you at the car in what?" He referred to his watch. "Two hours?"

"Should do it," I said, and rolled my eyes.

Martha was asking me questions, and I felt a pressure to take control, at least to locate the jewelry I'd promised. I picked a row at random and we thrust down it, jostling our way alongside cascades of mushrooms, reefs of broccoli, towers of sugared almonds, soap. When they stopped to look at a bunch of key rings carved from olive wood, I pushed ahead, squeezing though the throng, until I found a woman selling tiny beaded gold chains in both pendant and bracelet form. I talked to her for a bit. She was Italian, from Rome initially, but her boyfriend was French. She was here for the summer and then she didn't know. Maybe Morocco.

I found Iris and Martha again at a swimwear stand where a man with a money belt was telling them off for touching. They were diverted by a stall of striped cotton sarongs, but eventually I led them back to the jewelry. "Here it is!" I said.

"*Ciao!*" I said to the Italian woman. "We meet again!"

"Ah, hello again," she said, with just the right combination of both doubt and familiarity. One year, five minutes: same difference. "We do, yes."

They bent to look closely at the trinkets, while I stood back, occasionally pushed out of the way by an impatient shoulder or a swinging bag. I kept my eye out, but only casually. I thought I saw Roland and Layla in the next aisle, but when I moved my head to see through a hanging display of leather belts, they'd gone.

The girls bought more stuff after the jewelry: a phone case, a top, an ornament made out of crystals. But Martha, who was flagging, began to ask about my vintage shop (Les Vieux Amis: four stars on Tripadvisor). I had patchy signal and Maps didn't seem to want to download, but I'd remembered from the website it was near the church, so I led them in the direction of a bell tower poking above the rooftops, past the cafés that lined one side of the square and up a narrow pedestrianized road. It was pretty and shaded, the pavement strung with a run of bollards and plants in massive white urns.

At the top of a slight hill we reached a crossroads.

Martha nudged me and pointed. Rob was sitting outside a bar, drinking a beer. His bag was lying on the ground. His laptop was nowhere to be seen. He looked thoughtful, his elbow on the table, chin pressed in his palm, something enclosed, secretive, about the curve of his shoulders.

She took a step as if to go over to speak to him, but I pulled her back, suddenly wary or maybe just shy. "Let's leave him."

Les Vieux Amis was a few streets over, next to a flower shop. In the window were vintage leather boots, faded blue jackets, colorful cotton dresses. Lots of the things they'd said in the car they wanted.

We stared at the door: "Fermé—10–23 Août."

"Are you joking?" Martha said, not looking at me. "Are you *actually* joking?"

Iris cried, "But it was open last year in August, wasn't it?"

"Yes. It was open last year . . . Never mind!" The mood of a tour group depends on the mood of its leader; I learned that in Jaipur. I set off jauntily. "Let's find Le Petit Morceau. You'll love it. Everyone really went for it last year. Honestly. Trust me. I just need to remind myself how to get there from here."

I'd already worked out that the "lifestyle boutique"— another big hitter on Tripadvisor—was on the other side of the church. We took a narrow passage up to a main road, and were soon trudging alongside silky white walls, buttresses, high vaulted windows.

Jesus was stretched on a cross above the elaborately arched entrance, and below him, in a slice of shade on a marble step, surrounded by red confetti like droplets of blood, slumped Rebecca. She didn't see us approach. Her head was bowed, and she was fiddling with the leather on her sandal.

"Mother!" Iris bounded up the steps toward her.

"Oh, hello." Rebecca made as if to rise and then sank a bit lower onto the steps. Sweat marks bloomed under her arms, and her hair was flat, a couple of frizzy strands lying across her forehead. "Have you been successful?" And then, as they listed their purchases— necklaces, bracelets, key ring, lavender soap: "Oh, good." She cast her eyes up at me. "You have been clever. I was hopeless, I'm afraid. I didn't know where to start. I found it all so overwhelming." She rubbed her fingers across her forehead. "I was just lost down there. I'm just so hot."

"What have you done with everyone else?" Martha asked.

Rebecca let out a heavy sigh. "It was too difficult to keep together. And as you know, markets aren't exactly up Dad's *strada*. He's gone off to find a museum that's apparently got a couple of Cézannes. I left Clare at some stall trying on thousands of linen dresses—they all looked identical to me, but she's got money to burn, so it's not my problem. And the Lawrences decided to call it a day and have gone home for a swim." She rolled back her head. "Perhaps I should have gone with them. It's all too much in this heat."

Iris hooked her hand under her mother's arm and pulled her up to standing. Rebecca groaned. "First rule of getting old. Don't groan when getting to your feet," she said.

Martha said: "You need to show up more on the mat."

It wasn't exactly an impression of Layla, but the tone of conviction and the prissy way she pursed her lips brought Layla to mind.

Rebecca laughed.

Le Petit Morceau, when we finally found it, was smaller than it had looked on the website, but stylish enough, with that modern understated vibe, beige and white—candles, cushions, ceramics, all the *c*'s.

Anyway, who cared. It was open.

"Lovely," Rebecca gushed, with an enthusiasm designed to make me feel better. She peered through the window. "Lots of interesting things in here; I might find myself tempted. Oh—" she remembered. "Do you have my credit card by any chance? I couldn't find it in the kitchen."

"Yes." I dug it out of my back pocket and handed it over.

"I think I might leave you to it," I said.

"Of course." Rebecca rested her hand on my arm. "Thank you."

As soon as they had gone in, I set off back up the way we'd come toward the bar where the girls and I had spotted Rob. I began to imagine his face when he saw me, let myself think he'd be pleased. I'd order a coffee and sit down in the chair next to him and maybe we would kiss. I'd so vividly imagined this that when I reached the café and his seat was empty, for a moment I thought I had gone wrong, that this was a different crossroads. And I felt disconcerted, and a bit lost.

I texted him, and watched my phone for a bit, waiting for an answer. When nothing came, I put the phone in my pocket and wandered rather aimlessly back down to the market, looking out for him the whole time. I checked my phone again and when there was still nothing, I decided to go for a walk. Away from the market, toward the river, it was surprisingly quiet. A man cycled past with a dog in a basket. A heavyset woman walking ahead put down her bag of shopping to light a cigarette. I was in the shade of tall stone buildings; most of the shutters looked as if they'd been nailed up for years. You could tell you were getting close to the water because you could smell rotting moss, dank stones, muddy reeds.

The road bent and I saw a bridge ahead—a run of red railings, checkered clouds high above, the shrinking perspective of it. The light shifted in quality, became more glancing, glinting. I was hoping I could walk along the river itself, but when the buildings ran out, I realized I was higher up than I'd thought, that the shore was maybe thirty feet down.

The pavement had narrowed, and I walked along it to the middle of the bridge and then leaned over the railings to look down. The river was fast-moving, burbling around rocks, the weeds along the top of them streaming in one direction. The water was the dark green of old wine bottles, the rocks mottled gray, like porpoises or something. Straight ahead, the flow curved to the right, ran under a railway bridge, and disappeared beyond into trees.

I took a deep breath. I could feel my shoulders sink. Rebecca was right about the heat. It got under your skin and into your head. Made it hard to think. It was good to have more air, though it would be nice to be right on the edge of the water.

I began to walk back the way I had come, gazing below at the curve of beach between the river and the bank. I could see a figure in the shadow down there, at the base of the bridge, near some of those contorted trees that spend half their life submerged. Thinking there must be a way down then, I leaned forward, craning over as far as I could; no sign of steps, though perhaps they were on the other side. And actually, it wasn't one figure, but two. A man and a woman arguing. He was gesticulating and she was shouting, but suddenly he pulled her toward him, hunching over her, legs apart, like he was trying to lift her up. Her body slackened and they kissed for a bit, but then one of his feet slipped, a sandal sliding on wet pebbles, and she pushed him away. He staggered backward, and in that brief moment, I saw Phil's face.

I thrust myself back from the railing, close enough to the curb to feel the draft of a passing car on my back. Had he seen me? Surely not. I was too high up, and he was too preoccupied. Nevertheless, as soon as the road was clear I crossed to the other side of the bridge and began walking quickly away, in the opposite direction from the market, a need in my feet to pace it out, put some distance between me and what I had just seen. I'd known it was going on, but seeing it with my own eyes was something different. Jovial Phil and languid Clare, grappling with each other in daylight. Jovial, father-of-two, dad-on-holiday Phil. There was something so desperate, whatever was going on. So *belittling*.

My head was buzzing with all of this when I slowly became aware of the car. It was just a noise at first—a low, oddly persistent hum. I turned and saw a gray Jeep, driving behind me.

Driving slowly, menacingly.

I stopped walking and turned to face the road. My fists automatically clenched. As the Jeep crept past, I caught a glimpse of the figure at the wheel—hunched shoulders, a baseball cap pulled down low, but still immediately, chillingly familiar.

It took a moment for the truth of it, for the full horror, to sink in.

Him. No question.

Him with his head turned, and now, as the Jeep drew level, steadily looking at me, I felt sure, although the details were lost in the reflections off the glass and the shadows. My heart had started thumping. I felt my palms turn slick. I was waiting for the car to stop, the window to go down. For Sean to lean forward slightly in the driver's seat and greet me with a slow, knowing smile and the quiet but firm instruction.

"Get in."

Instead the Jeep crawled on at the same pace until it reached the end of the bridge, and then it turned right and disappeared.

Every one of my nerves was jangling. Shit. What had I done, let myself be exposed like this? I'd been wandering around the town, my head full of Rob, of Phil and Clare. What had I been *thinking*? Of course it was

Sean. The position of the shoulders, the way he held himself, the biceps below the arms of that tight T-shirt. How often had I seen him flex those muscles in front of mirrors? How many hotel gyms had I watched him patrol? Sean was never going to let me escape. He didn't care about the money. It wasn't about survival or the next meal. It was about the play, the trick itself. Catching people out, that's what he loved, cutting them down to size. That's what made him feel alive: other people's degradation.

He had traced me from Pugot to Castels, and he was ready to reel me in. But first he was going to toy with me—let me know he was there, play on my fear, confront me when he was ready, bring this game to an end on his own terms. Otherwise, I'd win. And he could never allow that.

And of course he had clocked me. He had taken a good long look, just to be sure. I was wearing sunglasses, but I was walking normally. I had done nothing to disguise myself, made no attempt to adjust. I had let my guard down. And now I would pay for it.

Alone on the bridge, with the car gone, I suddenly felt badly exposed. I needed people around me, a crowd to slip into. I needed to head back to the market and find Rob and his Fiat and go back to the house and leave the town behind. And then what? I had no idea. But at least I would be safer among people. Safer from immediate harm.

I turned around and, keeping to the other side of the

bridge from where I had leaned over and seen Phil and Clare, walked quickly back the way I had come.

I kept flicking my head around to check I wasn't being followed—to check Sean wasn't coming back for me.

Nothing the first time I looked.

Nothing the second time, either. There was no traffic on the bridge at all now. It was entirely deserted, eerily quiet in the still heat.

I kept going, breathing hard. A film of sweat had formed on my face and chest and arms. The end of the bridge was near now—just a few more yards.

And then, from behind me, came a faint squeal of tires.

I spun and saw the gray Jeep finish turning on to the bridge and, in a roar of acceleration, begin heading across it at speed.

I didn't look back at all after that. I just ran. I ran until I was off the bridge and then ran a few more yards and turned into the first side street—residential, with terraced stone houses on either side, their doors opening straight onto the pavement. I ran and kept running, my footsteps echoing, until I reached the top of that road and then crossed another, before diving immediately left into a small passage. I paused for a moment for breath, pressed against a wall, chest heaving. A cool breeze blew briefly. A delivery truck passed the end of the passage. No Jeep.

Barely recovered, I set off again, half running, half walking to the top of the passage, and out into a wide avenue—treelined, with municipal buildings and cafés on either side. There was traffic in both directions here, and people walking; a phone shop, shoes, a super-market. My lungs hurt and so did my calves. I was just walking fast now, scanning faces, checking cars, trying to think.

I slowed down as I reached a wide, squat yellow structure—the railway station. There was a newspaper kiosk in the forecourt and I stood behind it. A door slammed and a flock of pigeons flew up, scattering. I pressed my head into the wooden bulletin board. I could hear the rattle of a train and felt something in-stinctive leap inside me. But I had no means of buying a ticket—nothing with me but my phone and some change from breakfast. I didn't have Rebecca's credit card. I hadn't even brought my backpack. I'd left it in my room, along with clothes, the passport, the money. My *dignity*.

I'd broken the cardinal rule; never leave anything be-hind you can't walk away from in a second. I had left *everything*.

A group of women passed me then, coming from the station. English tourists—summer dresses, sunburnt shoulders, Birkenstocks, reading their phones for di-rections. I moved into their slipstream, walking closely behind them. At the edge of the market, I widened my stride, overtaking them, feeling the breath tight in my chest, and entered the first aisle. Hats, swimsuits, bas-kets, cheeses, honey.

And then, among the crowds of shoppers, I glimpsed a navy cap coming toward me. It bobbed and weaved through the throng. My stomach lurched and my pulse quickened. I stepped aside under an awning hung thickly with linen dresses, peered out nervously through folds of fabric.

And watched the cap pass—a child wearing it, on his father's shoulders.

I closed my eyes and took a breath. Emerging, I crossed quickly through to the stalls selling plants—an open area slung with pots of flowers, swathes of pink and orange and white. Beyond that was a van selling fish, and behind the van was a tree with a low wall built around it, painted white. I waited to check I hadn't been followed, peering down the side of the van, and when I was sure, I sat, tipping my head back to rest against the tree's trunk. Heat rose from my chest.

Time passed. The stall closest to me was beginning to pack up, a heavyset man in a sleeveless T-shirt loading buckets with a thud into the back of a truck. Poles clattered. My head throbbed. My blood pumped. It was unbelievably hot. I realized my throat was parched. The insides of my stomach were clenched together in a dry knot.

After a while I stood up again and began to walk in the direction of the car.

Rob was leaning against the Fiat when I got there, tipping his head back to swig the last dregs from a bottle of water.

"Lulu!" he said, pleased to see me.

"I'm late." I cleared my throat to move the crack in my throat. "I'm sorry."

He pushed himself away from the car. "The girls are grabbing something to eat with Phil and Rebecca. Clare got a cab home earlier. So . . ." He smiled shyly. "Just you and me, I guess."

"I just need to get some water."

"Of course." He tipped his bottle upside down to show it was empty. "Sorry."

There was a small supermarket a couple of shops down and I pulled a bottle of Evian out of the fridge, and paid for it with the loose change in my pockets. I could still see Rob from the register, and he was still standing by the car, gazing into space. As I came out, he turned and watched me as I walked toward him. My whole body was rigid with tension. I felt as if I were about to explode.

"Ali! Ali!"

I was only a few feet away when I heard the shout behind me, in warning.

"Ali! Ali!"

I spun around, my shoulders high, my eyes wide, and shouted, "What?"

A woman in her forties, short dark hair, pushing a buggy in the opposite direction, was looking over her shoulder at me. Except she wasn't looking *at* me, but *next* to me at the small boy lingering outside an ice-cream shop.

"*Allez, allez,*" the woman yelled again—come on, come on. Not an alert. Not a warning. Nothing to do with me at all.

The air squeezed out of my chest, and when I took the last few steps to Rob, I realized he was smiling with his forehead furrowed. He shook his head. "You OK?" he said.

"Yes. Fine."

The passenger door was open and I got in, sinking into my seat. It was baking. The car had been in full sun and smelled like plastic. I opened the bottle of water and drank nearly all of it.

Rob had gotten into the driver's seat. He pushed his bag down into the space at my feet and then, facing me, he put his hand on my arm to encourage me to look at him. He didn't say anything at first and then he gave a sort of half-laugh as if he were trying to sound gentle. "Listen, I have to know, is that your real name? Ali?"

It felt like a physical blow.

"What? Why would you—"

"The way you turned around just then, I just . . ." He bit his lip. "Look. Is there something going on I should know about?"

"Nothing's going on."

I clasped my hands together in my lap.

He carried on as if I hadn't spoken. "Maybe you think I'm being too . . . forward. It's only that since we . . . well, I just think . . . you can tell me the truth."

"The truth?" My nails were digging into the fleshy part of my palm.

"I've got a theory," he said. "You're a friend of Lulu's. She had agreed to do this fortnight, but then she had a better offer, an invitation, something she wanted to do more, and you stepped in to help her out."

"How very selfless you make this mythical me out to be."

"Well, maybe you did it for the money."

I turned to look at him properly. Risky, I know. But maybe I could brazen this one out. "I can see why you write fiction," I said.

A pause and then he laughed. "It's not a big deal, I just don't think you're a professional chef. I mean, most professional chefs know the difference between lavender and rosemary. And have seen a citrus reamer. And can peel a tomato. And . . . I don't know, seem a bit more together about it all."

I couldn't think what to say then, so I sat silently and simply looked at him with as close to a blank expression as I could muster.

He pulled his mouth into a line, then, quite curtly, tapped once on the steering wheel.

"OK. Fine," he said, and turned the key in the ignition. The AC roared and blew out an initial warm blast. "Let's go."

I waited until we had reached the first roundabout. The bag at my feet was open where he had shoved it in—the shiny top of the laptop visible, the notebook half sliding out. I nudged it with my foot. I wanted desperately to make it right between us.

"So, did you get some work done?" I said.

"Yeah." He was still looking away, his tone noncommittal, like he wasn't listening. He rubbed his lower lip with the middle finger of his right hand.

"Did you find somewhere cool and quiet you could properly concentrate?"

"Yes." His eyes flicked upward and right to the rearview mirror, and then across to me briefly before turning back to the traffic.

"Oh, that's good."

"Yup. I managed to knuckle down and get quite a lot done, so it wasn't a completely wasted trip." This time his right hand came to his throat and his fingers prodded there for a moment. "Yes, so not a completely wasted trip."

It seemed important to keep talking, to change the tone. "It's amazing to me you can just sit down and do it. You don't need index cards or Post-it notes, or any of the things I've always imagined writers being surrounded by—you know, huge piles of paper." With a rising flutter of my hands, I tried to demonstrate the piles, both the quantity and flimsiness of them.

He looked at me then and, holding my gaze, smiled, with a slight rock of his head. "Yeah, well. The laptop's an amazing thing." He shrugged, turning back to the road. "Plus, I've got my notebook."

He'd cooled—he didn't trust me—but I didn't trust

him either. He'd touched his lips and his throat. He'd used repetition and paused before answering. He'd played for time, avoided my eyes and then met them unblinkingly. He'd also looked up and to the right. It was all textbook stuff.

So. Yes. He was a liar too.

We drove the last bit of the journey in silence—over the bridge, up the hill, in and out of shadows. He pulled in onto the grass shoulder at the top, above the cattle barn. The engine died, but he didn't show any sign he was about to get out.

I bent forward to hand him his bag. The notebook had shaken loose and I picked it up separately, clasped it in my hands for a second, my thumbs rubbing the soft brown leather. And then I brought it to my nose and breathed in. "Ah. The smell of inspiration." I looked at him over the top.

"OK." He squeezed the bridge of his nose with the tip of his finger and thumb. "I'm not sure what's going on here. But I'm worried now we've had this conversation, you're going to fuck off, do one of those disappearing acts you mentioned. I just hope you don't, that's all."

He had swiveled his body, leaning back as far as he could into the car door. His intention might have been to put as much space as he could between us, but the car was small and his shoulders were twisted uncomfortably, and it only drew attention to how close we were sitting. His T-shirt was damp in patches—darker bands, across his torso, below his rib cage, and on his shoulders. I wanted to reach in and lift it where it was clinging to his skin.

"If I told you the truth," I said, "you wouldn't want anything to do with me."

The heat was pressing inside the car. A fly was buzzing against the windshield.

He said, "You could let me be the judge of that."

There was something in his expression that meant I didn't want to move. I let myself look at him again properly and I noticed how much I liked the shape of his eyes, how the lines curved out at the sides when he smiled. A lock of damp hair, a complete curl, was sticking to his forehead.

I could hear him breathing, a tiny judder on the inhale. His lips had parted. Sean had tracked me, first to Pugot, then to Castels. He'd *seen* me now. He was closing in—tomorrow, the day after—he would find me. Rob was getting closer to the truth. Whatever this was, it could go nowhere. It had no future. I was ruined. Yet the heat felt as if it were willing me on. I leaned slightly toward him and I thought if I carried on slipping in that direction, I would fall into him, like a tree cut at its roots, all buds and leaves and life, when it's dead but it doesn't know it yet. I could do it without thinking and I could tell, from the flush in his face, that he was waiting.

I got out of the car, and ran.

Chapter Twenty-Five

I was in my room in seconds, throwing things into my backpack—underwear, toothbrush, the trainers, a couple of jumpers. I unpicked Lulu's passport from behind the picture and fished out the bottle of money from the toilet tank. I squeezed it into the backpack but then it wouldn't close—the lid jabbing into the zipper. I rearranged the trainers and tried again and this time got halfway across before the zipper stuck.

I hooked it over my shoulder.

Quick scan of the room. Almost empty. Only the books by the bed. *Wall Game*: too bulky to take. I told myself it didn't matter. I tried not to care.

I lugged Lulu's suitcase downstairs and hid it next to the pool cleaner, pushing it as far back as it would go into the alcove and draping a deflated pool float over the top so it was half hidden. They'd think it odd if they found it. But when I texted Rebecca to tell her about the family emergency, I'd tell her she wasn't to worry about my luggage, that I'd make arrangements. And hopefully it would just sit there for a few months and eventually be forgotten.

I pulled open the door of the *pigeonnier* and stepped out. The heat hit, the pool shimmered. Roland was lying out there on his own, pale, hairless legs extended. He lowered the pages of his newspaper and released a little noise of greeting from the back of his throat. I nodded and he raised the paper again.

And I was through the gate.

I stopped still. My chest was heaving. I felt like I'd been running, though I hadn't. Not yet. I could see bodies up at the house, hear several voices. I hesitated only for a second or two, but it was just long enough to see Rob appear at the top of the slope. His head was turned—he was talking to someone in the kitchen—but he would be down here any minute. He was coming in search of me. I spun away and, head bent, began running, along the pebble track that curled behind the *pigeonnier* and then, under cover of the trees, across the grass to the boundary to the vineyard. I found a gap in the hedge and I was through, head ducked, stumbling through spaces between the vines and out the other side into the steep field. Keeping to the edge, I set off downhill, away from the disused barn, in a direction I hoped would eventually lead to the road.

I was in the full heat of the midafternoon, the sky an arc of merciless blue, the sun glaring. The world was silent, reproving. Even the crows dotted across the field ahead of me seemed motionless. My T-shirt under the backpack was already wet with sweat. The earth beneath my feet was dry and knobbly, and I tripped a couple of times.

I realized I was crying.

There was no escape, it turned out, from the life I'd made for myself.

I pushed the tears off my face. My hands were dirty. I could see a gate at the bottom of the field now, and the silver ribbon of the road.

I was in a slice of shade from a row of tall evergreens along the edge of the field. I took the last bit at top speed. The ground was littered with fir cones as well as great clods of dried mud, and I had to run it out on the flat, arms flailing, so as not to lose my balance. I imagined I could hear someone thundering behind me, but when I turned there was no one.

I opened the gate a crack and closed it behind me. I was on the lane now, farther down from the house, just before the bend at the bridge. I stood there, catching my breath, and then I turned right and kept on. I'd get to the village and find a bus, or a taxi, or maybe find Pascal and beg for a lift. I just needed a station, a ticket out.

I had no choice. I didn't want to leave the house, to abandon Rebecca or Martha . . . *Rob*. But they were on to me. And Lulu. Poor dead Lulu. Even if I hadn't been on the run from Sean, Lulu's death had changed everything. What future could I have? What had I even been thinking: normal life?

I'd reached the main road, with the avenue of trees. I turned right along it, walking on the shoulder to avoid the few cars that passed.

On the run again.

At Fairlight House, they called them abscondments. I'd be picked up by the police and there'd be stints at an attendance center before I'd be sent back. The Ormorods: they hadn't wanted me, not because I ate all their food, or broke windows, or got into fights; it was the running away they couldn't cope with.

I thought about the last time I'd seen Molly.

She was in her bathroom, in her Mickey Mouse pajamas from Primark. We'd been arguing. I'd teased her about her matching soap dish and tooth mug—cream with a blue floral pattern, pretend Victorian—and she'd said at least she had regular dental check-ups, had a *life*. Steven had called to her from the bedroom, and I'd gone downstairs to the lounge where I was sleeping and I heard him asking her how much longer I was going to be staying. He had left his wallet on the coffee table and I took out a twenty-euro note and his credit card and then I left the house.

I rang a few weeks later and told her I was sorry— but she told me not to ring again.

I stopped then, bent forward, hands pressing into my thighs. I closed my eyes.

It would be better for everyone if I were dead. If I had died instead of Lulu.

I could hear a car approaching, and I felt myself sway. I loosened my grip on my thighs, my eyes still closed. Was it Sean? Was this it?

The engine was louder now.

I waited for it to reach me.

Any second now.

I wasn't going back.

My eyes were shut tightly and I leaned farther down, felt my balance go, dizzy with blood in my head, spiraling on the inside of my lids. I teetered, waiting, ready to fall into its path.

It was nearly here.

Here.

At the last minute, I hurled myself away onto the shoulder.

Chapter Twenty-Six

The car had ground to a halt, a few yards ahead.

The door opened and Rob was running toward me.

I staggered to my feet. "Go away. Leave me alone."

"What are you doing?" he shouted, his face red and scrunched up. "What the fuck?"

He was trying to hold me, and I was struggling, batting him away. "Just don't. Please. Let me go."

He caught my arms, held them, stared into my face. "Lulu. *What?* What is going on? Where are you going?"

"I'm leaving. OK? That's all it is." I was crying again, and I yanked my arm away, began angrily brushing at the tears. "You don't need to know any more. Not now."

"Lulu. Please. Talk to me. It can't be anything so bad you can't tell me."

"You have no idea," I said.

A small van was coming up from the village. It slowed as it passed, the driver turning to look at us.

Rob glanced at it and then back to me. "Please, get

in the car," he said. "Just for a minute. I'll drop you where you want to go. Just get in."

"It's too late," I said.

"It's not too late."

"It is."

"It's never too late."

His voice was so gentle, so calm. I felt the fight go out of me. He was gripping my arm at the elbow and he steered me toward the Fiat. He opened the passenger door and gently lowered me into the seat.

When he was sitting next to me, both doors closed, he said, "I'm going to take us somewhere a bit less exposed." He drove toward the village, and I stared out of the window, unblinking.

He parked in the square, which was quiet at that time of the afternoon. He switched off the engine and turned to face me.

"So?"

The silence in the car was like a bottomless well.

I had a big unmanageable thing in my chest; I'd thought it was immoveable, that it could never be budged. But as I looked back at him, I felt it rush through me and into my throat, and my mouth made the shape of the words and then they were out there.

"I'm not Lulu. I wasn't before. And I'm not now. And I never have been."

He was looking at me intently.

"I didn't think you were," he said.

"I'm not a cook. I wasn't here last year."

303

"I also gathered that."

He was still waiting.

I said: "I don't want to tell you any more. I can't. It's worse. So much worse than you think."

He was half smiling now. "It can't be that bad."

I felt angry then. At him. At myself. "It is."

"So what? You're a friend of hers? She asked you to come in her place?"

It was hot now with the windows closed, and he turned on the engine to activate the air conditioning. Across the square two women were talking under the trees; an old man with a stick had stopped to poke the ground.

I shook my head. "I'm not a friend of hers."

He was frowning a bit now. "But she knows you're here?"

"No."

"I don't understand. Where is Lulu then?"

My shoulder was pressed against the doorframe, my head pressed against the window.

One of the women laughed. The old man bent down to pick up a coin.

I wanted to tell him the truth. I wanted to let it all out, to feel the relief of that happening, of it not just being mine anymore. I wondered if he might even understand. But I couldn't stop thinking about the spy in Rob's book, how she carried her secrets, her previous violence, like a stain. How you might have sympathy with her, but you weren't supposed to *like* her.

And I realized that I couldn't tell him, even now. Or ever.

I cleared my throat. "I've got mixed up in some bad stuff," I said. "I was connected with someone, a man, and—"

He interrupted. "The man on the boat."

"What?"

"At Sainte-Cécile-sur-Mer. I saw you on the beach. You were on your own for a bit. I noticed you because I thought you looked a bit lost—I mean, literally, like you didn't know where to go. But then you leaped into the water and swam out to a boat. There was someone on it—maybe two people. But I knew it." He smiled, nodded a few times, pleased to be right. "The woman on the beach. I told you I was good with faces. It *was* you."

"I don't understand."

"I was in a café; doing some work. You know, along the front there."

When I'd stood at the water's edge I'd looked across at Raoul's. Had there been a man sitting at a table on his laptop? Was that Rob? All that time ago, before the boat trip, before Lulu's murder. If I had walked back up the sand and sat down and ordered myself a coffee, maybe I would have looked across at him and we would have started talking. And Sean and his boat would have motored off into the bay without me.

"Yes," I said eventually.

He laughed, and lifted his arm as if he wanted to pull me toward him, but I pushed him away.

"I'm a fraud," I said.

"I still don't understand."

"I live by conning people."

He made a face, as if he thought I was being over-dramatic. As calmly as I could, I told him that a lot of what he thought about me wasn't true. I'd grown up in care, I said, and like many of the kids he'd got to know as a child, I was a bit of a fuck-up. I explained about dropping out of school and arriving in India and then running out of money. I told him I'd lived by my wits, hoping he would get the shorthand. But he was just looking at me, his mouth fixed in a smile, and so, to make certain, I said: "You know, ripping people off."

He didn't nod or shake his head, or make any sign that he understood where I was going with this. I kept on, then. I told him about meeting Sean and how his schemes were more sophisticated, and that we'd traveled west from India, to Morocco first, and then Spain, and then France. "And one thing led to another, and here I am."

He swallowed hard and tapped the steering wheel with both hands. "OK. I'm trying to understand. So somewhere along the way you conned Lulu into giving you this job?"

I let his words rest for a long moment.

"Something like that."

"And where's this guy?"

"I don't know. I've left him. Not that I was ever 'with' him. It was always professional."

He nodded then, rocked his head slightly. "OK."

I took a deep breath. "I'm sorry."

"I still don't quite get it."

"Please don't ask any more."

"OK." He let out a small laugh. His shoulders lifted and then fell; I realized he was struggling to maintain his composure. "So what about me?" He lifted the corners of his mouth, and feebly raised his hands as if already mocking what he was about to say. "Did this mean nothing?"

I wanted to smile, but my mouth was out of my control. I felt an obstruction in my throat.

Keeping his eyes on me, he carefully picked up my hand and held it in the gap between us. I remembered how he'd talked about the foster placements that had "worked" and the ones that hadn't. There'd been no judgment in his voice. He'd had only sympathy for the kids who were beyond help.

But then . . . Lulu.

I pulled my hand away. "So, can you let me go now? Please. You can go back and tell Rebecca I'm a fake, an interloper, whatever you want. Just give me a head start."

"What if I don't want you to go?"

"I can't stay any longer. It's all coming unraveled."

"Come back to the house."

"And what?"

"I'll pretend I don't know. We'll just carry on."

I turned toward him then, to explain how that just wasn't possible.

Bang.

A loud rap on my window—the crack of a signet ring on glass.

I leaped sideways toward Rob, my heart in my throat.

When I swiveled to look, a man was peering into the car, a familiar face with a goatee, grinning broadly.

I lowered the window, my heart still racing.

"Pascal!" I said. "Bloody hell . . ."

Pascal had taken a step back. "Sorry!" he said in French. "I didn't mean to frighten you! But I saw you from across the way and I wanted to tell you—I have some news about your friend."

My stomach dropped.

"You do?"

"Yes, I spoke again to Antoine. The man in Pugot was searching for his sister, Agnes, who had left home after an argument. And he found her. Antoine saw them together and spoke to them. So, not your friend at all. Mystery solved, yes? I'm so sorry for the misunderstanding."

I was computing all this as quickly as I could.

"No . . . that's OK. That's . . . fine. Thank you."

"So, OK, I'll see you." Pascal turned away, set off across the square, and climbed into the passenger seat of a waiting car, which pulled away.

"Did you understand that?" Rob said. "Your French up to it?"

308

I moved my head, half-shake, half-nod.

"OK." He glanced at me. "So, was that good news? Bad news?"

I brought my hand to my mouth.

"Good, I think . . . yes. Good."

Relief was starting to work its way through me. If Sean hadn't been asking about me in Pugot, maybe the man in the car in Castels hadn't been him either? The sun had been in my eyes. Was he thinner? Had he even been the right height? I closed my eyes to try to bring the memory into focus. Beyond that fleeting glimpse through the tinted window of a passing car, there was nothing concrete to suggest Sean had followed me.

I let out a long breath. It had all been in my head, the fear that he was coming—speculation, terrified fantasy, the product of my own guilt. I'd been tied to that man for more than three years, he had gotten inside of me and haunted me. For all I knew he had already given up, left France, gone to London. Or had never looked for me at all, cut his losses and let me, and the money, go.

And if that was the case, it made no sense to run. If I ran, I could be running toward him.

"Look," I heard Rob say, "my brother is away next week and I've told him I'll look after his house. It's in the middle of nowhere. Come with me. Whatever this is, we'll figure it out then."

I turned to face him. When I nodded, I saw relief in his face, and he pulled me toward him and kissed me, first gently and then much less gently.

Eventually, some time later, he started the car, drove off the deserted square, and turned back toward the house. We sat in silence nearly the whole way. We were crossing the bridge when he said, lightly, "By the way, I'm also a total fraud. In case that makes life easier for you."

"I don't understand."

He glanced at me and then away. "I'm not a writer. I wrote one good book. It was a fluke, or a con—it just happened to fit with what people wanted at that particular point in time. I don't have any talent, and I'm not cut out for this sort of existence. Phil has been watching me, making gibes. It's a nightmare. I haven't written a word since I got here. I haven't actually written anything in weeks. Months. I've got *nothing*."

He was talking fast—which is what people do when they're telling the truth. A writer's block: it made sense of the solitaire, the empty notebook. And it explained his body language earlier that day. He *had* been lying, only not in the way I had thought.

"So, we've both got secrets," I said. "We're both here on false pretenses."

As I said that, the full weight of what I hadn't yet told him swung back into my mind, and with it came a crushing sadness. Because I had to go to the police and then he would know the whole truth, and it would be over.

I stared out of the open window. Six days together. That was all we had. I would finish the job. Then I would put it behind me and do what had to be done. In the meantime, I had to pull myself together. When it came down to it, I told myself, he was just a mark.

Martha was at the front of the house when we walked through the gates, looking in the back of the Audi.

Her head emerged. "Oh, Lulu. Have you seen my gold cross?" Her fingers tapped anxiously against her breastbone. "I was hoping it might have fallen off in the car. Mum's going to kill me. She told me I shouldn't have brought it on holiday."

"Oh, no. I'll have a good look," I said. "Poor you."

She closed the car's back door, opened the front one, and began looking in there. "By the way," she said. "There're some people here to see you."

"People?"

"Um. The couple you were here with last year. What are they called? I want to say Olly and Katrina? They haven't got long. They were just passing, they said."

It was suddenly earth-shatteringly hot. The seconds split and divided and multiplied.

"Olly and Katya," I said.

My head was full of noise: the buzzing of insects, cicadas *tick-ticking*. The swifts were beating high, their screams thin and elated.

"What?" Martha was still buried in the front of the car.

Rob was standing next to me, his hand on my arm. He was saying something.

I said, "Her name's Katya. It's Olly and Katya."

Martha emerged. "Oh right. OK." She gestured vaguely. Anyway, they're in there. With Mum. I think."

"They're in the house. Now?"

"Yes." She laughed, as if I was being dim on purpose. "Yes. Olly and Katrina, Katya, whatever. They've come to visit you. They're here. Now."

Rob was repeating whatever it was he had just said. My brain had stopped working. I tried to force it back to life. "What?"

"I said we didn't buy milk, and we probably need it. Borrow my car. Drive back and get it. I'll explain."

He pressed the car key into my hand. "I'll cover for you," he murmured. And then more loudly, "If they've gone when you get back, well, that's a shame. But they did just drop in on the off chance. I'm sure they'll understand."

The key was warm in my palm. I looked at the gate, at the car beyond it. I imagined myself walking through it and getting into the car, turning it competently around and driving all the way to the village. And I imagined myself slumped in the driver's seat, unable to turn the key.

"We've got plenty of milk." Martha snapped shut the door of the Audi. "The necklace isn't in the car." She sighed. "Which is brutal."

Rob scratched the top of his head and left his arm up there, elbow out. At the back of his throat he made a noise, half-groan, half-laugh.

"Don't come in," I said.

He began to protest, but, ignoring him, I pulled my hair back into a ponytail, knotting it back on itself so it would stay in place. I put on my sunglasses and bit my lips and pinched my cheeks to get some color. It was five strides to the front door, and then along the corridor another four. I used them to adjust my gait to Lulu's; moved my weight to the ball of my foot, swiveled on my left heel slightly when I raised it. This wasn't like an encounter with Brigitte. Oliver and Katya; they had spent a fortnight in Lulu's company. The chances of passing for someone they knew so well were close to nil, but I lifted my chin, pulled back my shoulders.

People see what they want to see ... They don't like ambiguity. If something doesn't make sense, they try to supply the missing link.

"Ah, good. There you are." Rebecca was fussing with the coffee machine and she saw me standing in the doorway. "You've got visitors! Your friends, the people you worked for last year, have popped in to see you—Olly and Katya? She's gone for a quick swim and I'm making Olly a cup of coffee. He says he doesn't drink tea."

Out on the terrace, Phil was leaning across the table, trying to put up the umbrella. He was turning the handle, the white sails flapping outward, spreading, obscuring my view. I could see Layla and Clare a few chairs away. Martha had followed me in and was searching for her necklace under the table. "There we go," Phil said, getting his rhythm right. The umbrella filled the table and then suddenly lifted as the mechanism slotted into place.

The man facing me in shadow was already halfway out of his seat. I heard Layla ask something, some question. Rebecca called an answer. Phil sat down, releasing a sigh of satisfaction. The visitor moved toward me, from the patch of shade into the sunlight, and I met his cool, inquiring eyes full on.

For a moment everything stopped: the breeze, the drip of the coffee machine, the blood in my body. For one long pulse of silence, I could neither speak nor move.

He made no movement either, and for several seconds I stared at him, unblinking. He was squinting slightly. The umbrella, settling, creaked. Martha scrambled to her feet. Something fell to the floor in the kitchen with a clatter. Rebecca swore.

"Olly!" I said, moving forward. *It's a great help to believe in your story yourself.* "How lovely of you to visit."

He took a step back and I saw his Adam's apple move. His expression was quizzical, his eyes narrowed. "I didn't recognize you for a moment," he said, puzzled. "You look different."

His outfit—battered leather boat shoes, pinky-red shorts, a patterned short-sleeved shirt—were just what you'd expect a successful off-duty entrepreneur to wear. Ray-Bans hung around his neck on a neoprene strap.

"I've caught the sun," I said. "Maybe I've . . ." I twisted the ends of my ponytail ". . . changed my hair."

"That must be it." He was still holding my gaze and he shook his head slightly, still frowning.

"So, are you staying nearby?" I added quickly. "Have you found somewhere as nice as here, if that's possible?"

He ran his hand over the bristles on his chin. "No. We're closer to Avignon this year. Much smaller house. No guest quarters or we'd have nabbed you for ourselves."

He smiled then for the first time.

I was standing face on to him, my hands on my hips, to keep my ground. My legs were shaking. "But you thought you'd come and look me up?"

"We were on our way to Aix to collect Katya's mother, and discovered her train was delayed. We had time to kill and we were so near we thought we'd just see if you were at home." He shifted to draw Phil into the conversation. "We parked down the lane and were just having a little wander really—thought it might be too rude to knock. But Phil saw us, and . . ."

"I told them not to be so stupid and dragged them in. Any friend of Lulu's . . ."

"It's been lovely to have her. Makes such a difference to a holiday," Layla said, "having someone do all the everyday stuff. Just makes it a proper break."

"I couldn't agree more." The newcomer smiled and then pulled out a chair, gesturing for me to sit. I did so, and he stood over me, looking down, his hand resting on the back of it. I had to twist my head to look up at him. "She's quite the treasure."

"Refreshments coming through!" Rebecca bustled out with a tray containing mugs, sugar, a pot of tea, and the coffee. Rob followed, carrying a carton of milk. "Had milk all the time," he said. "Hi!" He lifted a hand in greeting and then looked pointedly at me. I gave him a reassuring smile and he put the milk down in the middle of the table. He did something odd with his hands, lacing them back on themselves and squeezing them together so that the knuckles clicked. He looked at me again, and when I kept my expression steady, he addressed the new arrival: "Nice to meet you."

He waited a couple of beats, and then backed sheepishly toward the safety of the house. I was relieved to see him go. I didn't need him. He would only make things worse.

The visitor had moved quietly around the table and had sat down opposite me, leaning forward on his elbows. "Such a lovely house," he said. "I'd forgotten."

"Isn't it?" Rebecca gushed. "It's so tranquil—for me that's the secret of a holiday, to be away from people and traffic, just to have peace and quiet."

He turned his smile on her. "So true. It's about recalibrating, isn't it? Giving yourself a bit of mental space."

"From what I've heard, your life must be even more frenetic than mine," Rebecca said. "But yes. Absolutely."

Clare leaned forward. "Did the drains smell last year?" she asked him. "We've had terrible problems."

Phil snapped, "Oh for goodness' sake. Can we just stop for one minute talking about the drains?"

Clare glared at him. "It's all very well for you."

"I don't remember a problem with the drains." The visitor smiled at her, before turning to me. "New sunglasses?" he said. "Suit you."

My cue to take them off. "Thanks," I said, not doing so. I was grateful for the brown tint, for the weight across the bridge of my nose. This interloper and I, we were the center of attention. It was like a performance, and I felt the pressure to give it my all. "We went to the market this morning," I said. "The one at Castels you and Katya loved so much. I even took them to the vintage shop we found, but sadly it was closed."

Martha was leaning against one of the large urns, watching us. "The disappointment was savage," she said.

"I'm not a big fan of Castels, I'm afraid," Rebecca said. "It was just terribly, terribly hot."

He wrinkled his nose, answering both of them: "August."

"So, was it July then," Martha said, "that you were here? Because the shop was open then."

He smoothed a section of table with both index fingers, and then looked up. "Maybe it was the last few days of July and the beginning of August. Not that it matters." He smiled benignly and then turned to address the others in their entirety. "So how are you enjoying Lulu's cooking? It's quite something, isn't it?"

There was a bit of fussing then, twittering, like when you walk past a hedge full of sparrows. "Delicious." "Very spoiling." "So lucky." It was quite touching, the effort they put into sounding enthusiastic. Phil said something about my duck confit, and Martha said she was impressed by my artistic flair, my "towers of bread."

Rebecca said, "I actually feel quite deskilled. I've forgotten even how to make a cup of coffee. I hope this is all right. It's not as strong as Lulu makes it. But then I'm a bit of a wimp."

He peered into his cup and took a sip. "It's the perfect strength. Just how I like it."

Rebecca smiled broadly. "Oh, good. I've passed muster."

Layla leaned across the table then, and asked him about his food business, whether Brexit was much of a problem, and he talked to her fluidly for a bit about exports and imports and tariffs, and she nodded in a way that made it look as though she were listening. When he paused for breath, she told him what she'd wanted to tell him all along—that there was an article in the *New York Times* he should read. It would "really open his eyes" on the subject.

I began to find it unbearable and stood up. "So,

Katya's having a swim," I said. "It's already so hot, isn't it? I don't blame her. I might pop down and say hello."

"Oh, take her a cup of tea!" Rebecca cried. "Before it gets cold. I might come down, too, as soon as I find my bathing suit."

He joined me as soon as I hit the grass. His mouth came close to my ear and I threw back my head as if I were laughing gaily, though he just made a noise, a vibration deep in his throat, an almost silent guttural roar.

I tried to pull away. "You came after me."

"Of course. Did you really think I would let you escape?" He spoke mildly, but he was holding my elbow with his spare hand, his fingers probing the tender flesh between the bones. "There was the money, of course. But also it was the principle."

"How did you find me?"

"Talk about hiding in plain sight. Respect due. A proper job! Wonders never cease. You, a private chef!" He was laughing, rhythmically, nastily.

"Fuck off, Sean."

I lifted my elbow to jab into his ribs, to force him away, but he dug his thumb in deeper, used it as a lever to twist my forearm out at an angle. "Calm down," he said, his face so close I could see the sun glinting off the red in his bristle, smell coffee and garlic on his breath. "Or I'll tell your new friends who you really are."

He stopped and let my elbow go as he bent forward,

toeing the ground. Something on the grass had caught his attention.

"I didn't guess. Not straightaway. I used my detective skills." He had unearthed the something with his foot. "The bus driver remembered dropping you off in Pugot. I asked around—a concerned brother, looking for a wayward sister—and found a guy with a grudge in a café who says you ripped him off."

He threw down the teacup and bent to pick whatever it was off the ground. I had time to see the glimmer of linked gold—Martha's necklace—before he snapped his hand shut and slipped it into his pocket.

"Schoolboy error, Ali. I thought I taught you better than that. You let yourself be noticed." He had stopped laughing. His forehead was furrowed, his nose wrinkled, as if my mistake was personal. "He saw you get in the car with this guy Pascal, who I discovered lives in Saint-Étienne. After that I worked out you had taken Lulu's job, and it was easy. I'm amazed, actually, that it's taken this long."

He strode ahead. The gate was unlocked, and he kicked it like you'd kick a ball. It opened with a clatter.

"Come meet Katya," he said, and there was anticipation in his face, a sort of vengeful glee.

Who was my replacement? I had only a few seconds to consider. But I knew as I followed him that I felt sorry for this unknown person, that it was dread for them that curled deep inside, and that that must mean I had in some ways managed to free myself. He preyed

320

on the vulnerable, on the insecure, and I knew now that I was neither.

She was in the deep end, the girl—the woman—floating on her back, her hair splayed, her pale limbs idly paddling. Her bikini was familiar, just like the one I used to have, a collection of triangles on strings. One black bikini is pretty well like another. That was the point: the anonymity of it. Her eyes were closed and she didn't hear Sean at first. For a terrible moment I thought she was dead, that he'd killed someone else, bringing her to me like a cat with a mouse. But he crouched, dipped his hand in the pool, and then brought it up fast, scattering her with water.

She spluttered upright, her back still to me. "*Oi!*" she protested, laughing. She splashed him back, and then, following his eyes, swept her hands against the water to twirl her body around.

The pool was in full sun, bright turquoise, loosely hooped with white. The ripples spread across from her arms, rocked against the edge. In the surface, the stone walls of the *pigeonnier* were reflected, skewed at an angle. Light glanced and bounced, shattered into a thousand pieces of glitter. Stare unblinking at water too long and it's like looking upside down into a mirror; you lose sense of where the sky begins and ends, of what's real and what's not.

For a few broken moments, I felt disbelief, both rigid, paralyzed, beyond emotion, as if something inside was crumbling. And then as the atrophy in my brain eased, as the blood began to flow again, I felt an overwhelming surge of relief, a sort of mindless, un-thinking joy.

The woman in the pool was calm, almost expressionless. She was biting the end of her finger, watching my reaction. Sean had sat down on the side, his legs dangling in the water, watching me too.

"How have you been?" she said.

That unthinking joy was only pure and unadulterated for a moment. It changed color, turned red, black. I just stood there, unable to do or say anything at all. My face felt heavy. I couldn't get my mouth to work. My throat was constricted. It was taking everything I had to stay upright.

"I'd forgotten how lovely this pool was," she said. "Sometimes when they're unheated they're too cold, but this is just the perfect temperature."

"Not too much chlorine either," Sean said.

"Yes, people often overchlorinate. Big mistake. At the same time those pools that are all natural and salt-flavored, I'm not so keen on them either. You get out smelling of crisps."

She swam to the side of the pool and used her arms to pull herself up. On the back of the sunlounger was a towel—one Rob had left earlier—and she lifted it and used it to rub her hair. When she finished, she dropped it in a heap on the ground where she stood.

"Look at her," he said. "She's lost for words. She doesn't know what to do with herself."

She was gazing at me with what looked like curiosity. She raised her arm and rested it on the top of her head. My legs felt like liquid. I thought I might be sick. I had the urge to collapse to the ground, or curl in a ball, or rush at her, push her into the water, and hold her under. *I wanted to kill her.* I was digging my fingernails into my palms. I tried to concentrate on the pain, to feel it as something sharp and real, to force the muscles in my face to retract.

I swallowed hard. "Forgive me," I said, and the words sounded almost normal. I took a couple of steps toward the closest sunbed and sank down. "You know, it tends to unnerve a person when someone they thought was dead turns out not to be. So." I raised my palms.

I had managed to keep the tremble out of my voice. I was light and air, not an internal *scream*. "So, you didn't die," I said. "You didn't murder her?" I wasn't addressing one question to her, one to him. I was addressing them both simultaneously, as if I already had an instinct of what was to come.

Lulu giggled. "It almost went horribly wrong. I was supposed to have just hit my head, but you saw me breathing, and Sean had to improvise."

"Which worked to our advantage," he said.

Lulu laid herself down on the sunlounger. She put on a wide straw hat and enormous seventies-style sunglasses so you could hardly see her face.

"We set you up," Sean said, almost kindly. "Do you see?"

He wanted me to ask questions. I was supposed to feed him the lines. I just couldn't. Not yet. I needed to breathe normally a little longer.

"Aren't you going to tell her?" Lulu picked up a bottle of Nivea suncream, squeezed some into her palm, and began rubbing it into her legs. "Explain what we did."

Sean still waited, something eager and hungry in his expression.

I lifted my chin, let out a long sigh. "You planned it? That night, when you met up after our dinner with Aunt Marie?"

Lulu flicked the lid of the suncream shut and dropped it to the ground. "Aunt Marie," she said mockingly. And I knew then that I had underestimated her.

I cast my mind back to that day on the beach at Sainte-Cécile. I was the one who'd spotted Lulu. Sitting up in the slatted shade at Raoul's, I was the one who couldn't wait to share my observations: the mani-pedi, the Longchamp bag, the three-for-two airport deal. Sean just sat there, while I tried to prove what I was made of.

"You already knew each other when I made that initial approach at the bar." It was a statement, not a question.

Lulu sat back on her elbows. "Now you're getting it. We'd met a couple of nights earlier at Le Club des Fous. You were ill. I watched Sean buying drinks on someone else's tab and confronted him." She reached her foot off the sunbed and poked his back with her toe. "And the rest, as they say, is history."

"Those few days when you stayed in bed," Sean pouted with mock sympathy, "I had to find some way to entertain myself."

I looked up at the sky, at its shiny, slippery blue, and then back at its blinking reflection in the pool. "Lulu wasn't the mark."

"No." Lulu had retrieved her foot. "You were."

I looked at her hard. "Are you going to tell me why?"

She sat back on her elbows. "Sean was going on about his partner and how well he'd taught you, and what a good reader of character you were, and I told him I'd got an A level in psychology and that I had trained as a professional actor. I might not be getting many auditions, but I bet him I could convince you. And I was right." She let out a throaty, open-mouthed laugh. "You were so quick to dismiss me. People see what they want to see. It made you feel good about yourself to think of me as lesser than you. Your problem—too certain of your own immunity. So . . ." She paused. "Gotcha."

"You did it literally *just for a bet*?"

"Of course not." She looked at me, again scathingly. "You're doing it again. I had several reasons. It suited me to disappear for a bit. Todd, my ex, was getting a bit persistent. I fancied trying on someone else's life. I needed a change, a different sort of excitement." She lifted one shoulder. "Maybe I got carried away."

I stared at her for a moment longer, and then I looked back at Sean, who, shoulders hunched, was dabbling his hands in the water, in stupid circles. He looked seedy, diminished, next to Lulu. Love weakens us all. He had fallen for her, told her the truth about himself on that first night, flaunted it, like a peacock splaying its tail feathers. If overconfidence leaves one vulnerable, so, too, does infatuation.

"Risky game," I said, "no? It might have pushed me into leaving."

I recognized the expression that fixed on his face then, the hardening of his jaw. It was the same look he had when a suspicious tour guide canceled a trip to the gem factory or when a sales assistant threatened to call the store detective. I thought how he liked to get one over on a certain kind of woman, and how wrong I had been to think myself special. I *was* that kind of woman. His games, his tricks; they were just another form of cruelty.

I let the air out of my lungs quietly. "You knew I wanted to leave you. You couldn't bear it. If I was going to leave, you wanted it to be on your terms."

He was still looking down at the water, dangling his feet, moving them again, rhythmically, from side to side. Lulu cupped her hands behind her neck and, eyes closed, raised her chest slightly toward the sun. Something had changed. Neither of them wanted to meet my eye. They weren't quite as pleased with themselves as they had been. It wasn't that they were sheepish. It wasn't quite that. But of course. I let out another short laugh. "The money. It was also about the money." I shook my head to convey disappointment. "You saw an opportunity to keep my half. What were you going to do? Give it to her? A sort of signing bonus?"

Sean inclined his head.

"Except—slight glitch in the system—I took the money with me." I laughed genuinely then.

"Thirty thousand euros!" Lulu said. "And you took my stuff."

I widened my eyes at Sean. *Thirty* thousand. So she wasn't in on everything.

"Including my passport, for fuck's sake. We weren't going to let you get away with that, were we, Sean?"

"We weren't."

"He said it'd be easy to find you, but we wasted so much time at first. You told the receptionist you were going to get the Eurostar."

"Double bluff? Triple bluff. I wasn't sure," Sean added.

"He thought you'd want to go back to Marrakech, only you wouldn't because you'd know he'd be thinking that. Then he thought maybe you'd go to Monte Carlo because you said you hated the thought of it. It didn't take many phone calls to rule that out. India— that was next on our list, but expensive to get there, and . . . well, you've got a sister? That's where Sean thought you'd end up. Honestly, this job, it's the *last* place we thought of looking. Even when we tracked you to Saint-Étienne, it took a while for the penny to drop. I mean, I'd texted the Ottys to say I wasn't coming. How did you swing it?"

"Your text didn't go through. They were expecting you." I lifted one shoulder in a sort of shrug. "So it was easy."

She laughed then, thinly.

Sean released a theatrical sigh. "So here we are. I want the money. Lulu wants her clothes . . ."

"And my iPad. And my fucking phone."

"Ah. Finally!"

I spun around. Rebecca was pushing open the gate. "Isn't it glorious here?"

She placed her towel and book on the sunbed next to me and walked slowly down the steps into the pool. "Oh," she said, sighing, when she was submerged. "Bliss. I needed that."

"We should get going." Sean removed his legs from the pool, dried them off with a quick flick of his hand, and stood up. He reached down to help Lulu off the lounger. "We mustn't abandon Katya's mother."

Lulu pulled on a pair of shorts and a threadbare white cotton top I'd bought several years ago in Anjuna market.

"Pretty blouse," I said.

"Thanks." She looked down to smooth the hemline, and then batted her eyes up at me. "It's new."

"Right." Sean hunched his arm over her shoulders. "Nice to meet you," he said to the floating Rebecca.

She splashed to the surface. "Oh, are you going? Do stay! Well, come again. Any time."

"We will."

"I'll see you out," I said.

We walked up the grassy slope in silence, stopping briefly to say goodbye to Phil, who passed us on his way down to the pool, and again to talk briefly to Layla and Roland in the kitchen. There was no sign of Rob.

I managed to get them along the corridor and out of the house, through the gate and into the road. I asked where they were parked and Sean gestured to the bottom of the lane, around the corner toward the bridge. "At the bottom there."

"I won't walk you down," I said. "I've got work to do."

Lulu brought her lips together. "Of course you do."

They looked at each other, and then at me, and Sean said, "So, here's what's going to happen. You're going to meet us later, with Lulu's stuff and the money. We'll meet you at the bottom of the lane. There's a gate, and we'll be waiting just inside the field. We'll be there at 11 p.m."

He looked behind me at the house as if taking it all in. "I'm expecting you to come with us," he added casually. "There's nothing for you here."

"What if I don't want to?"

"Ali. See sense. We could make your life so unpleasant. For one thing, I've got your passport. Play nice and you can have it back."

"I've got Lulu's."

"True. But it would be useless to you if she decided to report it stolen."

"Which I would," Lulu added.

"In that case," I said airily, trying to match my tone to Sean's, "I'll probably work out the last few days. It's only until Thursday and I am being paid."

"Ah." Lulu tutted as if she had bad news for me, and then stuck out her bottom lip. "Oh, babe. Actually, you're not."

I didn't know what to answer then, just stared at her. "Yes, I am," I said pathetically.

"Oh, bless. No. It's a direct transfer. The money's going into my account. I already got the first install-ment this morning." She put her head on one side. "All that hard work, all that slaving over a hot stove, and I'm the one making money. Who said crime doesn't pay?"

Chapter Twenty-Seven

It's strange how calm I was when I walked back into the house. There were so many things I could have been feeling: anger, humiliation, panic. But all I actually felt was relief. She wasn't dead. It was all that mattered. She was many things—devious, duplicitous, impressive, *annoying*. But she was alive.

In the kitchen, the fly zapper was crackling, another murder every thirty seconds. The house was quiet. Someone was watching something on the TV in the sitting room. Just to occupy my hands, I began to clear up. The coffee machine had been left on and the pot hissed steam when I ran it under the tap. The sink was full of cups, and I put them in the dishwasher.

"Have they left then, your visitors?"

I turned. Clare had walked in and was opening the fridge. She was wearing a white lace dress, similar to one I'd seen on Rebecca.

"Yes. They have."

"Sorry not to have said goodbye. I'm feeling a bit over 'people.'"

"It's been a busy day." I let a beat pass. "Did you have fun at the market?"

She had brought out a bottle of wine and was pouring herself a glass. She shot me a suspicious look.

I held her glance.

"I did, yes," she said eventually. She put the bottle back in the fridge and, closing the door with her elbow, said, "But, you know, when you've seen one French market you've seen them all?"

She sat up on the counter then and watched me. Finally, she said: "So, I wanted to ask you something . . . I don't suppose you want to sell me those vouchers?"

"Vouchers?"

"For the spa hotel in Nice?"

"Oh, *those* vouchers." I made myself sound surprised, but it had genuinely gone out of my mind. It had only been the night before but so much had happened since. It was like a con from another era. "For the Maison d'Anglais?"

"It's this weekend you had booked, isn't it? I could get a taxi to Avignon in the morning. I've looked it up and from there there's a direct train."

"They're not cheap," I said doubtfully. "And I was thinking I might see if they'll transfer them to another date."

She waited, swinging her legs with an expectant

smile. She was so used to getting her own way I had an urge to say no, just to put a stop to the trend.

"The smell of my en suite bathroom is really bad," she said. "For all fucking Phil says there isn't a problem, I'm not sure that room is actually habitable."

"I'm sorry about that."

She was picking at a cuticle. "Anyway, I think one week in the bosom of my sister's family might be enough." She looked up. "What do you think?"

I leaned against the sink and smiled companionably. "OK," I said. "It's a deal. You're good to have come and I'm sure Rebecca really appreciates it, but I can see, yes, sometimes you need to get on with your own life."

She went upstairs to pack and I stood in the kitchen, working out where everyone was. I could hear Iris's and Elliot's voices in the sitting room. Maybe the others were at the pool. Rob? I didn't know. I would delay as long as I could. I put on another pot of coffee and sat at the table while I waited for it to drip through. I tried to clear my mind. I made a good cup of coffee now, I realized, got the strength just right. Not, of course, that there was a right and wrong strength, but I'd learned to make it how Rebecca liked it. I'd responded to her cues and altered my behavior. It was a satisfying, strangely comforting thought.

The pad of feet in the corridor. Layla walked into the kitchen and, seeing me, faltered. "Oh, sorry," she said unnecessarily. "I was just getting some water."

She filled a glass from the tap and, after she'd drunk it, she leaned into the counter, looking out to the garden. "What are people's plans; do you know?" she asked.

I said I didn't, and she stayed where she was for a couple of minutes, not speaking, and then Roland came into the kitchen and the two of them quietly conferred. Should they go down to the pool? Would that be the friendly thing to do? Or would people want to be on their own for a bit? Eventually, after a bit more murmuring and a couple of throat-clearings (from him), they decided it would be a good idea to "make themselves scarce" for a while.

They went upstairs to change into their trainers and went for a walk. I realized after they'd gone how on edge they both were, with their "people's" and their gulps and it struck me that part of it was that it was difficult being guests. I felt sorry for them then. Layla always having to know better than everybody else— perhaps insecurity. And Roland's tendency to back her up all the time: he just loved her. They loved each other. It's so easy to think you know people when you don't. Sean turned people into types, a series of predictable reactions, and I'd followed his lead. When I'd thought Lulu was dead, I'd realized she wasn't a construct we could work with, but a real person, with a network of friends, a family. Now I realized even that was patronizing. She was nothing like the person I'd thought she was. She was clever, sophisticated, canny. *She* had played *me*. I didn't know how I could have imagined I was good at psychology, when I didn't even understand myself.

I realized I'd learned a lot. I cared about this job. I wanted to succeed at it. And I cared about the people I worked for. I'd been using my skills to get close to people, to make them like me, and it struck me like a bolt that it didn't have to go anywhere from there. It had been enough on its own.

I took the coffee I'd made down to the pool, but I stopped at the gate. Rebecca and Phil were lying on adjacent sunbeds, heads turned to face each other. They were speaking softly. Rebecca was prone, with her arms tucked protectively underneath herself, her back curved, but Phil's were trailing on the ground. She was talking and his answers were more monosyllabic, high murmurs at the back of his throat. At one point he lifted his hand and moved a lock of hair away from her face. A breeze ruffled the water and I saw his shoulders contract in a shiver as if he were cold, but he didn't get up.

I turned then and took the coffee back up to the house. I walked around the ground floor. Each room felt like home now, a place where something had happened. And then I went upstairs and knocked quietly on Martha's door. When I poked my head in, she was lying on her bed, watching something on her phone. She sat up when she saw me. "You haven't found my gold cross, have you? No?" She sank back down. "*Shit.*"

I stepped in and closed the door.

"How are you?" I said. "We haven't had a chance to talk properly today. Are you OK?"

"Oh, I'm fine. Yeah."

Perching on the side of her bed, I said tentatively, "Oh, good. I wondered, have you . . . have you managed to speak to the father?"

She frowned, looking confused. "What father?"

"You know . . ."

"Oh, you mean Liam?" She wrinkled her nose. "No. I haven't, which is proper shady; I'm beginning to think he's an actual arsehole."

"I'm sorry."

"It's OK, though. My period's come. Didn't I tell you?"

She stretched out her arms and gave a self-conscious half-yawn, as if belatedly realizing this might have been an omission.

I smoothed the sheet with my fingers and then looked up at her, smiling. "No. You didn't."

"Yeah. This morning. So, the good news is, I'm not pregnant. Or maybe I was. But I'm not now. Should I be sad? I don't know. But I'm not. Sorry." She looked at me full on this time. "I should have told you."

"It doesn't matter."

"But yeah, I'm going to a gig when I get back with

my friend's brother. We've been speaking, so . . ." She grinned. "So, actually, fuck Liam."

"Absolutely." She wasn't even hiding his identity, which made me feel happy. "But also in future, maybe don't."

"You're funny."

I found Rob in the garden on a chair under a tree. At first he didn't see me and I watched him lift his hands and make a sort of languid stretch, before returning them to the keyboard. I held back. I was still the person who had walked away from a murder, taken on what I thought was the identity of a murdered woman. Were the facts any different now that we knew she was alive?

It was late afternoon now and it was cooler where he was sitting, the ivy in the upper branches creating a deep shade. When he caught sight of me standing there, he got to his feet, casting the laptop aside. "I've been worried," he said. "What's been going on with those people? What happened there? Please explain. I thought you were about to be found out. I don't understand."

The ivy smelled dark and bitter. The cicadas were strident, like a chorus.

"Yeah, the thing is," I said, "those people—they weren't quite what they seemed."

"What do you mean? Why did they come?"

"I guess they wanted to intimidate me."

"That's horrible."

"I guess. Yes."

"So, tell me. Explain."

A leaf fluttered down from a branch. The rim of his ear was in a dapple of light. I felt the space between us widen. I wished he were a little less like the kind of person you had to be to succeed in the world, and a little more like me.

"It's complicated," I said.

He let out an exasperated noise then and shook his head. "Oh, for God's sake, stop saying that . . ." He sat back down, scratching his cheek with the back of his thumb. "Christ. I was about to say Lulu. You haven't even told me your *name*?"

I took a deep breath. I'd been hoping it would be easy, that I could skate over the full truth. Lulu was alive. I could just patch something together and he would never have to know what I was capable of doing, or who I really was. But I realized in that moment that if I didn't tell him, I was going to lose him anyway and that maybe if I were going to change, make a life for myself, I didn't have a choice.

"Ali," I said. "My name is Ali."

"I knew it!" he said. "I was right." His face softened then. "Ali," he said, his eyes on me, as if he were saying my name for the first time. "So?"

I thought then that maybe it would be OK, maybe the story itself would appeal to him. Maybe he could even use it in his own fiction.

I took a deep breath. "Something happened that day you saw me in Sainte-Cécile-sur-Mer. That woman today, Katya, she's actually Lulu. We'd only just met her; she was a mark. We were going to get money out of her, but the con went wrong and she fell and Sean killed her. He put a towel over her face and smothered her. Or I thought he had. I was traumatized, terrified, and I ran and got her luggage from her room and one thing and another and I ended up here, pretending to *be* her. I thought I could hide from Sean, that I would be safe, but in fact it turns out I'd gotten everything wrong. I was the one being tricked because they turned up today and she was alive. Do you understand? Do you see?"

Because he wasn't getting it, his expression was still confused, and he was smiling as if the whole thing was somehow ridiculous.

"Do you see?" I cried out again. "I thought she was dead."

And he stopped smiling then and he stood up and put his arms around me. I hadn't realized I was crying, but I must have been because he was kissing the tears off my face, and it was like something had been awoken in me then, a hunger or a desperation. I felt like I could lose myself in his body. Or maybe it was more that I could find myself.

Chapter Twenty-Eight

It was very quiet as I bumped the suitcase along the side of the swimming pool. The moon was splintered across the surface of the water. Bats swooped above me. My shadow seemed monstrous. The house was dark and shuttered, but I expected at any minute to hear shouts, running steps. I rolled the bag to the edge of the terrace, scraped it past the wall into the rough area beyond, and across the ragged ground to the trees. No one came.

At the top of the escarpment, I kicked the bag so that it somersaulted and then slithered ahead of me to the field below. Harsh grass grazed my legs as I scrambled down after it. I righted the bag at the bottom. One of the wheels didn't seem to work too well now. I brushed some of the mud off the nylon casing and dragged it behind me, up and over the furrows, sometimes on two wheels, sometimes one, until I reached the turnout at the far end.

In the distance, a dog barked once, twice, and then fell silent. Unseen creatures crept between clumps of foliage. The sky was ghostly white at the edges of that big moon, but fell away into blackness. The land seemed huge and alien, a wilderness of different densities, towering shapes, and thick shadows. I was very aware of the curvature of the earth. The row of trees where I'd just stood was a looming black mass.

No sign of Sean and Lulu.

I shivered, rubbing my arms, though it wasn't cold. I wasn't sure of the time. I'd left my room at a quarter to eleven. I guessed it had taken ten minutes to get down here. Five minutes to wait, at most.

I was listening out for the sound of a car. I'd first hear it when it crossed the bridge; I'd catch the double bump of the wheels, the creak of the undercarriage, the throaty choke of acceleration. When I heard that, I'd have a few minutes to collect myself.

"You came." Sean's voice was almost in my ear.

"Fuck," I cried, jumping back. "Fuck."

He was three feet away, next to the gnarled trunk of a tree. He took a step forward, his body detaching from the knot of branches.

For a few beats he just stood there, legs apart, staring at me, then he said: "Are you alone?"

He was wearing a black T-shirt and black trousers, like some kind of commando.

"Of course I'm alone. I want to get this over with. I've got what you wanted." I pushed the suitcase handle

341

toward him. The bag toppled forward, landing on the earth with a crunch.

"Lulu will check it over when she gets here. We parked up the road. She's on a call. What about the money?"

I put my backpack down on the ground, unzipped it, and brought out the plastic bag. "It's here. All of it—minus a hundred euros that I needed for expenses. Yes, so just a hundred euros short of *the full 60,000*. I gather Lulu doesn't know about Dutroix's share?"

He rubbed his hands together, shrugged up his shoulders. "Maybe above her pay grade."

I held the bag of money tightly to my chest as he reached out for it. I shook my head. "That night I was ill and you went up to talk to him," I said. "What happened? Why have you still got his share? Did you hurt him?"

"Come on, Ali. This is me we're talking about. I didn't *hurt* him. For 30,000 euros? What do you think I am, a monster?"

I made a face to say, your words not mine.

"Ali." He sounded hurt. "How can you even think that? I got up there that night. He'd fallen off the roof, fixing a broken tile or something. He'd gone to hospital. What am I going to do? Leave the envelope on the bar? Seems he was suffering from a concussion so, you know how it is, opportunities sometimes fall into your lap. Come on. Ali!"

He was coaxing now, cajoling me as he'd done so

often in the past. "You and me, that's what we do, no? If we find ourselves in a situation, we work it to our own"—he made a movement with his hands, like climbing steps—"advantage."

I put the bag of money on the ground. "You should have told me."

"I was going to. As soon as I'd got rid of Lulu. I mean, fuck. She's persistent, you know? I got caught up in the *drama*." He rolled his eyes to imply I'd understand, and then bent down, picked up the plastic bag, and cradled it under one arm. "As soon as we're on the road, we'll see her on her way. I've had to play the game because, man, she's a ballbuster. I'm looking forward to it, being you and me again, to a bit of peace. You're coming, aren't you? We're still the dream team. Nothing's changed."

The way he smiled, slightly lopsided, the crinkle between his eyes, the sense of conspiracy. I could feel myself slipping into his power, being drawn to him, even as I tried not to. No one knew me like he did.

"Come on," he said, picking up the handle of the suitcase with his spare hand. "Let's go. We can meet her on the corner."

He began to walk off, dragging the case behind him, but after only a few steps, stopped, realizing I hadn't moved.

The moon illuminated his face. An owl shrieked.

"So, what? You going soft?" he said.

"No. Of course not."

"You've got a scheme up there, then?" His tone was hostile. "I thought so."

When I didn't immediately answer, he said, "Respect, Ali. I'm only interested. I'm not trying to cut in on anything. We can hook up again later when you're done. I know you. You'll have found something on those jerks."

Time did a somersault on itself. I felt we were back at the beginning, when he was interested in my take on the situations or people we encountered. He'd listen with the same half-smile, as if he'd already made up his own mind, but he was open to minor adjustments. I remembered the challenge of it, how I'd want to impress and how when I did, even in a small way, it felt like a win. We were in a dusty field in the bottom half of France now, not on a golden rooftop in India. But I needed him to listen. I wanted to see the expression on his face shift, some sort of validation.

I wasn't soft. I did deserve respect.

I fiddled with my feet. The toe bar on the right flip-flop was coming loose from its hole and I poked it back in. The moon was behind me and my own shadow was a definite purple shape, like the negative of a photograph.

"My employers." I pointed toward the dark tower of trees, to the shuttered skeleton of house beyond. "They've all got secrets they'll pay good money to keep hidden."

I heard him shrug, the fabric of his shirt shift. A clod of earth crumbled under his shoe. "Of course."

"Even the teenagers," I said. "They've got a lot

invested in being the kind of people their parents want them to be. One of them has failed her exams; one has had an affair with an older man. Another has smuggled weed into France. They'll pay to shut me up, and they've got massive bank accounts." I shrugged.

He was nodding regularly, in a practiced, vaguely bored kind of way.

Outside the hotel in Jodhpur, there was a street hawker who'd start small with key rings made from elephant tusk and build up until he was chasing you down the street with paintings ripped from the walls of temples.

"I know who the older man is, by the way. He's actually a teacher at her school." I made a face, and Sean nodded, grudging respect.

"As for the adults, their relationships are precarious, and the murky stuff underneath—well, they wouldn't want the kids finding out. I mean, it's shady, man."

Sean didn't say anything. In the darkness, the planes of his face cast his features into shadow.

I felt myself swallow. "One couple in particular," I said. "The husband took the wife's speeding points so she wouldn't lose her license. She's a doctor. He's a lawyer. You know, like proper professional people. They broke the law. They could lose their jobs if that came out. So." I raised my eyebrows, and Sean nodded.

"Yeah, I can see," he said politely. "That's worth a bit."

"Yes, it is." Even to my own ears, my voice sounded thin.

"OK, then." He bent over to touch the handle of the suitcase and lifted it upright with a little jerk. "You've got big plans ahead."

I looked at the thin curved line of his mouth. He hadn't spoken with irony or sarcasm. His tone was flatter than that, as if he wanted to leave me a small piece of dignity.

Leaning on the handle of the suitcase, he craned his neck to look up the lane. "I don't know what's happened to Lulu."

It was being dismissed that stung.

"And also," I said, "I've got the beginnings of a Big Store."

His lips parted as he turned. He always loved a Big Store. In the moonlight, his skin looked silvery, his features molded from molten bronze. I felt it then, like an electrical charge.

"Go on."

I could feel the old excitement rising in me too. I spoke quickly. We didn't have long. "I met this rich woman called Sophia Bartlett who's looking for a house for her parents to stay in for her wedding. She's baited. I've told her *my* house is usually booked years in advance, but that I might have a cancelation. I've got the Domaine to myself on Friday. She gave me her business card and I thought I'd give her a call, reel her in. She's so desperate she'll hand me the full amount up front. What do you think I can ask? Ten thousand euros?"

I watched him consider. And then nod. He asked questions then. How long did I have sole access to the house? Did I have paperwork I could print out? Was I thinking cash?

He nodded at each of my answers. He approved of my thinking, of my methods. "Letterhead? Nice." He wasn't trying to muscle in. His interest was professional.

"That sounds extremely promising," he said. "Well done."

"Thanks."

"Good luck with it."

There was the sound of an engine, the slam of a car door. Lulu was striding toward us. "Hurrah," she said. "You're here. All sorted? Have I given you enough time?"

She seemed very angular and solid next to me and Sean. I'd started to think of us both as part of the night, as ghosts. Her hair was in tight braids and she was wearing a T-shirt, one of mine, and a pair of stone-washed jeans I hadn't seen before. Between the pale bones of her throat glinted Martha's cross.

"Have you checked my stuff's all here?" she said, addressing Sean.

"It seems to be. I haven't done a full inventory."

"Is it?" To me this time.

"Yes."

"Here's yours." She was holding a thin plastic bag and she threw it at my feet.

I picked it up and checked the contents. My passport was there, some underwear, no sneakers. Lulu meanwhile was unfastening the outside pocket of her case. "OK. Passport. Phone," she said. "I'll have to take your word on everything else."

"Right." Sean moved to stand next to her. "I guess we're done here."

The two of them faced me, straight on.

"For now," he added. "We'll be seeing you again soon."

I felt myself shiver and I pressed my hands deep into my pockets.

I was aware of the skeletons of the trees, the tracery of the bushes, the cavernous shadows along the edge of the field. Lulu was still holding her phone, tapping it in the palm of her hand, like a Victorian teacher with a cane. A breeze rustled in the branches, a few leaves at our feet skittered. The screen was sending flashes of light onto the necklace at her throat.

"OK." I pulled my hands out of my pockets as if I were about to hug him. I don't actually think I was going to. But I'd been too abrupt, and as I pulled my hands out, a small piece of paper fell to the ground.

I stepped forward to pick it up, but Sean beat me to it.

I looked up. "Can you move your foot?"

"Should I?" he said. He was looking carefully at my face. "What's it worth?"

"Nothing." I rocked back on my heels, shrugged as if it didn't matter.

But he could tell.

He stretched back his shoulders and then slowly bent down, moved his foot and picked it up. He made a performance of holding the card out and looking down his nose at it, as if he were wearing spectacles. "'Sophia Bartlett. Content Designer,'" he read out loud and then, looking up, he said, "She the woman you're going to 'rent' the house to?"

"Yup, that's her," I said, still casual. I put my hand out and smiled. I was aware the smile didn't reach my eyes.

"How about I keep hold of it for now," he said.

"How about you give it back?"

He stuck out his lower lip, considering. I told myself his reluctance was posture. Just for show. Any minute, he was going to laugh and return it.

Lulu was looking from one of us to the other.

"Please, Sean," I said again.

He considered me. His forehead was creased, his mouth rigidly closed. A muscle went in his cheek. I'd like to think he was weighing it up: respect and affection, residual loyalty, all those long hours we'd spent together on the retirement circuit, the low points, the high points, the sacrifices and the scrapes, versus what? Boredom. Greed. The desire to own or destroy anything solid and glittering that was created despite him.

He let out a long shuddering sigh, as if he was

disappointed in what he'd seen. "Nah," he said finally. Even the act of looking had been a piece of stagecraft. The delay gave the illusion of hope, sharpened the knife. He looked again at the card, and then up at me. "Think of your life as being like a franchise. You may think you've set up on your own, but there is always someone else—me—pulling the strings. So, yeah. This little scam of yours—I quite fancy running it myself."

He put the card in his top pocket and looked over again at Lulu. "Let's go," he said, picking up the suitcase and wheeling it toward the parked car.

I wasn't sure whether to follow. It would look pathetic, a final loss of face. But I did anyway.

Sean put the bag of money and the suitcase in the boot and opened the passenger door and got in. He closed the door and stared ahead, refusing to catch my eye. Only Lulu lingered. Her mouth was tipped down at the corners in a self-conscious display of pity. "Oh, dear," she said. "Did that not go as you wanted?"

"It doesn't matter," I said.

"Are we good?"

"Of course."

"Bless," she said.

She put her arms out, and I took a step toward her and sank into them. Her back was narrow, her ribs prominent. We really were about the same shape and size; I had time to observe that. One of her braids brushed my cheek. Her breath warmed my neck.

I pulled away first. "Sorry," I said. "I am fine."

"He has to win," she said. "You know that, don't you? It's just a thing with him. He's not going to let you go."

He still wasn't looking at us. I held her gaze for a few moments; then I nodded.

She crossed to the other side of the car, opened the door, and got in. I stood there, hands thrust deep in my pockets, watching. When she started the engine, the insides of the thicket were blasted with light. She turned the car competently, considering the narrowness of the space, and I waited, expecting them then to accelerate off. But they didn't immediately. Just for a few seconds, the car idled, parallel with where I was standing, the headlights illuminating the first few yards of road. Sean's eyes were cast down, his features lit by his phone. He might have been setting the GPS, looking at Waze or something. I slunk back, closer into the hedgerow, my feet sinking into old leaves, vegetative fragments. Some long thorny tendril snagged the back of my T-shirt.

The human face has forty-three individual muscles, which together are capable of more than 3,000 expressions. I put my hand up to cover my mouth, just in case he saw. It's not just the zygomaticus major that activates when you smile.

Epilogue

In the French penal system, a fast-track investigation, or *enquête de flagrance*, occurs when a crime punishable by imprisonment has just been committed, or—get this—*is in the process of being committed*. In other words, when the culprit, the author of the misdeed, is caught in the act.

On the third Friday in August the Castels police, acting on an anonymous tip-off, entered the Domaine du Colombier just as Sean and Lulu were showing Sophia Bartlett and Quentin Trevisan, her fiancé, around the house. An envelope of cash was sitting on the kitchen table, next to a counterfeit receipt for the two-week rental made out on letterhead stolen from the upstairs "snug." The Ottys, the most recent renters, had been gone less than twenty-four hours, but the couple, in the words of the investigating officer, had made themselves "quite at home."

Rebecca Otty was back in the UK when the arrests

were made, and spoke to the police by Skype. She gave evidence that Lulu and Sean had visited the house in the previous week to scope it out, and that, while there, they had stolen a valuable gold necklace. Quoted in the *Mail*, she expressed herself baffled by the whole episode. Most of all, she said, she felt sorry for the innocent woman forced by "evil Sean" and "the gold-digging chalet girl" to take Lulu's place as private chef. She had been "quite a darling." No one in the house that week would hear a word against her, including her husband, who'd been won over by "her excellent duck confit." "It just shows you can be taken in by anyone," she was reported as saying. "Even when they're just like you."

Sophia Bartlett, the intended victim of the scam, also didn't understand why she'd let herself be duped. But it had been very hot the day Ms. Fletcher Davies had approached her in the local shop, claiming to be an acquaintance. She hadn't recognized her, but had thought nothing of it. "It's not the sort of face you remember," she told the prosecution. Alarm bells should have rung, but she and her fiancé were so desperate to rent a house—"there was just *nothing* available"—they'd let down her defenses.

At trial, Lulu claimed to be innocent of all the charges laid against her, to have been acting under coercion. The expensive Swiss lawyers hired by her parents argued successfully that she had fallen under the spell of Sean Wheeler, a charismatic scoundrel she'd met only a fortnight before, and that she was an unwilling accomplice, but by no means the "author" of the scheme. Her acting skills were to come into their own. On the witness stand, she came across as vulnerable, mortified, *innocent*. She was let off with a fine.

Sean's passage through the French courts was bumpier. He was accused not just of theft, trespass, and fraud at the Domaine, but also of similar crimes connected to the building he'd appropriated, my "shop," in the Marrakech medina. The French architect from whom he'd extracted a down payment had come forward after reading about him online. Sean was found guilty on all counts and sentenced to five years. He was also fined 80,000 euros. Not that Sean would have cared about that. It was never about the money with him.

I hope he thought about me the moment he heard the *gendarmes* at the gate. I hope he thought back on how carefully I'd framed him. It's the little things that trip people up—their small vanities, their petty venialities. I could have handed him the Sophia Bartlett scam on a plate. But I knew he wouldn't have gone for it straight. It wasn't enough on its own. He needed to think the con was mine, something he had taken *from me*. It was a simple process, to reveal the details of the plan, so proud of myself, so desperate for his approval, and then to make it look as if I'd dropped the card with her phone number on it by "accident." And then all that good acting as I pleaded for it back—so much of it in the eyes. After that it was a done deal. It was, as I've said, never about the money with him. It was about having one over. He knew that. I knew that. So, yes, I'm confident he'll have worked out what I did. I only wish I'd seen his face when he did.

I live with Rob in his flat in Dalston now. It's all pretty domestic. We've even got a baby, Janey, nearly three months old. She was conceived at the Domaine—and to be fair it was a tactical pregnancy, a way to keep him—but now that she's here, none of that seems to matter. We're not married, neither of us is quite ready for that commitment, but I don't think he's going anywhere and nor am I. Definitely. A child, a family of my own, well, it turns out it's all I ever wanted.

The flat's on the small side, and Molly's pressuring us to move down south. You get a lot more for your money in Morden, she says. Outside space, and you're only ten minutes from Ikea. She's pregnant herself now, and I try to see her as much as I can. I'm mending bridges, but it's a slow process. I've paid back the money, and I've saved all Janey's newborn clothes to pass on, but I know Steven doesn't like me. He talks about "drawing lines" under things, which I know means he'd rather Molly didn't have to think about her past. Thing is, I *am* her past, so obviously that makes things tricky. She is always kind to me, though she keeps a lot back; that's her way of dealing with it, I guess. Anyway, putting all that aside, we've no plans to move. I want Janey's childhood to be as stable as possible. I know she's little, but they pick things up, don't they?

Rob's book came out and did really well, even if it didn't "trouble" the bestseller lists. He used quite a lot of my story, specifically the early days with Sean, transporting them to 1970s Berlin so I'm not immediately recognizable. He wanted to wheel me out for the publicity—the real-life "inspiration" for his plot, etc.—but I put my foot down. It's awkward enough as it is with Phil and Rebecca. (She's back in publishing incidentally, riding high, though at a different company.) As far as the Ottys are concerned, Lulu was a friend who persuaded me to take her place, and I had no idea what she was planning. They try to gloss over the things that don't quite fit—the misunderstanding, for example, over Clare's hotel vouchers. Rob, who knows everything except the details of my last con on Sean, says I'd been in an abusive relationship, that I was a victim too. Not that he's completely averse to a little exploitation of his own. He's been pressuring me to let him use the Lulu part of the story for his sequel. So far I've held out, but I'm not sure how long I'll last. I find him hard to resist. I think often about Sean's definition of the perfect hustle: working out what it is a person wants and fulfilling that desire. The funny thing is that's also what you do when you care for someone. Love, the greatest con of all.

It's odd, the straight life. It's hard to relax. I sometimes miss the buzz. I was at the library today, and the light came sharply through the windows, catching in the librarian's eye. Janey was in my arms, and she was letting out these little coos, drawing lots of attention. I carry a big bag—I was going to say old habits die hard, only anyone with a baby needs a big bag—and I boldly put the books I wanted into the outside pocket. No one noticed, what with Janey being so adorable (a baby: the perfect misdirection). But then, as I've always said, no one ever notices me.

At the bus stop, my phone rang. It was a mobile number I didn't recognize. A woman with a Geordie accent was following up on my recent accident. I checked my emails. HMRC had an urgent rebate for me if I clicked on the link. They're everywhere, we're everywhere, though you don't need me to tell you that. Sometimes I imagine a row of teenage boys in a call center in South Korea, their screens a mess of numbers and data. Other times, I wonder if it isn't more personal. I think of the woman with the Geordie accent: is it real or is it fake? Is she running a scam from a kitchen in Newcastle or a basement in Vladivostok? Is she on commission? Does someone stand behind her with a knife?

I'm never going to be dependent on anyone again, that's my resolution. I love Rob. I really do. But I'll always have an escape route. I've taken out a lease on a little shop down near Columbia Road Market. I sell a load of old junk—house plants, Moroccan ceramics, vintage French pots—at vastly inflated prices. Now that *is* a con!

It's not enough to live on, so I have the odd extra iron in the fire. When we first got back from France, I wrote to Liam Merchant, the teacher who toyed with Martha, threatening exposure, and, long story short, he left several hundred pounds in cash in a paper bag at a designated drop-off point. The idiot. Occasionally I ping him another email. If nothing else, I reckon he'll keep his hands off schoolgirls if he knows I'm watching. I keep tabs on Layla and Roland too. He's representing the plaintiff in a big city fraud case—the stakes are getting higher. At some point, I might get in touch. It will be useful if I ever need a lot of money in a hurry. Which I might.

Last I heard, Lulu was living in New York, in a flat on the Upper East Side, writing a book; recipes intertwined with memoir. She's become quite the influencer. Rob was a bit miffed when he heard about her deal. But I don't begrudge her. You have to respect the way she operated both Sean and me, wrapping him around her little finger, and playing up to my prejudices. Maybe in other circumstances, we might have been friends.

Sean is still at Baumettes Prison in Marseille, running a racket from the inside: cash, dope, mobile phones. A bunch of inmates uploaded selfies to a Facebook page—as a taunt to the authorities—and, despite the black band across his eyes, I recognized his face. I expect he's quite enjoying himself. The gentleman of crime lording it up among his underlings. I'm safe for now. Four years of his sentence to go, according to my calculations.

Of course, I've got more to lose these days—a boyfriend I love and a child I'd literally kill for. Vulnerability is never good. We've got a guard dog. One of Molly's puppies. Only small, but as Layla said, Jack Russells are fighting dogs. They can be quite tough.

He raised the stakes, Sean, when he pretended to kill Lulu. For six days, I lived with her death. It rocked me to the core, I'm not going to pretend it didn't. But the thing is, I *survived* it. I stared death in the face, and if that changed me, well, I'm sorry. Sean has no one to blame but himself.

What did he say about women being underestimated? "No man ever thinks a woman can get one over on him." Well, I did. And nothing will stop me doing it again.

They look innocuous enough, Jack Russells. But appearances can be deceptive. *Sharp teeth*.